LOSING SLEEP

a sweet romance

HILLARY SLAUGHTER

To Lindy-

Thank you for being my book person and the best older sister a girl could ask for. Love you, girlie!

Chapter One

I EXHALED AND ALLOWED my breath to guide me as I shifted from upward dog to downward dog, following the instructor on my laptop. I pedaled my feet, working through the tightness in my calves as I waited on my yoga mat for the next pose. I strained to hear what the instructor said with the volume as close to mute as I could get it and still hear.

I should be sleeping, but old habits, particularly those honed during childhood thanks to a flighty but loving mother with a tendency to favor adventure over making it to school on time, died hard.

It was 5:30 in the morning, and I had the day off. I didn't need to be awake this early. I didn't need to cram in a calming workout before spending hours on the phone with angry customers. But instead of allowing me the rare experience of sleeping in, my mind was running circles as I worried about the day ahead and the week-long trip to celebrate my friend Tory's birthday. I was already packed, for the most part. I only needed to toss my shower items into my duffle bag, and I would be ready to go. My roommates had agreed to watch my dog, Ruby. My mom knew where I would be and could call if she needed me. There wasn't any reason for the nervous energy coursing through my veins. And yet, here

I was in leggings and a tank top, sweat beading my forehead, doing yoga in my bedroom because I couldn't get my brain to turn off.

"Step your right foot forward into a high lunge and raise up to warrior one."

Focus, Audrey.

If I could stay present on my mat, maybe I could stop worrying about my upcoming drive with one of Tory's friends, a man I'd only met in passing. Not to mention other fear-inducing thoughts like flat tires, my mom having another accident, animals darting in front of our car, and being too late to celebrate Tory's birthday tonight, in addition to worries I refused to think through enough to label. After all, if I didn't worry about it and try to account for it, who would?

The slight jingling of dog tags was the only warning before a small, furry body decided to join me on the mat. Ruby pressed against my right ankle, looking up at me with interest in her dark chocolate eyes.

"I'll walk you after this video is done," I promised, shooing her away with a wave of my hand. My little brown dog didn't budge.

Ignoring her, I moved to warrior two, opening my arms and staring over my right shoulder. Ruby took this as her cue to settle in, lying on top of my foot.

The next pose had me shifting forward, twisting so my left hand rested on the mat next to my right foot, my right arm extended. I gently nudged Ruby away. She in turn dug at my hand to get me to wrestle, her wriggling body hitting against me. As a shih tzu-mix, she wasn't large, but she could still throw off my balance.

I tightened my abs and grounded down through my feet to keep from falling.

"Stop, Ruby! We'll play in a minute," I whispered, humor and exasperation lacing my tone. Ruby just blinked at me before sitting back on my foot.

I continued through the yoga flow with mixed success. While this wasn't my most relaxing yoga practice, Ruby served as an excellent distraction from the anxieties circling through my mind until it came time for the balance poses.

With the help of a local yoga instructor, I had been working on my headstands for months and was close to finally being able to balance. As I tightened my core and kicked up my legs, Ruby knocked into me, nudging at my hands. The jostle was enough to send me crashing down with a loud thud. I groaned and rolled over onto my back in defeat. Seeing my collapse as victory, Ruby licked my face, her tail thumping with excitement as I stared up at the ceiling and light blue walls.

"Knock it off," I said with a laugh, tucking loose tendrils of brown hair back behind my ears. It was impossible to stay mad at my exuberant dog.

"Audrey, you okay?" a quiet voice called through my bedroom door.

"I'm fine," I said with a wince. My collapse had been loud enough to wake my roommates. "Still getting the hang of headstands."

My door cracked open to reveal Chloe on the other side, her pixie cut sticking up in random spikes around her head, her face creased with sleep lines from her pillow.

"Why are you doing headstands at"—she glanced at her phone—"5:50 in the morning?"

"Because I wanted to start my day with a new perspective?" My voice pitched high at the end, doing little to disguise my worry. Already, my list of concerns was returning, filling my head. My fingers itched to jot everything down, make a checklist, take some form of action.

She rolled her eyes. "And you couldn't wait to gain this new perspective until later in the day because...?"

I sighed. "Because I'm too anxious to sleep and thought yoga would calm me down. Unfortunately, this one,"—I gestured at Ruby, who was now lying innocently in a ball on my yoga mat—"decided it was playtime."

Chloe stepped into my room and settled on the floor next to me, wrapping an arm around my shoulders.

"I wondered when it would hit."

"I'm going on vacation. I'm not supposed to be anxious. I'm supposed to be relaxed and excited and—"

"I don't think 'supposed to' applies here." Mallory, my other roommate and landlady, stepped into my bedroom with a yawn, sitting on my other side. "Last time I checked, there's no 'supposed to' guide for going on vacation the day your ex-boyfriend marries your ex-best friend."

And there it was. The reality I was attempting to ignore.

"It shouldn't affect me. I'm not invited to the wedding. I haven't seen either of them in over a year." I actively avoided both Lyle and Emily even on social media, but that was beside the point. My stomach still tightened every time I thought of them and the happy life they were building together.

"They betrayed you and are getting married. That's got to hurt," Mallory said, brushing her blonde hair out of her face and watching my reaction carefully.

Tears stung my eyes as I tried to push down my emotions. No matter how many times I told myself I was better off without either Lyle or Emily in my life, a part of me still missed how my life used to be. I missed the security that came from knowing someone, even a self-obsessed guy like Lyle, loved and chose me above everyone and everything else. It was a level of security my life seemed destined to lack.

Sure, my mom loved me, but she never chose me first. She was always chasing something: the next adventure, the next get-rich-quick scheme. Then finally, when she'd opened her life and heart to dating again, she'd chosen Dave. While the two were perfect for each other, it had left me aching and questioning how I fit into the life they'd built together. Left me questioning where I belonged.

Chloe gave me a squeeze, bringing me back to the present. She jumped to her feet with an energy similar to the cartoon characters on her pajama shorts. "If ever there was an ice-cream-for-breakfast situation, this is it."

I laughed and shook my head. "I'm about to spend five hours in the car with one of Tory's friends whom I barely know. I'm going to need a lot more than ice cream to get me through."

"Pepsi and ice cream for breakfast, then," Mallory said, following me out of the room. "You can make a float."

While sugar and caffeine would help, I had a sinking feeling the challenges of my day were just beginning.

Later, after both Chloe and Mallory had left for the day, a knock sounded on the front door. Ruby sprang from the faded plaid couch and rushed over to greet our new guest. I followed her, glancing through the peephole and taking in the tall guy with a well-trimmed beard, dark hair, and a large grin.

When Tory had first invited me on this trip, I'd tried every excuse I could think of, including undependable transportation, as a reason to stay home. Growing up, vacations had hardly been relaxing, thanks to my mom and her tendency to forget things like booking hotel rooms ahead of time and making sure we had enough money for food on the road. As an adult, my vacations had been sparse, mainly consisting of trips to visit my mom, stepdad, and half-sisters. The few trips I had gone on with friends had included Emily, something I actively chose to ignore.

Tory, who had known me since college, saw straight through my tricks. She insisted I needed to come on the trip to celebrate her birthday and distract me from thinking about Lyle and Emily's wedding. Her solution to my car concerns currently stood outside my door, an hour late.

Maybe I should have opted to drive my own car, Jovi, instead. Named after Bon Jovi because my car was "Livin' on a Prayer," at least it would have left on time and wouldn't have involved spending hours in the car with a stranger. And if Jovi broke down on the side of the road somewhere, I'd have an excuse to stay home instead of navigating a weekend of awkward social interactions, celebrating Tory's birthday with her boyfriend, Trent, and all of her friends.

I opened the door and forced a smile as I took in my ride's forest-green t-shirt, the outline of a mountain and the words "Not all who wander are lost" emblazoned across the chest.

"Hi, I'm Audrey. You must be Greyson." I hoped my voice sounded welcoming instead of pinched and stilted from nerves.

"Everyone calls me Grey. Sorry I'm late." He offered me his hand, and I took it hesitantly, his calluses rough against my palm as I gave it a quick shake.

"Nice to officially meet you. Hope you're ready for the drive to Island Park." I kept my tone bright, pausing in hopes he'd explain why he was late. Instead, he just grinned.

"Did you know Island Park has the longest main street in the world?" He spouted the trivia with clear enthusiasm, as if that explained his tardiness.

"I did. They have a sign." I waved him inside the apartment, trying not to stress about the change in plans and how it would have been nice to have a warning that Grey would be late. Since waking up far too early this morning, I'd had ample time to think through our travel plans and build my own mental timeline. Grey had destroyed it before even arriving on my doorstep, and it left me feeling twitchy as I fought back flashbacks from my childhood and the countless times Mom had changed plans without telling me.

Relax. You have plenty of time to get to the cabin to celebrate Tory's actual birthday tonight.

While the trip would last about a week, today was Tory's birthday. She'd started the drive early this morning, determined to spend as much time as possible at the cabin with her boyfriend, Trent. I was driving up today with Grey instead of waiting to go up with the rest of the group tomorrow because I wanted to be with Tory on her birthday. Or at least, that was the official answer. Unofficially, Tory had decided I shouldn't be home today because it was Lyle and Emily's wedding day.

As I stepped back to let Grey in, I didn't move quickly enough to block the doorway. Seeing her opportunity, Ruby bolted, making a beeline for the open door and freedom. Before I could react, Grey dropped to his knees on the laminate, arms extended.

"Hello, sweetheart! Aren't you a pretty girl?" Grey gushed, offering his hand for Ruby to sniff.

Distracted from her escape attempt, Ruby took one whiff of the newcomer and immediately rolled over for a belly rub.

Grey gave her a few scratches before picking Ruby up and following me inside. Once I'd closed the door, Grey set Ruby down, and she trotted over to her food bowl as if nothing had happened.

"You ready to go? We don't want to be too late getting to the cabin," Grey said, checking the time on his phone. "Driving in the woods at night gets creepy fast."

I scowled, annoyed that his comment made it sound like our delay was *my* fault. "I've been ready for the last hour."

"Perfect. Let's go. Do you need help with your bags?" Grey turned towards the door, pausing at the duffle, yoga mat, and backpack I had stacked in the entry.

"I've got it," I said, waving him towards the door.

I gave Ruby one last pat, my fingers sinking into her fur for just a moment as I let her warmth comfort me before taking a deep breath and straightening. I could do this.

"Be good for Chloe and Mallory," I called to Ruby as I grabbed my stuff and followed Grey out the door.

A knot of panic tightened in my stomach with each step I took. This was a bad idea. I just knew it.

Chapter Two

AFTER DEPOSITING MY DUFFLE and yoga mat in the trunk, I climbed into Grey's black SUV, setting my navy-blue backpack on the floor next to my feet. I cringed at the wave of heat that greeted me as I settled into my gray pleather seat. The summer heat was already out in full force in Utah County. That was one positive about this trip—Island Park, Idaho would definitely be cooler than Pleasant Grove, Utah. I could already feel sweat beading at my hairline as I buckled my seatbelt and waited for Grey to turn on the AC. The car smelled faintly of fast food, but it was clean and well maintained.

"Road trip, road trip." Grey settled into the driver's seat and grinned. "I've never been to Island Park. You?"

"A few times. It's a beautiful area." I buckled my seatbelt and fisted my hands in my lap, resisting the temptation to throw the door open and run upstairs to the safety of my apartment.

Forget about adventure and escape. I could avoid my problems from my bedroom just as well as in a cabin surrounded by nature. If I stayed, I'd have easy access to restaurants and the internet, not to mention I could hit up some yoga classes at the rec center. I'd just avoid social media, with its photos of Emily and Lyle's happy day. I could even distract myself with work. The phones were guaranteed to be busy with a recent product launch, and I doubted my team would be sad if I canceled my time off request—

The car rumbled to life, and I flinched as music blasted from the speakers.

"Sorry about that." Grey turned down the music, backed out of the parking lot, and pulled onto the road. Just like that, my last chance for escape vanished. "I forget how loud my music is sometimes. Though I feel like I should warn you—Tory gave me a heads up about your musical tastes, and I'm not sure how I feel about letting you control the radio." He quirked an eyebrow, humor lacing his tone.

"What do you mean 'she warned you'?" An insult to my music could not be ignored.

"She said your tastes are...'specific.'" He pitched his voice higher on the last word in a poor imitation of Tory. "She didn't give details. I'm more of a classics man, myself." He adjusted the volume, bringing the music back to a blaring level.

I listened to the music pounding out of his speakers, recognizing the melody. "Motley Crüe is fine. Though personally I prefer Supertramp. Their sound is more my style."

"You know classic rock?" Grey fiddled with the volume again, making it so I didn't have to yell to be heard over the bass.

"What? Girls can't like classic rock?" I shrugged, trying not to laugh at the shocked expression on Grey's face. I'd gotten that reaction more than once from men when they learned what I liked to listen to.

"Based on Tory's description, I thought you'd be into some new age, Indie meditation stuff, not classic rock." Grey shrugged, his eyebrows pinched as he tried to process this new information.

"Tory has teased me about my music tastes since the day we met. Something about quiet people having secretly loud passions," I said, humor lacing my tone as I thought back to my second year in college when I'd been randomly assigned Tory as a roommate. Little had I known she'd turn into one of my best friends, even if she made side comments about my music.

Tory had quickly gotten over those comments when we'd used classic rock dance battles to alleviate stress after long days of work and class. There really was a rock song for every scenario. Rough day at work? "Working for the Weekend" by Loverboy should do the trick. Bad break up? Pat Benatar had your back. Need a good workout beat? AC/DC all the way.

Though I had yet to find the perfect music mix for fixing a broken heart.

As the familiar beat vibrated through the car, I felt my tension ease. I kicked off my flip flops and settled against the headrest, familiar streets passing outside my window soothing me as we headed towards the freeway. I could do this. I could relax and have fun, let go of my worries and be in the moment.

"I should have known Tory was messing with me," Grey said, turning onto the freeway. "She hates my music choices too. Says I play my music too loud, has since the day she moved in next door."

I snorted a laugh. "Sounds about right. She hates loud noises. Back in college, I took her with me to a concert once. I'm never making that mistake again, at least not without earplugs for her."

Thoughts of Tory had me reaching for my phone. But instead of a text from my friend, my phone vibrated with a notification from my office's messaging system. I read the message, stifling a groan. The question was from Angela, a college student on my team who used me as her answer source instead of the database of approved responses that could be tricky to search. I bit back my annoyance and typed a quick response before switching to my texts and pulling up my conversation thread with Tory.

ME: *We're on our way. Happy birthday! Hope you're ready to celebrate.*

TORY: *The celebration has already begun. [winky face emoji] Drive safe. See you soon!*

TORY: *And don't murder Grey.*

I rolled my eyes. My phone buzzed again, and another message from Angela stared back at me.

ME: *I'm on vacation. Ask Drew.*

I could answer her questions, but it would be better if she reached out to our supervisor. He had the title and extra pay to deal with Angela and her requests. I just had the technical knowledge and years of experience. Not that it had mattered when they'd interviewed for the supervisor position three months ago, picking Drew with his charm and connection to the owners over me.

You could always quit.

The thought had crossed my mind on more than one occasion of late. After all, working a call center job was hardly my idea of a post-college dream job. One of my yoga instructors had recently mentioned that I'd make a good yoga teacher, and I couldn't get the idea out of my head. Though getting certified would take time and teaching yoga wasn't exactly an easy career choice.

Working at the call center was steady and stable. I felt comfortable and needed. Even if they needed me a little too much at times, messaging me when I was off the clock like right now.

ANGELA: *He's not at his desk.*

ME: *I'm also not at my desk.*

ANGELA: *But you're still responding.*

I hesitated, biting my lip, before typing my response. I pondered the ramifications of what I wanted to say. While I knew my job was secure and that I was entitled to time off, it was hard to turn off the work part of my brain. I was going on vacation, however begrudgingly. If I answered Angela's questions now, it wouldn't be long before the rest of the team would be messaging me. Taking a deep breath, I typed:

ME: *Not anymore. I'm off the clock starting now. Talk to Drew.*

I hit send and then went into the messaging app settings, silencing my notifications. They still had my phone number if it was a real emergency. I dropped my phone into the backpack at my feet and shifted to stare out the window, clasping my hands together in my lap to resist the urge to pick up my phone and turn my notifications back on.

"I can only imagine what that was like." Grey's words pulled me from my thoughts, and it took me a moment to remember our conversation thread: taking Tory to a concert.

"Let's just say Tory does better in quiet, open spaces like the mountains. She always thought it was funny that I liked such loud music since I'm such a quiet person," I said, allowing Grey's comments to distract me from my nerves about being away from work.

"It's the quiet ones who have the most to hide. I'm too loud for anyone to say that about me."

"Or quiet people are more observant and know everyone's secrets." I quirked an eyebrow and forced humor into my voice, pushing away thoughts of work and doing my best to keep the conversation going.

Grey pursed his lips, thinking for a moment as he tapped his fingers on the steering wheel. "Makes sense. What secrets are you hiding?"

I shook my head. "They wouldn't be secrets if I told you."

"Fair enough," Grey shrugged. "Is one of them the reason why you're already shoeless in my car?"

At that, I did laugh, surprised to find my anxiety dissipating with each mile we drove closer to the cabin. Maybe I really did need a break. "That's no secret. I hate shoes, and the less I have to wear them, the better."

There was a reason yoga was my go-to form of stress release. It involved exercise and didn't require shoes, even if the music lacked a decent beat.

"I bet you kick them off under your desk at work, don't you?" Grey's question felt like more of a statement, and I was amazed at how quickly he could read me.

I wiggled my toes, taking in the rough texture of his floor mats. "Guilty as charged. I spend all day sitting at my desk. Why should I torture myself further by wearing shoes?"

We drove for a moment in silence, the familiar businesses and billboards of Utah County slipping past my window as we got closer to the Point of the Mountain. I quickly calculated when we'd arrive at the cabin and breathed a sigh of relief. If we drove straight through and made minimal stops, we'd get there around 5:00, just in time to celebrate the last few hours of Tory's birthday and well before dark settled in, with its increased risk of hitting wildlife on the road.

As if sensing my plans, Grey spoke, "Do you mind if we stop for lunch? I was going to grab something before picking you up but didn't want to be even later."

"I ate before you came, but I guess we can stop. I wouldn't mind a Pepsi." I tried not to think about the added time in the car, but hoped a stop now would mean fewer stops later.

"Perfect! I know just the place." Grey didn't hesitate before flicking on his blinker and taking the next exit.

Chapter Three

When Grey had said he knew the "perfect place," I'd assumed he meant a fast-food joint with a drive thru so we could get back on the road quickly. Instead, he drove to a burger place that, while delicious, was notorious for its slow service.

"I've been craving cheesy fries and a shake all week. Don't tell my gym buddies." He said as he climbed out of the car, pausing before closing his door. "Just kidding! I don't have gym buddies. It's difficult to find guys with the skills needed to maintain this type of physique." He patted his stomach, which was average in shape and size, far from the six pack of the gym rats I knew.

I forced a smile, slipped on my shoes, and followed him into the restaurant, shivering at the blast of AC that greeted us along with the friendly worker at the counter. I placed an order for a drink, my stomach full of lunch and the nervous knots I'd been battling all day. I tried to let go of my mental travel timeline. There was still plenty of time to reach the cabin before dark, and this way I'd have even more caffeine to help me through.

We placed our order and settled into a booth near the door, drinks in hand. The red vinyl stuck to my legs as I slid across the bench. Hits from the early 2000s played on the speakers, and memorabilia from local high school sports teams dotted the walls.

"I know you've been friends with Tory forever, but that's all I've got. What's your story, Audrey?" Grey asked as he settled across from me, his expression open and interested.

I bit my lip, trying to ignore the unsettled feeling that always came with one-on-one attention from someone I didn't know well. It was an instinct I'd developed as a child. If I didn't let people close, I didn't need to be disappointed when I had to move again or when the friendship didn't last.

"I have a degree in business and have worked at the same company for a few years. I'm on the customer service team, though I keep getting promised a leadership position if I can hang on a little longer. You?" I rushed to tack on the last word, cringing at how awkward I must sound and wishing, not for the first time, I had someone to help me navigate social situations.

While Chloe and Mallory frequently reassured me that I didn't come across as awkward, it didn't stop me from second-guessing everything I said when getting to know someone new. My mom was skilled at making literally anyone feel at ease when talking to her and I had not inherited her ability. It was part of why I'd dated Lyle. He could take the attention, navigate the social situations, while I hung back in my quiet comfort zone.

"That all sounds very professional and frustrating. I'm not nearly that put together. I work for a construction company, though we'll see how long I stay." He flashed me a grin before launching into the story of how he got his job.

I nodded and hummed at the appropriate moments, sipping my Pepsi, the carbonation burning as it slid down my throat. My mind scrambled to come up with comments and questions, anything to add to the conversation in front of me. But everything I thought of felt forced.

How long have you been at your job? I was pretty sure he'd already answered that question and I'd missed it.

Why construction? Sounded too basic and slightly judgmental.

Is your beard as soft as it looks? That was just weird.

So I kept quiet, grateful he seemed content to carry the conversation with an occasional question for me. I responded and returned the questions, but that was the limit of my conversational prowess.

About the time I needed a refill, Grey's meal arrived, bringing with it the smell of fried food and making me almost regret that I hadn't purchased second lunch. But I knew if I ordered food now, we'd definitely be late getting to the cabin. I ducked out of the booth, taking an extra moment at the soda machine before returning to our table, counting my breaths to distract myself from the self-consciousness I always felt when talking to people I didn't know well.

Despite his near constant talking, Grey managed to finish his meal, and we were back on the road in twenty minutes. Unfortunately, I had overestimated my bladder capacity, and the two Pepsis I'd drunk at the restaurant caught up to me just over an hour and a half later. I shifted uncomfortably in my seat as I tried to listen to Grey's monologue about the restaurants we passed. I wasn't sure why this had become his topic of choice, but I was too busy not knowing what to say to add to the conversation.

I'd never been an adept conversationalist. At least not like my mom. On more than one occasion she'd told me to just ask people questions, reminding me that everyone loved to talk about themselves. For that approach to work, I had to think of good questions to ask. One instance in college when I asked a cute boy who was sitting alone if he'd farted was all the evidence I needed that I wasn't made to be social. Listening and staying quiet was so much easier.

That was one part of why my relationship with Lyle had worked. Like my mom, he enjoyed talking, and I was good at listening. Of course, it could also be part of why it hadn't worked. Maybe Lyle had gotten tired of having a girlfriend whom he was always talking for and wanted someone who could speak for herself. Emily, with her extroverted personality and big smile, fit that bill better than I ever would.

I pushed the unwanted thought away, trying to ignore the now familiar twinge of inadequacy that haunted me every time I thought about my last relationship. In playing it safe and picking someone who could give me security, I'd been burned in the worst possible way. I really was better off now, but that didn't fully erase the doubt and regret.

"Personally," Grey said, his monologue quickly becoming the soundtrack of our trip, "I'm a big fan of fried chicken, but there are few places that do it right. It needs a good crunch without—"

Spotting the Brigham City exit, I broke in. "Do you mind if we stop? That last Pepsi was one too many." My voice hitched with desperation, and I didn't care. If I didn't find a bathroom soon, I'd have a different reason to be self-conscious in front of Grey.

"Sure," Grey said, the change in plans doing nothing to dampen his enthusiasm. "I should probably get some more gas. Meant to fill up before picking you up, but you know, things happen."

I still didn't know what "things" could have happened to make Grey an hour late, but if his lack of preparedness meant I got to pee, I'd take it.

I rocked in my seat, feeling like my bladder would explode as Grey navigated off the freeway. He pulled into a gas station and parked in front of a pump. I dashed from the car, nearly forgetting to slip my shoes back on as I rushed into the convenience store.

"I'm going to grab some snacks once I'm done filling up. You want anything?" Grey called after me.

"I'm good." I yelled over my shoulder, grateful for the kind offer but also desperate to make it to the bathroom.

I hurried into the restroom, relieved to find an open stall even as a terrible smell greeted me, bits of toilet paper and paper towels scattered on the floor. The restroom wasn't the cleanest I'd ever used, but I couldn't afford to be picky at the moment. At least it meant I wouldn't have to continue dancing in my seat on the drive.

I finished quickly in the bathroom, trying to breathe as little as possible. I stopped in the hall outside the bathroom for a moment, grateful to breathe the stale convenience store air. Now that my bladder was empty, I needed a moment to mentally prepare for the next several hours in the car with Grey's rambling. He was like an overexcited, friendly puppy, eager to share his every observation and inviting my own comments. Unfortunately, I had little to add to the conversation, and despite my love of loud music, I also appreciated the quiet.

I walked towards the exit and found Grey waiting for me in the convenience store near the cash register, a white shopping bag in hand, his ever-present smile flashing through his beard.

"I know you said you didn't want anything, but they had a buy-two sale going, and based on your shirt, I thought you could use this." He held out a Pepsi, and some of my misgivings faded.

I glanced down at my blue "With enough Pepsi I can rule the world" shirt and returned his smile, touched at the thoughtful gesture. "Thank you."

My mom was the only other person who had ever bought me Pepsi. It had become our thing when I was in high school. Whenever I had a hard day, I'd text her and come home to a bottle of Pepsi waiting for me in the fridge. I'd settle at the counter with the bottle in hand and Mom would sit on the stool next to me, pausing for a moment between work and dates and everything else that always took her attention. Instead, she'd focus on me and whatever I had to say. Every time I felt the familiar burn of carbonation, it took me back to those moments—moments when I'd known everything would be okay because my mom was there.

"Gotta keep my road trip buddy happy," Grey said, pulling me from my thoughts with a wink as he led the way to the car. "If you're going to be stuck with me for several hours, you're going to need the caffeine."

Laughter tinged his tone, and I felt some of my hesitations about this trip fade further.

As I climbed into the car, I stashed my drink in the cupholder, kicked off my flip flops, and leaned back in my seat, closing my eyes. My early morning was catching up to me, and a nap would help the miles pass faster. A brief span of quiet with only Toto playing in the background hinted that my nap plan might work. Then Grey's monologue picked back up. I tensed, a knot forming in my shoulders as I listened to his poetic description of a burger joint I knew was not that good, though he made it sound like a culinary masterpiece. I'd give him this—the guy was definitely a glass-half-full kind of person. I was sure under other circumstances I would have found him friendly and nice. Maybe even charming. My lack of sleep and remnants of anxiety about the trip meant I found his quirky conversation less than fascinating.

When he switched to discussing chicken nuggets, I reached my limit.

"You know you don't have to talk constantly, right?" I mumbled the words under my breath, assuming the music would drown them out. Of course, that wasn't the case. Leave it to me to say the wrong thing and offend my ride with hours still left in the drive.

Grey stopped talking for a moment and I could hear his fingers tapping the steering wheel to the beat of the song. "You know, I've heard rumors that talking constantly isn't necessary for survival, but I don't want to risk it."

Instead of offended, he almost sounded entertained, as if he found my surly response humorous.

"Keeping this up won't guarantee your survival either," I said, regretting the words as soon as they spilled out, but unable to take them back. Surely there was a kinder way to tell someone to shut up that didn't involve threatening murder. It felt like another moment that could be held up as evidence for my lacking social skills. I curled my toes into the floor mat, the coarse texture grounding me as I pretended my cheeks weren't on fire.

Grey guffawed, and I opened my eyes to see him shaking his head, laughter lines deepening around his eyes, surprise filling his features.

"You don't sugar coat things, do you?" His voice lacked judgment, filled instead with curiosity.

"Normally, I'm pretty nice. But hours in the car listening to someone talk incessantly about food changes a woman. Do you do anything besides talk, eat, and talk about eating?" This was why I didn't interact with new people. My filter broke, and I never knew what would come out of my mouth.

Just ask them questions about themselves, indeed. My mom's advice had gone awry once more.

At work, I was able to bite back my thoughts in the name of professionalism and keeping a stable job. Out in the wild, meeting people and attempting a social life, all bets were off. It still amazed me that I'd managed to convince Mallory, Chloe, Emily, and Tory to be my friends. Though Emily's friendship hadn't lasted.

When I'd dated Lyle, he'd regularly shared his shock at the things I said. It left me feeling uncertain and ready to retreat back into my safe introvert shell. If Lyle were here, he'd point out how I was butchering the exchange. Yet, Grey's reaction was completely different. He almost seemed relieved to have me talking, no matter the snark level.

I pushed the doubts away and refocused on Grey and the conversation in front of me.

"I also enjoy eating while talking and talking while eating. Some would argue these are the same, but I disagree. It all depends on which is your priority in the moment." Grey didn't miss a beat, one of his eyebrows quirking up in a challenge as if daring me to argue with him.

I paused, surprised at his quick comeback, and bit back a smile. "It may be time to look for alternative hobbies."

"Maybe you can help me with that. What are your hobbies?"

The question caught me off-guard. It was a perfectly normal and natural direction for our conversation to take, yet I was left scrambling. Once upon a time, before Lyle had destroyed my heart, my list of hobbies had seemed endless. Hobbies had been something my mom and I shared. She'd jump from one source of entertainment to another, taking me along for the ride. I'd picked up each interest, hoping this one would be the one to hold her attention and lead to a career and routine. They never had, but many of the interests had stuck with me, acting as entertainment on the nights mom was out late working one waitress job or another. Between classic rock, baking, and hiking, I stayed busy. But those were activities that didn't fit into a life that revolved around Lyle, so one by one, they'd faded from my world, and I hadn't found the energy to bring them back.

Now, my life seemed to revolve around yoga, sweatpants, and binging shows. And the occasional phone call with my mom, in which she told me to "loosen up" and "live a little," the sounds of my seven-year-old half-sisters filling the background.

"How are my hobbies going to help you expand yours?" I asked, dodging the question.

"You seem to have such well-informed opinions on my hobbies. I figured you must be well-adjusted and heavily involved in all kinds of uplifting endeavors based on your commentary." Grey glanced my way, and I schooled my features, refusing to let him see that he'd gotten to me.

"You're mocking me."

"Correction," he held up a finger to underscore his point, "I'm teasing you, and you started it. Also, you still haven't answered my question." Grey looked at me, challenging me to prove him wrong.

"I like baking." It wasn't a complete lie. I still baked, mostly chocolate chip cookies when I had a free moment on Sundays, but that counted. Right?

"Doesn't count. It involves food."

"Who made you the hobby judge?"

"My car, my rules."

I shook my head, rising to the bait. It had been a long time since I'd bantered with someone other than my roommates, even if he managed to entertain and annoy me simultaneously.

"I walk my dog every day." It wasn't quite the same level of physical fitness and activity as hiking, but I did it regularly.

"You don't have a yard, so walking your dog is a necessity, not an area of interest." Grey's tone was light, non-judgmental, and yet it still poked at me.

"I like music and yoga." The words tasted sour and desperate on my tongue as I stared at my hands, twisting them in my lap. Why I needed to prove to this bearded man that I had a well-rounded life was beyond me. Yet, I refused to acknowledge that the bulk of my time away from work was spent pretending I was fine with how my life was playing out.

"I'll allow that. Though, two hobbies are hardly an indicator of a well-rounded human. I, at least, have three: 'talking, eating, and talking about eating.'" Grey quoted my logic back to me, and I looked up to see him raise a finger for each hobby, wiggling them in triumph to underscore his point.

"You just said anything food-related doesn't count, so that leaves you with only one." I reached over, folding down two of his fingers, leaving only the index finger waving back at me. This was perhaps the oddest argument I'd ever had, and yet, I didn't want it to stop. Even if it left me feeling slightly off kilter.

"The good news is you have yet to ask me for my hobbies, so chances are good I've got a couple of secret weapons up my sleeve." Grey brushed at one of his shirt sleeves, indicating hordes of hobbies lurking just beneath the green fabric.

His tone softened. "We might even have a full conversation for some of this drive as opposed to one based on my rambling and your monosyllabic responses." Grey quirked an eyebrow and his lips pulled into a small smile as he waited for my reply. It seemed he could read my discomfort and was doing his best to both call me on it while coaxing me out of the aforementioned introvert shell.

His words stung as I realized their accuracy, digging up personal doubts that had haunted me most of my life. Grey's entire conversation may have been flat and focused on a single topic, but my responses hardly provided the material for a stimulating conversation. I was used to fading into the background letting others—my mom, Lyle, Emily—shine in the spotlight. I didn't know what I'd find if I let the beam shine on me too brightly for too long.

I took a deep breath. I could give Grey this much. I could try to join the conversation.

"Sorry." The word came out soft and hesitant, but I pushed forward, ignoring the doubts that continued to niggle in my brain. "You may have noticed, I'm not really an extrovert. I'm much more comfortable at home with my dog and a yoga video than in social situations."

I fidgeted with my seatbelt, pretending the confession didn't stick a bit in my throat as I gazed out the window at the passing mountains. It looked like we were driving through the canyon instead of heading back to the freeway, which made no sense. I pushed the thought aside, certain I must be turned around. I had only been up this way a handful of times. Going up the canyon was hardly the fastest way to get to Island Park. Though maybe Grey knew a shortcut I was unaware of.

Grey reached over and gave my arm a reassuring squeeze before returning his hand to the steering wheel. I startled at the warmth and comfort that came from the simple gesture. Grey's kindness and patience when I was clearly struggling to find my footing unnerved me. I typically surrounded myself with loud, bold personalities. People like my mom, who allowed me to fade into the background.

"I get that. But you know, 'Not all who wander are lost.'" He gestured at his shirt, with its faded words and outline of mountains.

"That makes no sense." I bit back a laugh, completely thrown off by the random change of topic. Grey was good at keeping me on my toes, and I couldn't quite decide how I felt about it. The smile hovering at the edge of my lips told me I might like it more than I realized.

"Maybe not, but it kept you talking and meant I got to bring in a fun fact you probably don't know." Grey shrugged, clearly unbothered at the random change of topic. It was the type of comment that would have left me stumbling over my words and second-guessing everything I said well after the conversation was over.

"What's that?"

"This lovely quote, which some may argue is overused, is from *The Lord of the Rings*. Though technically, the exact quote is 'Not all those who wander are lost.' But it's close enough."

"Seriously?" The information surprised me. I assumed the quote had come from some t-shirt company trying to make a quick buck from outdoors enthusiasts.

"Are you questioning my J. R. R. Tolkien knowledge? It comes from *The Fellowship of the Ring*." His lips pursed, daring me to question him.

"As someone who's never read or watched *The Lord of the Rings*, I'll take your word for it." I held up my hands in a placating gesture, my lips tipping into a smile.

Grey groaned and put his hand over his heart in mock outrage. "It's a classic! I'm not sure I can continue this drive with someone so unfamiliar with such a staple of modern culture."

I shrugged. "It's a story about mythical creatures walking in the woods for days trying to throw a ring into a volcano. What's classic about that?"

He shook his head, his hand clutching at his heart now in exaggerated distress. "If you'd read or seen *The Lord of the Rings*, you'd understand just how wrong you are, Audrey."

"I'll take your word for it." I leaned back in my seat, watching humor dance across the lines of Grey's face.

We drifted into a comfortable silence for a moment before Grey glanced my way, giving me a wink and a cheeky grin.

"Wasn't that conversation nice? And we didn't reference fast food once. The question is, how do we keep this going? I'm more than happy to rank my favorite taco places."

I slouched in my seat and gave an exaggerated groan before I straightened with an idea.

"I'll keep talking on two conditions. First, you don't make fun of me if I say something stupid, and second, you promise not to discuss food unless we're discussing where to stop for dinner. Deal?" Under normal circumstances, I wasn't opposed to a good foodie conversation. But after listening to Grey discuss food for the bulk of our drive, I needed a change of topic.

Grey tapped his fingers on the steering wheel, seeming to consider my terms before flashing a smile, white teeth contrasting with his dark beard and tanned skin. "Deal, but with one exception...which I'll explain later."

I didn't like leaving our deal so open-ended but decided to play along. Searching for a question, I quickly dismissed the first options that came to mind. Asking him about why he was late felt accusatory, and asking his favorite color would hardly lead to a full conversation. Instead, I started with the obvious. If Grey wanted conversation, I'd give it to him. He just couldn't blame me if it was a bit stilted and predictable. "What are your hobbies?"

"I'm so glad you asked." Grey scrunched his face, tapping a finger on his chin as if pondering before responding. "I like hiking and fishing. I wouldn't say that I'm a movie buff, but I do enjoy movies. I also like long walks on the beach and getting caught in the rain."

I laughed at the botched Rupert Holmes song reference. "I think the lyric you're looking for involves pina coladas and rain, not beaches."

"True, but I don't drink alcohol, and I think pineapple is nasty, so I figured I might as well combine two dating profile clichés into one for a fun new twist."

"Your answer was well-thought-out." I could appreciate his cleverness even if his wit kept me on my toes. A not altogether unpleasant experience, if I was being honest.

"That's what happens in the age of internet dating: you get good at answering questions about yourself. I think I have profiles on nearly every dating app available."

"I've never tried online dating. Does it work?" I'd heard enough horror stories to scare me away from the possibility. Yet I was also curious. Now that I was done with college, the internet seemed like the only viable option for meeting people, especially since I didn't drink or go to clubs. And if I didn't count road trips with near strangers to celebrate a friend's birthday.

"I'm still single, so what do you think?" He looked over and winked at me, and I couldn't keep a smile from my lips, his conversation distracting me from the passing scenery outside the car.

"I've heard many success stories," I observed, giving him the same argument I'd heard from my mom every time she tried to get me to join an online dating service. After all, it had worked for her. Why wouldn't it work for her introverted, comfort-zone-bound daughter?

"I've decided those are unicorns," Grey said with complete seriousness.

"Excuse me?" I turned to face him fully, surprised.

"You know, the rare exceptions to the rules that everyone references but aren't actually the norm," he said with a shrug.

"If that's the case, why do you keep online dating?" I watched him, genuinely curious.

"Because, who knows? Maybe I'll get to be the exception one day."

The sincerity in his tone made me pause, speaking to a longing I tried to keep hidden, especially in the wake of Lyle's rejection. It was the longing of a little girl who would have given nearly anything to live in the same home for longer than a year and for her mom to work normal hours that didn't require babysitters at all hours of the night.

"What if you're not the exception? What if you're the rule?" My questions came out soft, hinting at vulnerabilities I kept buried deep.

"Then I guess I'll keep waiting for my unicorn while I get caught in the rain on long walks on the many beaches filling the landlocked state of Utah."

While Grey's response was the quietest I'd heard him, there was a level of hope and sincerity I couldn't ignore. Maybe there was more to Grey than I realized. And maybe, if I remembered this moment of vulnerability, I might just survive this car ride after all.

Chapter Four

OF COURSE, MY SURVIVING the car ride assumed that it would end at some point, preferably before nightfall. I quickly learned Grey's one exception to the "no food talk" rule. I'd been so absorbed in our conversation around hobbies and online dating that I hadn't asked Grey about the shortcut I assumed we were taking up the canyon. Turns out, it wasn't a shortcut. Grey had taken a detour up Logan Canyon to visit what he informed me was his favorite place in Cache Valley: an outlet store connected to a local dairy company.

"I'll wait here," I said, unwilling to get out of the car. If he knew I was waiting, it might even speed up his shopping.

"We were so close, I couldn't not stop. My life is sorely lacking in various cheeses and shelf-stable chocolate milk. Have you ever had their cheese curds? They're life-changing. Now, come on." Grey climbed out of the car and waved me towards the store.

I did my best impression of a stubborn child, shaking my head with my arms crossed over my chest.

"Are you lactose intolerant?" Grey leaned into the car, watching me from the open driver's side door.

"No..." I trailed off, not sure where he was going.

"Do you hate cheese and other sources of joy?" He quirked an eyebrow, his lips tipping up into a smile that promised mischief.

"No."

"Are you afraid of outlet stores that promise deep discounts and other forms of delight?"

I gave a frustrated laugh. "No! But I also would like to reach the cabin before dark."

Bad things happened on mountain roads after dark. Animals darted out onto roads and accidents happened, resulting in injuries, scars, and leaves of absence from work so I could take care of my mom while she recovered. I pushed the thoughts away, refusing to dwell on those dark days. The accident had happened over a year ago, and Mom was fine now, even if I still carried some of the emotional scars.

"I hate to break it to you, but the fastest way to get back on the road is to come with me." Grey took a slow, measured step away from the car, starting to inch the door closed. "Otherwise, I have a tendency to get distracted by all the cheese and milk flavors. I could be in there for hours, debating purchases."

"Hours?" My voice held a shrill note that I couldn't quite erase. "You take *hours* shopping for cheese?"

"And flavored milks." Grey threw me a wide grin and closed the door, sauntering to the white storefront attached to the factory. It looked like something out of the Swiss Alps, with its green shutters and bright red and white flowers.

I fumbled with my seatbelt, slipping on my shoes and scrambling from the car. I hoped Grey was joking about needing hours to make his purchases, but I also had a sinking suspicion he would take his time shopping just to push my buttons. My flip-flops slapped against the asphalt as I chased after him, catching up to him as we reached the automatic doors. They whooshed open, welcoming us into the store with a gust of AC-cooled air that made me shiver.

Grey grinned at me, extolling the virtues of various cheeses as he grabbed a basket. I slipped my phone out of my leggings pocket to text Tory, moving in the opposite direction from Grey. I hoped my presence in the store would be enough to remind him we had a schedule to keep.

ME: *Is it murder if I make it look like an accident?*

TORY: *I'm not a lawyer, but best guess, yes.*

ME: *What if he had it coming?*

TORY: *What is this, a remake of* Chicago? *Was he popping his gum too loud? Or did he lie to you about having another wife?*

ME: *I'm serious. He just took an unannounced detour for cheese.*

TORY: *Is it good cheese? There is always time for good cheese.*

ME: *I don't know. We haven't tried any yet. But that's beside the point!*

TORY: *Enjoy the journey! We're just sitting on the couch in the cabin, staring at each other. You're not missing much. I think Trent is going to break out the old video game console soon.*

I sighed and put my phone away, tapping my fingers on my thighs as I pondered an even later arrival time at the cabin.

"Do you ever stop sighing?" Grey asked as he stopped next to me, perusing the contents of the shelves behind me. They contained jams, nuts, and a few other locally sourced non-dairy treats. "Or is your allergy to spontaneity acting up?"

"I can be spontaneous," I stuttered, my cheeks heating with embarrassment. "I'm on this trip with you, aren't I?"

"A trip that was planned weeks ago is hardly spontaneous. Honestly, the most spontaneous thing I've seen you do so far is pee outside of your allotted time for a bathroom break." He grabbed a bag of taffy from the shelf behind me, adding it to his basket before turning to examine the fridges that lined the back wall of the store.

I glared at him, scrambling for a comeback as I watched him walk away. I took a moment to take in my surroundings, observing the simple layout of the small store. In addition to the shelves I stood next to, it contained a single row of freezers and some pallets against a wall. The biggest thing in the room was the checkout area, and that was because it had an ice cream counter attached.

A blonde woman in a teal romper nearly ran me over with her cart in the cramped space. I took a step out of her way and moved to browse the milk section, both amazed and wary of the variety of flavors in front of me.

"Bet you ten bucks you won't try the root beer milk." Grey's deep voice rumbled in my ear, sending shivers down my spine and making me jump.

"What?" I whirled around to find Grey standing directly behind me. His basket was already overflowing with milks and cheeses.

"Root beer milk. It's better than you think." He waggled his eyebrows and held up a light-brown carton of milk.

"At this point, almost anything would be better than what I think of root beer milk. It sounds disgusting." I took a step back, shaking my head as he continued to offer me the carton.

Was the milk fizzy like root beer? How would someone combine soda and dairy outside of a root beer float? My questions were endless, but I wasn't curious enough to find the answers. I'd learned a long time ago it was better to play things safe, even in simple decisions like trying new foods.

"Trust me, it's good."

"I'd much rather get something safe like chocolate. Or maybe I'll branch out to cookies 'n cream." I reached for one of the more familiar flavors.

Grey quirked that infuriating eyebrow once more. I wanted to shave it off. "Chicken."

"Excuse me?" I said with surprise. I didn't want to try a new milk flavor. How did that make me a chicken?

"You're afraid of a little carton of milk. *Bock, bock.* Chicken." Grey flapped his arm not holding the basket like a bird wing, emphasizing his point.

Suddenly my mind was filled with all the times I hadn't tried something. I hadn't gone to friends' birthday parties because I knew mom couldn't drive me and make it to work on time. I hadn't tried out for the school play because Mom didn't have the money to pay for costumes. I hadn't interviewed for a new job because the change in hours and location were inconvenient for Lyle. I almost hadn't come on this trip because it was so far outside my comfort zone. Was this what I wanted, a life defined by the things I didn't do or say?

I bit my tongue for a moment before grabbing the carton of root beer milk out of his hand and adding it to his basket. "Fine, but you're buying it, and if it's gross, you owe me a chocolate milk too."

"You might be surprised! Besides, 'not all who wander are lost.'" Grey grinned and headed to the cash register to check out.

"That still makes no sense!" I called after his retreating back, shaking my head and walking to the exit, careful to erase the smile from my face before Grey could see.

I stood by the door, arms crossed over my chest as I waited for Grey, who was taking his time chatting to the elderly cashier ringing up his purchases. I was irked that I'd let Grey get to me, doubts already filling my mind as I waited. Yes, I was afraid to try a weird milk flavor. What if it was gross and I had that aftertaste stuck in my mouth the rest of the drive? In my mind, root beer and milk were two things that had no business being combined. At least I had the gas station Pepsi to dispel the flavor if needed.

I followed Grey to his car, trying to ignore the aroma of farm that seemed to linger in the air everywhere in Logan. He had several bags filled with food, and it took him a minute to find my root beer milk. He handed me the unassuming light-brown carton with a mug icon on the front before unlocking the SUV and stashing his bags inside, slipping the cheese into a small cooler I hadn't realized was in his trunk.

"You have to drink the whole thing, and then I'll give you this." He held up a second carton, this one darker brown with a chocolate bar on the front.

"Fine, but that means we're going to be making another bathroom stop sooner than planned."

"I'm not in a hurry. You?" Grey stood with his hands on his hips, almost challenging me to contradict him.

Technically, I was in a hurry, and it had nothing to do with not wanting to miss Tory's birthday. It would still be her special day, even if we got there after dark. Personally, I did not want to be in the car dodging animals on the road when night fell, but Grey didn't need to know that. No one but Mallory and Chloe knew just how much driving at night, especially in the mountains, freaked me out, and I planned to keep it that way.

Instead of answering, I took the first carton of milk and shook it, assuming it needed the flavoring mixed in. Pulling open the tab on top, I raised the carton to my lips and hesitated just a moment more before taking my first tentative swallow. Flavor exploded across my tongue, reminding me of childhood summers. I paused, processing the flavor. It was surprising: creamy and rich and far better than I anticipated.

"It tastes like a melted root beer float," I said, surprised at how much I enjoyed it.

"Right?" A grin stole across Grey's face, the smile perhaps the biggest he'd given me since we'd started this drive. It stole my breath for just a moment as I took in the pure, simple joy on his face. "It's basically magic in a milk carton."

I quickly finished my carton, eyeing the front of the store. "I might need a few more of those." I admitted begrudgingly. "Though we also need to get on the road..." I trailed off, torn.

Grey waved to the store. "Be my guest. I'll wait here."

I hesitated only a moment before walking back into the store, this time with my own basket. I grabbed a mix of milk flavors: root beer, cookies 'n cream, strawberry, and orange. If being brave had worked out well once, I hoped it would prove worthwhile again. On a whim, I threw in a bag of cheese curds.

When I got back to the car, Grey was in the front seat on his phone, brows pinched, a look of concern on his face as he typed out a response.

"Everything okay?" I asked as I stashed my milk in the back next to his bags and then climbed into the front seat, cheese curds in hand, and kicked off my shoes.

"Yep. Just a question from my brother." He deposited his phone in the cupholder, making sure the screen was locked first.

"Well, in that case, I have snacks for the next leg of the journey." I held up the bag of cheese curds, feeling weird offering a bag full of cheese as a road trip snack.

"Yes! These are seriously the best. Have you ever had them?" Grey took the bag and opened it, offering me first dibs on the assortment of oddly shaped orange pieces.

"No. I thought cheese only came shredded, blocked, or sliced." I grabbed one of the smaller pieces and began to chew. A slight squeaking sound filled my ears, and I froze, the sound stopping too. As soon as I started chewing again, the sound returned, and I couldn't fight back a smile of surprise. "It makes noise!"

Grey laughed, dispelling the last lingering hints of worry from his face and settling the bag of cheese on the center console before pulling onto the road. "Squeaky cheese, it's a thing. And it means these are fresh. Try eating them in a day or two and the squeak will be gone."

"That's crazy. I feel like this is something from a cartoon, not real life." I could easily picture this featuring in an episode of *Scooby-Doo*.

"Sometimes fact is crazier than fiction." Grey popped a piece of cheese into his mouth, and I could hear it squeak from across the car.

A crumb from the cheese had dropped into his beard, a bright orange dot contrasting with the dark strands. While his beard didn't qualify for mountain man status, it was long enough to hold the cheese hostage.

"You've got a piece of cheese in your beard." I gestured towards his chin, not sure what the etiquette was for helping someone remove beard food.

"How do you know I'm not saving it for later?" Grey raised an eyebrow before reaching up in an attempt to brush the crumb from his beard. He missed completely.

"It's a little more to the right."

He made another attempt, managing to move the crumb closer to his mouth.

"Here. Let me."

I reached over and brushed at his beard, knocking the crumb free. His beard was softer than I'd imagined, and the warmth of his breath made my skin tingle. I quickly drew my hand back, startled by how much I liked the sensation of touching him.

"Got it." My voice came out breathy, my cheeks heating.

Grey gave me a knowing smile.

"Thanks for the help—and the cheese curds." He grabbed another curd, popping it into his mouth.

Grey drove through Logan, using his phone to navigate as we started back on our trip, taking an alternative route instead of backtracking down the canyon towards the freeway. Everything was back on schedule and going according to plan. I'd even convinced Grey to let me control the music, connecting my phone to his car's speakers through Bluetooth, a luxury I only dreamed of when driving Jovi.

I was attempting to come up with more questions to ask Grey when a light appeared on his dashboard and the car pulled to the right, an unexpected flapping sound starting.

"Uh-oh," Grey mumbled, pulling into a nearby gas station parking lot.

"What do you mean 'uh-oh?' We don't have time for 'uh-oh,' not if we're going to make it to the cabin before dark." I could hear the squeak of panic in my own voice and hated it. But I was unable to control it as memories of the phone call following my mom's accident filled my mind. I'd had no idea a deer could do so much damage.

Grey put the car in park and turned to me, regret in his expression, and my stomach plummeted. This wasn't good.

"We're about to test my limited car repair knowledge and see if I remember how to change a flat tire."

Chapter Five

Hours later, I sat in the waiting room of a tire shop, waiting for Grey to finish talking to the worker at the counter so he could fill me in. We'd managed to change the tire, thanks to a couple of YouTube videos and a friendly trucker who stopped at the gas station. He was more than happy to point out the cause for our delay: a large nail protruding from the tire, most likely picked up at our last stop. My role in the effort had been to remove all our luggage from the trunk and stack it in the backseat, careful not to squish our cartons of milk. Thanks to the summer heat, I worked up quite a sweat, which now resulted in a chill-inducing damp shirt as I sat in the overly air-conditioned building, my backpack at my feet.

Red vinyl seats and pictures of tires and cars filled the tire shop, the smell of rubber adding to my headache. It had been building since we'd discovered the flat tire, but I'd been unable to find any pain killers in my backpack. I clutched my now half-finished Pepsi like a lifeline, hoping the caffeine would kick in soon. I sat next to one of the large windows filling one wall of the shop, cars passing on the street outside, trying not to think of the minutes ticking away as we waited.

I gave a sympathetic smile to a mom sitting in the corner, trying to keep her three little ones entertained. A man on a laptop worked in a chair not far from me, typing furiously. I debated pulling out my book from my backpack but prayed we wouldn't be here long enough for me to need entertainment beyond what my phone could provide. Too bad spontaneous tire shop yoga was probably frowned upon. Otherwise, I'd be stretching out, attempting to alleviate some of the tension in my neck and shoulders that had been building since we'd discovered the flat tire.

My phone started ringing, and I answered it as soon as Tory's name filled my screen. I'd forgotten to call with news of our latest delay.

"Where are you guys?" Tory asked, concern lacing her tone. In the background I could hear Trent yelling something unintelligible, along with the sounds of a video game. "I know you got a late start, but you've got to be getting close."

"About that...remember our detour to buy cheese? Well, somewhere along the way Grey picked up a nail in one of his tires, and now we're stuck in Logan waiting on repairs."

I waited for Tory's reaction as I watched Grey gesturing to the worker, frustration clear in his stiff shoulders and furrowed forehead. It took Tory a moment to speak. The sounds of shifting and then a door closing were followed by silence, hinting that she'd left the cabin basement in order to have this conversation.

"So you're stranded in Logan?"

"Yep, and based on Grey's facial expressions, I don't think we're getting out of here any time soon. I'm so sorry, Tory! We wanted to be there for your actual birthday, but I don't know if it's going to happen." My eyebrows scrunched, worry lacing my tone as I gave a play-by-play of the exchange.

The worker Grey had been talking to, a blond guy who looked like he was still in high school, disappeared into the garage portion of the shop, leaving Grey alone at the counter. Grey hesitated for a moment before storming over to where I sat, slumping into the chair next to me. The vinyl squeaked as he settled in and scrubbed a hand down his face, fatigue etched into his features.

"Let me put you on speaker so you can hear the latest," I said, already dreading what Grey had to say. I held the phone between Grey and me, biting my lip as I waited for his news.

Grey leaned close to me, and I tried not to notice his musky smell. It provided a nice break from the odors of the tire shop, and I wanted to drink it in, allowing the scent to erase my headache and transport me away from here.

"They can't patch the tire, and based on the wear on my other tires, they're recommending I replace all four. However, they don't have the tires in stock, and the closest shop with enough of the tires I need is in Salt Lake City. They can have someone drive them up, but they won't get here until tomorrow at the earliest." Grey's hair and beard stuck up in odd directions from where he'd been running his fingers through it. It was the first time I'd seen his calm demeanor shaken this entire trip, and it did little to ease the anxiety I'd been fighting since we'd pulled into the gas station parking lot.

"But what are we supposed to do until tomorrow? Tory's birthday is today. I guess we could find a hotel..." I trailed off, trying not to think of my savings account. I had not budgeted for an impromptu stay in Logan. "Or maybe one of my roommates can come pick us up, take us home."

If that happened, I would not be returning on the trip. I'd stay home, go back to work, and spend my evenings avoiding social media and doing more yoga than was probably advisable. One of my instructors had asked if I could sub for her one day this week. I'd never taught a class before, but maybe I'd be brave and give it a try.

Based on the number of notification bubbles on my work messaging app, my coworkers wouldn't be disappointed to hear my vacation had been cut short. It had taken all my self-control not to open the app while we sat in the tire shop waiting for news.

"Don't worry about my birthday. We'll more than celebrate when you get here," Tory reassured.

"You guys could stay with my grandparents in Hyrum," she suggested after a pause. Her grandparents lived a short distance away in one of the smaller towns in Cache Valley.

I immediately shook my head, though Tory couldn't see me. "We wouldn't want to inconvenience them. They'd have to come pick us up and—"

"They'd love it, and you know it." Tory cut me off. "You remember how excited they were every time we visited during college."

I pictured Dot and Hank and the little white house Tory and I had escaped to whenever finals and boy stress had gotten to be too much. It was cozy, with two small spare rooms barely big enough to qualify as bedrooms, but at least it was clean and free. Not to mention Dot was one of the best cooks I'd ever met. My mouth watered as I thought about the cookies she always seemed to be baking. Also, her pancake breakfasts were rock-ballad-worthy.

I looked at Grey, who shrugged as if to say, "What do we have to lose?"

I bit my lip before nodding. "Fine, but only if you're sure they'll be okay with it."

"They'll be thrilled! It's been way too long since grandkids came to stay with them. You haven't met my grandparents yet, Grey, but Grammy will probably stuff you full of baked goods while Gramps tells you stories about me as a kid, complete with embarrassing photos. I'll call them now." Tory hung up without saying goodbye, leaving us alone to process our change in plans.

Everyone else in the shop remained quietly occupied as Grey and I sat in strained silence. Easy listening music played from speakers overhead, just loud enough to be heard but too quiet to make out the lyrics.

"I'm sorry about the delay. If we hadn't stopped..." He slumped deeper into his seat and stared at the floor in complete dejection.

I leaned my head back, the chair squeaking as I shifted in my seat. I stared up at the fluorescent lights, processing our situation. I shouldn't blame Grey for our current predicament. It could have happened to anyone. But that knowledge didn't fully stop the stress bubbling in my gut.

I took a breath and tried to release the tension between my shoulder blades, turning to look at Grey, who was hunched over, elbows on his knees, head resting in his hands as he stared dejectedly at the floor.

It's not his fault, I reiterated to myself, sad to see such a happy, energetic guy worn down by something outside our control. I needed to shift my focus. There was nothing we could do, and there were some positives in the situation.

For starters, we wouldn't be driving on winding mountain roads at night. And we'd still get to visit the cabin, just a day later than planned. While I was sad to miss Tory's actual birthday, I was certain she'd pack the remaining days of our vacation full of activities. Not to mention, I'd get to see Hank and Dot again, two of the most delightful humans in the world. We'd be okay. It was a change in plans, but I could pivot. Probably.

"You could have run over a nail literally anywhere. It could have happened at the burger place or the gas station or on the freeway. We're just guessing it came from the cheese shop. It's not your fault." I worked to keep my tone reassuring, hoping to alleviate some of his frustration.

He turned to face me without sitting up, his elbows still on his knees. "True, but I'm still sorry. I'm sure spending the night in Hyrum was not high on your priority list when you planned this trip."

I shrugged, trying to let go of my timeline once again. This trip was proving to be an unwanted lesson in flexibility. "Maybe not, but there's nothing we can do about it now."

Conversation faded between us, and I scrambled to think of something else to add. A snort escaped at the first thought that came to mind. Grey quirked an eyebrow, waiting for me to explain the sound.

"Believe it or not, this isn't the worst trip delay I've ever experienced." My lips tipped up in a slight smile as I became lost in memory. "My mom is spontaneous, to the point of it being problematic sometimes when I was growing up. She loaded me into the car one evening with little warning when I was probably ten, talking about visiting the Grand Canyon. We lived in California, so the drive was going to take half a day or longer."

I trailed off, still amazed I didn't have more stories like this when I thought about my mom and her tendency to act first and think later.

"What happened?" Grey straightened, watching the memories play across my face in what was probably a kaleidoscope of expressions.

"We made it about an hour into the drive before we ran out of gas. Mom had to push the car the last few yards to the gas pump." I shook my head, my smile more one of sadness now than fondness. "She'd forgotten to fill up before we left. When we reached the pump, she had just enough money to get us home. Don't ask me how she thought we were going to make it to the Grand Canyon."

I gave a shrug, downplaying the memory as something simply humorous rather than one of countless stories about how Mom's lack of planning bit us. Understanding and compassion filled Grey's expression, a combination I wasn't prepared to navigate.

"Anyway," I rushed to change the topic, ready to escape the trip down memory lane, "if we're being honest, going on this trip wasn't high on my list of priorities. Tory had to pull out all the friend guilt to get me to come. If it wasn't her birthday trip, I probably would have backed out long before you showed up on my doorstep."

"My dad used to say the best stories start where the best laid plans fall apart." A small, sad smile tipped the corners of Grey's mouth. "I can't count the number of times he was right about that. Although spontaneous trips to the Grand Canyon might have pushed the limits on that a bit."

He wasn't wrong. The memory wasn't entirely painful. Mom had let me pick out treats from the gas station, and we'd spent the drive home eating candy bars and laughing about our misadventure. At one point, Mom had even stopped at a park well past dark, grabbing a blanket from the car and spreading it in the grass. We'd laid there, attempting to star gaze, despite light pollution, until I could barely keep my eyes open.

Before I could respond, my phone vibrated with an incoming text. I held it up so Grey could see Tory's message too.

TORY: *My grandparents can't wait for you to come stay. Gramps is already on his way to pick you up!*

"I guess that settles it. I hope Dot and Hank like cheese curds." I attempted to joke, and Grey cracked a half-hearted smile as we settled in to wait for our ride.

Chapter Six

LESS THAN AN HOUR later, Grey and I found ourselves stuffed into the cab of Hank's truck, an old pick-up that looked to be a relative of my own car, Jovi. I sat squeezed in the middle, doing my best to take up as little space as possible on the cracked upholstery. Grey sat pressed against the door like he was ready to bolt from the car at the first opportunity. Unfortunately, the cab was too small for us to keep from touching, and our thighs pressed together as we rode, every bump and jostle pushing us closer together. It was also too small for me to take my shoes off, though my toes itched to be free.

"Don't worry," Hank said with a pat on my knee as we left Logan behind, the busy streets transitioning to fields. "That tire shop does good work. They'll get you back on the road first thing tomorrow."

Hank was a tall, thin man wearing a faded green baseball cap and blue overalls. His white beard, a new feature since the last time I'd seen him, would have made Santa Claus proud. He drove slowly along the roads to Hyrum, not seeming to notice the number of cars passing us. Instead, he turned up the volume on a local radio station, country music crackling from the speakers. We passed fields and houses, the space a breath of fresh air after navigating the congestion of the Wasatch front on the freeway.

"Dot is beyond thrilled to have the two of you staying with us. You would think it was Thanksgiving or Christmas with how she's rambling on. She's running around like we've never had guests before." Hank gave an exasperated shake of his head, but the grin tipping up his lips hinted at his own excitement as we turned onto Hank and Dot's street.

It was a quiet, tree-lined road with few houses, fields creating distance between each home and its nearest neighbor.

"We're just grateful you'd open your home to us," Grey said.

We pulled up in front of Hank's house, and I was immediately hit with a flood of memories. My own grandparents, while loving, lived states away and only visited for holidays and big life events. Tory had grown up an hour away from her grandparents, frequently taking weekend trips to visit them and help on the farm. Even when she'd moved to college, she'd made time to visit Hank and Dot. It was on those trips that I'd come to see how a family could be. Hours spent working, laughing, and teasing resulted in a community and closeness I could only dream of. Even now, with my much younger half-sisters, I sensed my mom getting that type of family. Unfortunately, now that I lived in Utah and they were still in California, the closeness didn't include me. My childhood memories would forever be a mix of loneliness and anxiety peppered with impulsive fun, nothing like the happy, steady consistency of so many of my friends' families.

One of the reasons Emily and I had become such close friends was because of our similar family situations. She'd grown up with a single—though much less impulsive—mom. She'd understood my struggles in a way no one else had, which had made losing her friendship even more difficult.

Pushing aside wishes for what could have been, I followed Grey out of the truck and to the large front porch lined with a flower garden full of bright blue and purple blooms. Dot stood next to two wooden rocking chairs on the porch, arms flung open in greeting, a giant smile emphasizing the wrinkles lining her face.

"Audrey." She wrapped me in a firm hug, her head barely reaching my shoulder. "It's been a long time. How are you, my dear?"

I returned the embrace, emotion gathering in my throat at the contact. I could feel the anxiety in my chest ease the slightest bit as I breathed in her familiar vanilla scent. It was like she'd been baking and decided to dab the spice behind her ears before putting the bottle away.

I cleared my throat before speaking, not wanting my emotions to show. "I'm good, Dot. Thank you for letting us stay here."

Dot waved a hand, dismissing my gratitude. "It's what family does. Now, introduce me to your man."

"Oh, we're not—"

"I'm not her—"

Grey and I spoke over each other, racing to get out the words and clarify Dot's confusion.

"Tory mentioned him when she called. Told me all about how you'd found a man who pushes your buttons and helps you get out of your comfort zone. I'm so glad! You've been single for too long. That Lyle boy was an idiot." Dot rambled on, seeming oblivious to my protests—and Grey's. Instead, she wrapped Grey in a hug, her head just reaching his chest.

From her permed short white hair to her knit purple cardigan and small, stooped frame, Dot radiated homey and friendly, which made popping her bubble difficult.

"Dot, I don't know what Tory told you, but Grey and I aren't dating." I gestured vaguely between us. "We're..." I wasn't really sure how to describe what we were. Acquaintances? Friends? Road trip buddies?

Dot took only a moment to process the information before shaking her head, her grin growing wider. "Really? This old brain of mine struggles sometimes. I must have misunderstood Tory when she called."

Grey quirked an eyebrow. "If you could jump to that level of misunderstanding, it makes me wonder what Tory said."

"Oh, now that you ask, I don't remember. Sometimes it's a miracle I remember anything at all. Don't get old, it messes up everything." Dot waved away the question, but I didn't believe her for a minute. Dot was sharper than women half her age. Tory had said something that led her to think we were dating, but knowing Dot, she'd never break the confidence and tell us. "I'm sorry about your car, but I'm grateful for the company. I made cookies, and there's no way Hank and I could eat them all."

Dot led us into the kitchen, where the aroma of baked goods and several wire racks filled with peanut butter cookies greeted us. The kitchen looked exactly as I remembered: off-white Formica countertops, dated appliances, and faded yellow wallpaper. Yet, despite its clear age, the kitchen was cozy and well-cared for. It was the kind of kitchen that had seen decades of homemade bread and canned peaches.

"Speak for yourself, woman. I could eat all of these, no problem," Hank joked, coming up behind Dot to wrap his arms around her waist and plop a kiss on top of her head.

"Oh you," Dot said as she broke out of his embrace and moved towards the avocado-green fridge. "Grab yourselves a cookie or two. Do you want milk?"

"I'm good with just a cookie, thank you," Grey said, grabbing one and giving me a wink. "But maybe Audrey wants some. Especially if it's root beer flavored."

I rolled my eyes, pretending Grey's familiar comment didn't faze me, though a small smile tipped the corner of my lips.

Dot's face pinched in confusion as she pulled the jug of milk from the fridge and held it up for me. "I don't know about root beer milk, but I've got two percent."

"I'm good, thank you." I shook my head, my stomach too tied in knots to enjoy food at the moment. My body and brain had yet to fully let go of the nerves from our trip so far. I was struggling to let go of my timeline and embrace the change in plans. Being here in this familiar setting with Dot and Hank should help my nerves settle soon. "I don't want to spoil dinner."

Dot returned the milk to the fridge with a nod. "I expect both of you to eat at least two cookies after dinner. Life's too short not to enjoy dessert."

"Don't worry, I'm sure they'll eat a dozen—or more. Who can say no to your cookies?" Hank asked, carrying a stack of white plates to the table and setting them down with a gentle clank. Dot's cookies really were the best.

I hadn't noticed that two pizza boxes and a salad already sat on the worn wooden table.

"We didn't mean to interrupt your dinner," I stammered, realizing anew just how much we must have inconvenienced this sweet couple.

"You didn't. I picked up the pizza while Hank got you. We divided and conquered!" Dot said as she carried over glasses and a pitcher of water, the ice clinking against the glass. "Though, I couldn't help but order two kinds. We used to do it to keep picky eaters happy, and old habits die hard."

She waved for Grey and me to take a seat, and we settled into chairs next to each other, across from Dot and Hank. The old chairs creaked as we sat, the worn, striped cushions doing little to pad our seats.

Hank reached for the closest box, serving himself a slice before passing it to me. At the familiar aroma of pizza, the knot of anxiety that had been sitting in my stomach since we'd discovered the flat tire dissipated and my stomach growled as I grabbed a slice of pepperoni pizza. Everyone served themselves, the only sound the noises that accompanied dishing up and eating food.

"Grey," Dot said, "tell us about yourself. It's not every day we get to play host to a handsome young man, particularly one who's friends with our Audrey. We think of her as another granddaughter, you know."

I paused my eating, letting her kind words wash over me.

With how infrequently I'd visited them growing up, I doubted my own grandparents would have exhibited this level of curiosity in Grey. The one time I'd taken Lyle to visit, they'd spent the time asking me about my mom and half-sisters, only caring to learn the basics about Lyle when I'd mentioned how long we'd been dating.

When my mom had gotten pregnant with me, my grandparents had stepped in to help as much as they could, but they'd had other children to worry about, their situation already difficult enough to make ends meet. It didn't help that my mom's independent streak had often caused her to clash with her parents as she'd insisted she could do things on her own instead of accepting their help, which had often come with strings attached. This meant my grandparents had quickly become infrequent figures in my life, the bulk of their visits happening over holidays because that was how often my mom could handle being around them.

Dot's words left me feeling warm and loved, though I struggled knowing how to react. I wanted to wrap Dot in a hug and hold on tight, but I also knew she wasn't *my* grandma. While she spoke the words, did she really mean them?

"What would you like to know?" Grey asked, setting down his slice of pizza to give Dot his full attention.

"Why aren't you dating Audrey?" Dot asked, brow quirked, a look of complete innocence filling her face.

I inhaled sharply at Dot's question, sending water down the wrong tube and triggering a coughing fit. Grey patted me on the back as I sputtered, trying to catch my breath.

"You okay there, honey?" Hank looked at me with concern.

I nodded, my eyes watering.

"That's a good man you've got there, Audrey. Watching out for you like my Hank does for me." Dot's eyes fairly sparkled as she looked back and forth between Grey and me.

"Oh, he's not...we're just..." I broke off, not sure how to explain my relationship with Grey. Acquaintance felt like the wrong word, but could I claim him as a friend? We really didn't know each other that well, but at the same time friend felt insufficient for describing what we were. Was there a word for bonding with someone while on a road trip on which all my plans had to be thrown out the window?

"I do my best to watch out for my friends," Grey said, coming to my rescue. He gave my hand a reassuring squeeze, underscoring his words.

While the contact was brief, it caused warmth to fill my chest. I wanted to grab his hand again and twine my fingers with his. There was something grounding about Grey's touch. I wondered if I sank into it, made it a more regular occurrence in my life, if it would chase away my worries and help me let go more.

I turned towards Grey, my eyes catching on his, and I paused at the genuine kindness I saw in their depths.

"You two are too cute!" Dot said, bringing us back to the moment. "Are you sure you're not dating?"

I reached for my water, using the drink to distract me from the confusing mix of emotions I was experiencing. While I felt some humor and lingering nerves, I'd also felt a zing of attraction and perhaps something even more as I'd looked at Grey. It had been a long time since a man had looked out for my needs, and the sensation was both foreign and welcome.

"We just met this morning," I said, needing a change of topic. "My car couldn't make the trip to Idaho and Grey agreed to give me a ride."

Dinner passed quickly after that, with Dot asking questions about our trip. We all pitched in to clean up dishes, despite Dot's insistence that she and Hank could handle it. Grey wouldn't hear of it, slipping on a floral apron and stationing himself at the sink to wash dishes. Something about a large bearded man wearing a frilly pink and yellow apron set my toes to curling and my lips to smiling.

I settled in next to Grey, drying the dishes and stacking them on the counter for Hank to put away. As I finished the last plate, I stifled a yawn, my early morning and the long hours of travel catching up with me.

"Let me show you two to your room. You must be tired." Dot paused, seeming to consider us for a moment. "The two of you don't mind sharing, do you? Since you're friends, I hope it won't be an issue."

My foggy brain barely registered her words, instead fast-forwarding to images of the comfy, if cramped, twin bed I'd slept in on my previous visits. It was covered in a dated, homemade quilt and a mountain of pillows. I couldn't wait to bury myself in it.

Dot bustled past us, leading Grey and me to a staircase I knew from experience branched off into a bathroom and two tiny bedrooms barely big enough for twin beds. We paused near the front door to grab our bags and then headed down the narrow hallway. The worn green carpet brushed my toes as I walked, and I examined the family photos on the walls as we passed. I recognized several of the faces, including Tory and her parents and siblings. The pictures had been updated since my last visit, with a few new faces added to the mix.

"Thankfully, we just got a new bed for the spare room. Otherwise, the two of you would be sleeping in the little twin beds our girls used as kids."

Dot continued talking, gesturing to the different pictures we passed and explaining who occupied the various photos that filled her home. But my mind had snagged on one detail: the word *bed*, as in singular. It seemed odd that Dot would only replace one bed when I considered that the beds Tory and I slept in on our previous visits had probably been equally old and worn. Maybe Dot and Hank were staggering the expenses, redoing one room and then the other in their tiny farmhouse. I hoped they'd save the kitchen for last. There was something quaint and welcoming about the dated room.

When we reached the end of the hall, I paused in confusion. I clearly remembered there being three doors: two that led to separate bedrooms and a third leading to the bathroom. Instead, only two doors greeted us.

"It cost a pretty penny, but the renovation was worth it, in my opinion. Making a bigger bedroom that could fit a couple, as opposed to two tiny bedrooms, just made sense. I know it sounds silly, getting rid of a bedroom, but both my girls have already come to visit for multiple days with their husbands, which never used to happen when we only had the tiny bedrooms."

My mind whirled as I tried to digest what Dot was saying. Bedroom. As in singular. Dot's comment about sharing now made perfect sense. There was one room to sleep in, which meant one bed for Grey and me to share. While I liked Grey and we got on well enough, we were far from any relationship status that would make sharing a bed comfortable or welcome. I wanted to tell Dot I'd sleep on the tiny couch in the front room—anything to avoid sharing a room—but the words were trapped in my throat.

Dot flung open the spare room door like a game show host revealing the grand prize. The room on the other side was far from spacious, though it did boast more room than the previous spare rooms. Not that we could really tell because filling nearly the entire room was a giant bed covered in more pillows, lace, and frills than I'd ever seen in a single space. I nearly choked again as I took in the pink monstrosity, the biggest bed I'd ever seen before in my life. The strap of my duffle slid off my shoulder, underscoring my surprise as the bag hit the floor with a thud.

"We decided to splurge and get a California king. We figured it would encourage the girls and their husbands to visit more often if they knew we had a comfortable bed waiting." Dot fairly glowed with pride and excitement as my hopes for a restful night disappeared like dust in the wind.

Chapter Seven

I COULD ONLY STARE, my chest tightening as I took in the bedroom. The bed and a single dresser with a lamp on top were the only pieces of furniture in the room, and I was unsure how the dresser drawers could possibly open, crammed into the space as it was with the bed. Narrow strips of exposed carpet on two sides of the bed provided the only walking space.

Grey stepped into the room, pressing against the pink striped wallpaper to fit. "It's a... beautiful bed." He cleared his throat, doing his best to look at anything besides the bed dominating the room.

I snorted and covered it with a cough as I followed Grey into the room, placing my bag and backpack on the bed and trying to ignore the dread pooling in my stomach. We both hovered in the doorway, only a few inches separating us as we continued to stare at the bed. "Beautiful" was not the word I would have used. It looked like a Victorian child's dreams had thrown up.

"I'm glad you love it! We even added a door into the bathroom to make things more comfortable." Dot gestured to a door hidden in the corner that I'd missed upon first inspection. "I know it's not ideal, the two of you sharing a room, but it's what we have. The couch in the front room is too small and lumpy for anyone to sleep on, unless it's Hank after a fight."

She gave us a mischievous smile before stepping back into the hall.

"If you two need anything, just holler. And don't worry, the walls are thick." Dot gave an exaggerated wink and closed the door behind her with a click.

I lost it, nervous laughter bubbling out as soon as the door was closed. I was one setback or unexpected twist away from losing my sanity completely. Also, if Dot knew we were just friends, what was that last comment?

"What does she think we're going to do? Even if we did want to get intimate, there's no way we could find each other in all those pillows." My voice came out high-pitched with a slight edge as I gestured to the bed. Bed *singular*, something I kept repeating to myself as I tried to find a solution for our current predicament.

"I'm sure we could figure it out, if we really wanted to," Grey said, his eyebrows dancing suggestively.

"Watch it, Fabio, or you'll find yourself smothered by one of these pillows." I picked up a square pillow completely covered in lace and brandished it towards him.

Grey fought back a grin as he held up both hands and backed up the couple of inches he could manage in the tight space. "So, you're going to murder me. Glad we cleared that up."

"Orange isn't really my color." I shrugged, as if that was the only reason not to kill another human being.

My laughter faded as I looked around the room, my shoulders tense as I considered how to handle the situation. "There's only one bed."

No matter how many times I said or thought it, it didn't get any better. In fact, it got worse. Much worse as I considered sharing a bed with Grey, who probably was a sleep-talker or sleep-snuggler. Was that a thing? Lyle definitely hadn't been a snuggler, and he was my only point of reference in that regard.

Maybe I really could sleep on the floor. I'd pick a strip of carpet that didn't block Grey's access to the bathroom, and we'd be fine. I probably wouldn't get much rest, but who needed sleep anyway? I could sleep in the car tomorrow, assuming I could convince Grey to play the quiet game.

Grey nodded. "I think we've established the singular bed. It honestly might be the biggest bed ever made. I can't imagine how they got it in here."

"But there are two of us."

"Right again. I think we can add math whiz to your list of hobbies."

I ignored the jab, my thoughts still focused on the problem in front of us.

"We can't both sleep in the bed. I'm not...we're not..."

I gestured vaguely between the two of us, hoping Grey would pick up on what I couldn't quite find the words to say. Would Hank and Dot notice if I slept on the couch? I could set an alarm to make sure I was up and ready before they woke up. Though, if Hank still kept farm hours, I might have to sleep in my clothes for tomorrow so he wouldn't guess I spent the entire night on the couch.

Grey held up a hand, stopping my awkward stammering. "We're adults. I think we can share a bed and keep our hands to ourselves. Besides"—he gestured to the narrow strips of carpet we stood on—"I think we can both agree sleeping on the floor is not an option, and after

Dot's glowing description of the couch, I wouldn't make a pet dog sleep there."

I bit my lip, recognizing the truth of his words as he shot down each solution I'd thought of. He was right, but I didn't have to like it.

"If it makes you feel better, that bed is big enough an entire scout troop could spread out and not touch. I think we'll be okay sharing." Grey watched me as he spoke, a smile hovering on his lips. "I'll even build a pillow wall if you promise not to smother me with it."

"Fine, but just know if you try anything, all bets are off. I might even change my mind about how I look in orange. And I don't care if you're a sleep-snuggler, I have a pillow and I know how to use it." I poked a finger into his chest to underscore my point. It sent a spark of warmth up my arm, and I immediately drew back my hand. The attraction that had been building between us all day surfaced again, sending heat into my cheeks. It had been a long time since I'd felt this way. I wasn't quite sure what to do with the feeling, especially in light of having to share the bed with this man, whom I found equal parts attractive and annoying.

"Sleep-snuggler? Is that a thing?" Grey raised an eyebrow at me, his voice clearly filled with humor.

I picked up a bigger pillow, this one covered in pink satin, and brandished it at him threateningly.

"Fair enough," Grey said, holding his hands up in surrender. "Want to take the bathroom first?"

I nodded and grabbed my stuff, struggling past the bed and managing to get into the bathroom. The space was tight, with just enough room for the sink, toilet, and standup shower. The clean lines and modern fixtures testified that the bedroom wasn't the only room in the house to have received a facelift since my last visit.

I quickly washed my face, brushed my hair, and changed into pajamas: a worn teal lounge suit I'd owned for years. I hesitated a moment before stepping out of the bathroom. Except for my roommates, I never let anyone see me without makeup. It had started as a hobby, one of the many my mom had experimented with in her constant quest for a career. From there it had grown into a way to cover my insecurities until it had become a form of armor. It had shielded me from Lyle's comments about my flaws and from setbacks at work. But tonight, letting Grey see me without it couldn't be helped.

I ducked into the room, grateful to find Grey had turned off the overhead light and flipped on the standing lamp tucked against one side of the bed. He'd also built the promised pillow wall and piled the remaining pillows on the floor, making an obstacle course for anyone needing to use the facilities.

"You done?" Grey asked, grabbing his bag and moving to squeeze past me into the bathroom.

"Yep. Be careful not to get lost in all that extra space," I quipped, settling my bags on the dresser and keeping my face turned away from Grey until I heard the door close, the lock clicking into place.

I clambered over the wall of pillows and settled under the covers, shifting to get comfortable. I stared up at the ceiling, the anxiety of sharing a bed with Grey chasing away the exhaustion that had been settling into my bones before Dot had revealed the bedroom situation. The fact that I was sharing a bed with Grey after having sworn off dating seemed to prove the universe had a messed-up sense of humor.

This trip seemed destined to shine a bright spotlight on all my flaws and the reasons why I was better off alone, safely home in my comfort zone. If I survived this trip, I would swear off all travel for the rest of eternity.

The sounds of Grey shuffling around in the bathroom were faint, and I attempted to fall asleep, closing my eyes and hoping for oblivion. Maybe if I was asleep before he joined me in bed, it would make this whole situation easier.

Instead, my mind raced, refusing to shut down and allow me the rest I needed. At least we weren't driving to the cabin in the dark. However, we still had several hours to drive tomorrow, and who knew when the car would be ready to go?

What if we got trapped here all day?

My thoughts continued to spiral, counting everything that had already gone wrong and the many things that still could go wrong between now and the end of this trip.

I opened my eyes, staring at the ceiling, wishing not for the first time I had just stayed home. Though if I had, I would have missed out on root beer milk and Dot's peanut butter cookies. While those bright spots didn't fully make up for the disaster our trip was proving, they did calm the circling thoughts of frustration I was battling.

The bathroom door opened, and Grey stepped out, wearing blue flannel bottoms and a faded grey t-shirt. I closed my eyes, pretending to sleep, and felt the bed shift as Grey climbed under the covers. A moment later, I heard the click of the lamp switch, and the room was plunged into darkness, Grey's breathing the only sound.

I lay there, pretending to sleep for a moment, before opening my eyes and rolling onto my side to face Grey. Light from the moon seeping in through the curtains provided the only illumination. While I couldn't see Grey over the pillow wall, knowing I wasn't the only one navigating all our trip setbacks brought a sense of unexpected calm. Something I was extremely grateful for since the tight bedroom quarters meant yoga was out of the question.

"Hey, Grey," I whispered, not wanting to wake him but hoping he wasn't asleep yet.

"Hey, Audrey," he whispered back, the bed shifting as if he'd rolled over to face me too.

The dark provided a sense of anonymity that encouraged me to speak. The house outside the bedroom door was quiet, telling me Hank and Dot had likely gone to bed too. Or maybe that was the thick walls deceiving me.

"How are you so calm about the tire situation?" The words slipped out before I could second-guess myself. It wasn't even my car, and the what-ifs had been multiplying in my head since the moment we'd pulled over with a flat tire.

"Because I'm here with a beautiful, smart woman who keeps me on my toes and makes this adventure memorable." His voice rumbled into the quiet of the bedroom, and I wished I could see he face and read his expression.

"Be serious!" I said, considering throwing a pillow at him but not wanting to sacrifice even a piece of our pillow wall.

"Who said I wasn't serious?" Humor laced his tone. Then Grey paused, taking a moment to further consider my question.

"What other option is there? I could be angry and raging about how frustrating and unfair everything is, but that won't fix my car. Sometimes these things just happen. You can plan and prep for every worst-case scenario and yet, your car still breaks down. Your brother still badgers you to move to Oregon despite you having repeatedly told him no. You're still an hour late picking up your carpool buddy." He paused, and the silence felt heavy with anticipation. Finally, he spoke, his whisper feeling louder than a shout as the words registered. "Your mom still has a health scare and begs you to take her to the doctor even though you're 99% sure it's all in her head and the result of her anxiety."

I released a breath. "That's why you were late today?" My voice was whisper-soft as guilt settled in my stomach. I'd been so frustrated with Grey and his delays. I had no idea there was more to them than a guy who struggled with time management.

"It happens almost every time I go out of town. It didn't used to be this bad, but since my brother, Mason, moved out of state...she's gotten worse."

There was an ache in his voice that spoke to my heart. I wanted to comfort him, to provide some reassurance that he wasn't alone in navigating the challenges of anxiety, and yet, what did I know about comforting an anxious parent? My mom was spontaneous and without fear. I was the worrier in my family. I could only imagine what it was like worrying about the worrier.

Not knowing what else to do, I reached over the pillow wall, wanting to offer comfort but unsure if he would welcome it. His fingers brushed mine and I grabbed his hand, giving it a comforting squeeze and holding on. "That must be difficult."

"She refuses to see a therapist, so there's not a whole lot I can do. Just try to help her calm down and pray the people waiting on me understand. I haven't been on vacation in over a year. Not since Mason moved."

I flinched at his words, recognizing I'd been less than patient with his delay earlier. I currently felt about the size of an ant as I thought about how I could have been more patient and understanding. Instead, I'd lashed out at Grey and judged him for something completely out of his control.

We lay in silence for a moment, his hand in mine, as I thought about his description of his mom. Was that what my future held if I continued to let doubt and anxiety rule my life?

"Is there anything that helps her?" My voice came out raspy and breathless. I was desperate for something positive to hold onto.

I felt the bed bounce, as if Grey had shrugged. "Just time. If I can sit with her, listen to her fears, hold her hand, she usually calms down. It's part of why Mason moved. He couldn't handle it, the pressure of always being on call. Even now, he's mad I'm here. Mom keeps calling him, but there's only so much he can do from Oregon. But she won't call me while I'm driving, afraid I'll get into a wreck or something. I've texted her at all our stops, but that doesn't stop her from worrying."

Grey's expression as he'd read the texts on his phone earlier in our trip made more sense. He'd said the message was from his brother, a statement that had meant more than I could have guessed.

Questions filled my mind, none of which I felt comfortable asking.

Quiet settled around us, and yet, I felt desperate to keep the conversation going, to continue getting to know this side of Grey. The vulnerable, genuine side. Yet, I worried about saying the wrong thing, pushing this moment from tentatively comfortable to unbearably awkward.

After a moment, I settled on sharing what little I knew about coping. "I probably understand where your mom's coming from more than most. That's part of why I do yoga. I need something to control my anxiety."

"Makes sense."

I fell quiet, still holding Grey's hand, worried anything I said would be wrong, but knowing I needed to say something. The quiet between us felt loaded, filled with unspoken words.

"I'm sorry I was short with you earlier. I had no idea." The words were halting at first and then spilled out in a rush, as if racing to escape before I could change my mind. I held my breath, waiting for Grey's reaction. The words felt inadequate but₁ spoke volumes about how I felt. I was sorry for the situation, but more than that I was sorry for how I'd reacted and behaved when he'd first picked me up. I knew better than anyone how situations outside of one's control could change life's trajectory.

His voice was gruff when he spoke. "Apology accepted. Don't worry, though—it takes a lot to offend me."

Now was the perfect time to open up, to share with him about my mom's accident and how it influenced my reactions to him and this trip. But I couldn't do it, choosing to play it safe with my response. I owed him vulnerability and honesty but felt too raw to give it just now.

I squeezed his hand, trying to say more with the simple gesture than my words ever could.

"That's an admirable quality. I wish I was that way." Instead, I jumped to conclusions when rides were late and threw off my plans. Plans that, admittedly, I hadn't bothered sharing with anyone else.

"I've decided we're all just humans, doing our best to survive, trying to help as many people as we can along the way." Grey's deep voice carried with it a wisdom I envied.

"Wandering out there in the world and hoping we don't get lost?" I quipped back, remembering the saying from his shirt.

"Exactly. Where did you learn to be so wise?" Humor laced Grey's tone, and I felt it soothe something deep and jagged in me. Something I hadn't realized had been aching from the moment I'd first snapped at Grey, setting us on an unintended path of animosity.

"Some nerd who likes *The Lord of the Rings* taught me a thing or two when he drove me up a canyon on an unexpected adventure." I reached for my own sense of humor, needing to say something that would ease us back into familiar comfortable territory. I wasn't ready for more vulnerability tonight. If I wasn't careful, Grey would have me spilling all my secrets, including dark corners of self-doubt better left buried deep.

"Sounds like a smart guy. Think I'd like him?"

"I don't know. He has a weird obsession with talking about fast food."

Grey snorted a laugh, giving my hand a squeeze. I didn't pull away. Instead, I lay there, holding Grey's hand and listening to him breathe until exhaustion finally won out and silenced my swirling thoughts.

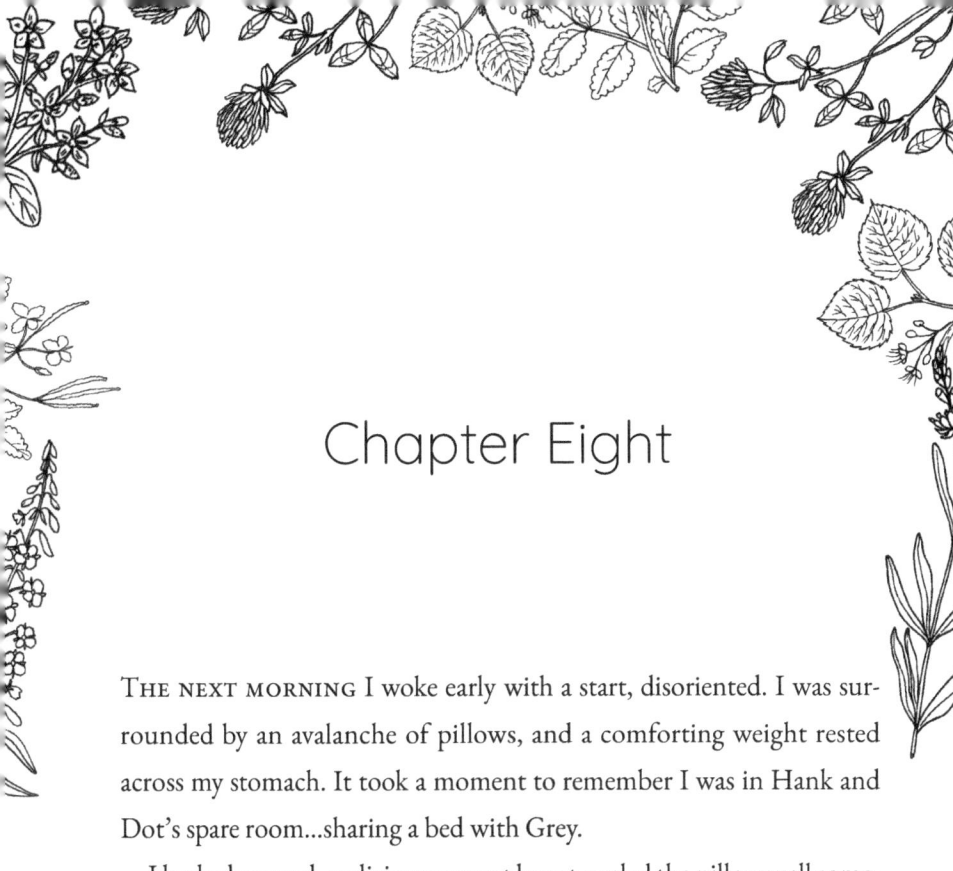

Chapter Eight

THE NEXT MORNING I woke early with a start, disoriented. I was surrounded by an avalanche of pillows, and a comforting weight rested across my stomach. It took a moment to remember I was in Hank and Dot's spare room…sharing a bed with Grey.

I looked around, realizing we must have toppled the pillow wall sometime during the night. While a few pillows still separated me from Grey, they hadn't been enough to stop his arm from settling on my waist.

While the sensation was new, it was also unexpectedly comforting knowing he was near. Unfortunately, biology and my worry about being seen without my makeup on meant I couldn't enjoy the sensation for long.

Moving carefully, I rolled away from Grey and attempted to tiptoe into the bathroom. If I moved quickly, I could get ready for the day before Grey saw the mess I was first thing in the morning. In the rush to get out of the room, I forgot about the mass of pillows we'd tossed on the floor. I stepped on a small, pink lacy pillow, losing my balance. I teetered for a moment before the pillow sent me toppling into the wall with a thud.

Grey jerked up, confused as he looked around the room. His beard and hair stuck up at odd angles, adding a layer of dishevelment that was oddly attractive. I stared at him for a moment, appreciating how his edges softened first thing in the morning, before I remembered my own bed head.

"Sorry!" I spun around and booked it to the bathroom, grabbing my bag from off the dresser, and slamming the door behind me. If my tripping into the wall hadn't done the trick, that sound would definitely have fully woken him up. I deposited my bag on the floor and stood there for a moment, taking in my appearance in the mirror and processing what had just happened as my breathing slowed.

Hopefully, Grey was groggy and disoriented enough from being startled awake that he hadn't noticed I resembled a wild animal first thing in the morning. I wasn't talking about a cute, fuzzy chipmunk. I looked more like a deranged, electrocuted squirrel, with creases from my pillow covering my face and my hair forming an odd sort of halo around my head. Far from the put-together exterior I tried to present to the world. After all, if I looked like I had my life together, no one would guess at the tumult of nerves and self-doubt I was constantly battling.

Working quickly, I changed into a pair of black leggings and a green tank top, perfect for a quick yoga routine before spending the rest of the day in the car. I then scraped my hair back into a messy bun and applied my makeup, knowing I'd have to repeat the process after I exercised and showered.

I checked my appearance in the mirror one more time before stepping back into the cramped spare bedroom. Grey was exactly where I'd left him, though he looked a little more awake.

"How'd you sleep?" Grey yawned and stretched, the muscles in his arms and chest rippling and bunching as he moved.

I forced myself to look away, startled to discover just how attractive I found the sleepy man in my bed. "Fine. Good, actually," I stuttered, trying to gather my thoughts. "You?"

"Like a rock. This bed may be monstrous, but if Hank and Dot's kids don't use it, I'm happy to. This mattress is amazing." His voice had a slight rasp to it, like he was still clearing the sleep from his throat.

I nodded in agreement, trying not to dwell on how pleasant it had been waking up next to him in the very comfortable bed. "Do you think we could convince them to get rid of a few pillows?" I looked around at the carnage on the floor and bed, pillows and lace covering nearly every inch of carpet.

"I bet they wouldn't notice if we just took one or two or fifty with us."

I snorted a laugh. "What would you do with fifty lacy pillows?"

"Donate them to a good cause, like a retirement home for serial killers who also collect creepy dolls and clowns," Grey said, his expression completely deadpan.

I shook my head at the absurdity, my lips tipping up into a smile. "Somehow, I think Dot would notice."

"Fine. You look ready for the day. Got a hot date?" Grey quirked an eyebrow as he gestured to my workout attire. "Personally, I'm going to look as homeless as possible for the rest of this trip. I might even squeeze in a few more minutes of shut eye."

I shook my head, ignoring the second half of Grey's comment. "I thought I'd do some yoga before breakfast. Other than that, I'm going to be trapped in the car for several hours with a near stranger."

I tacked on the last part more for me than for Grey. Maybe if I reminded myself about how little I knew Grey, I could squash the seeds of attraction that had started sprouting yesterday after our late-night conversation.

"I'm hardly a stranger at this point. I mean, we did share a bed." Grey waved grandly around him, and my face flushed.

"For convenience."

Grey sat a moment longer before heading into the bathroom. "True, but that doesn't change the fact that I'm going to miss the bed head. It was cute."

My mouth fell open at his final comment, my hand reaching up to check my hair was still safely secured in its bun. No matter what Grey said, I looked better this way. More presentable. More professional. More desirable. Or that's what I'd always assumed. Did Grey really mean what he said? Was it possible he could somehow like me, even when I wasn't perfectly put together?

The cool air filled my lungs as I stepped out onto Dot and Hank's back porch. What their house lacked in space was more than made up for by the size of their porch and yard. I could imagine Tory spending summers here, running around for hours, uninhibited by stress or worry. The images were a stark contrast to my own childhood where constant worry plagued my steps. The life of an only child being raised by a single parent who wasn't much older than a child herself.

I rolled out my purple yoga mat on the porch, grateful I'd thought to pack it with me. My muscles needed to stretch and move after the long hours in the car and sitting in the tire shop yesterday. The breeze teased whisps of hair from my bun as I sat cross-legged on the mat with my eyes closed, taking a few deep breaths to ground myself before beginning the practice. I was just moving into mountain pose when the screen door slammed, letting me know someone had joined me.

Peeking one eye open, I found Dot standing in the doorway, hands on hips, wearing a faded pair of jeans and a floral-patterned button-down shirt. Her white hair ruffled a bit in the breeze, and a wide grin stretched across her face, deepening the wrinkles around her eyes and mouth.

"What on earth are you doing out here?"

I opened both eyes and gestured to my mat. "Yoga. Figured I'd get a workout in before we hit the road today."

"If I were in your shoes, there's a different kind of workout I'd be doing this morning." Dot gave an exaggerated wink, and my cheeks instantly flamed.

"Dot! It's not like that," I squeaked out as I pushed away images of waking up in bed with Grey, his arm around my waist. While we hadn't done anything, the sensation had been unexpectedly nice—something I refused to examine too carefully. After Lyle, I'd sworn off men, at least until I felt more healed and capable of handling the vulnerability of letting someone in.

Dot waved aside my protests as she sank into one of the wooden rocking chairs on the porch. "It might not be like that now, but I'm sure that handsome man in your bed would be more than happy to change things."

"We're practically strangers," I blurted. I did not need to think of Grey in bed, sleep-rumpled and gorgeous.

"Every relationship has to start somewhere. Hank and I were strangers once, and now look at us." She waved around her, taking in the little white house surrounded by fields. "All it takes is one shot, and a love story can begin."

Giving up any hope of yoga, I sank into the remaining rocking chair, the stiff wooden back serving to ground me in the moment.

"I don't think I know yours and Hank's story," I said, curious to hear how this amazing couple had found each other decades earlier. It was the kind of marriage I had dreamed of but feared would always be out of reach. I had lost count of the number of bad dates Mom had experienced before finally finding Dave, and I wasn't sure my heart could handle another rollercoaster like my relationship with Lyle.

Dot's smile turned dreamy and distant as she became lost in memory. "It's pretty simple, really. I was a city girl who wanted a change of pace, so I took a job at the college. Hank was a farm boy who came to college to get a degree before taking over the family farm. I swore left and right I'd never marry a farm boy. I told everyone who would listen that country life wasn't for me."

"I'm guessing Hank didn't listen," I observed, pushing off with my left foot to send my chair rocking. The gentle motion was soothing, and I reveled in the moment of calm after the hectic day yesterday. The temperature was cooler than I was used to in Utah County, and I wished I'd thought to bring my jacket outside with me as the breeze danced along my arms, raising goose bumps.

"Good thing too, or I probably would have married Elton Kingsley or someone equally as boring from my hometown." Dot gave a shudder, and I couldn't help but laugh at her expression, a humorous mix of disgust and horror.

"So how did he convince you to give a farm boy a chance?" I leaned forward, planting my feet to stop the rocking motion, engrossed in Dot's story.

"He was taking an English class and claimed he was no good at writing papers. He insisted he needed a tutor if he was going to have any chance of passing. What I hadn't realized was he'd overheard me telling a coworker that I'd been top of my English class in high school. When I heard him moaning about his fate, I offered to help, but I made it clear I was only his tutor, nothing more. Well, as you can imagine, Hank can be crafty when he wants to. He said he needed all the help he could get and got me to commit to tutoring him every Friday night for the rest of the semester." Dot became silent, lost in memory as she rocked on the porch, a soft smile touching her lips.

"I'm guessing you didn't stay just a writing tutor for long." This was the part of any relationship that fascinated me. The moment it went from friends to more. For my mom and Dave it had been on a date to the movies. I remembered because after listening to Mom recap the date when she got home over Pepsis, that was the night the uncertainty I'd felt about our future and where we'd be living in six months finally loosened its grip. I'd relaxed enough to enjoy the last few years of high school, finding the courage to apply to college out of state.

I still couldn't point to the moment it had happened for me and Lyle, though I knew exactly when it fell apart. Now I doubted I'd ever find someone willing to take that step with me again. It had taken me almost 25 years to find someone willing to commit to me like Lyle. With my social ineptitude, it would likely take at least that long to find someone else willing to take a chance on me.

"One week he asked if we could take the tutoring session to a local diner because he hadn't eaten dinner yet. The next week, we went on a picnic. Before I knew it, we were no longer talking papers. Instead, I was hoping the cute farm boy in front of me would hold my hand and kiss me goodnight." Dot's cheeks had a pink hue to them, and I wanted to bottle up this moment and the softness in her expression as she reminisced.

"And I've been convincing her to let me kiss her goodnight ever since." Hank's deep, raspy voice cut across the moment, and I looked up to find him standing on the porch steps, hands in his overall pockets and a giant grin on his face.

"Hank, you're craftier than I gave you credit. Does Tory know?" I asked, grateful for humor that helped cut through the tender emotions Dot's story had brought to the surface. They were emotions I did my best not to dwell on because they led to wishing and wanting and heartbreak. If I didn't hope for the same happiness in my life, I couldn't be disappointed when it didn't happen.

"How do you think we convinced her to come spend summers with us? She thought it was her idea, but all it took was telling her how much the dogs missed her company, and that girl was begging her parents to let her stay," Hank said with a wink.

I laughed, picturing all too well a young, over-eager Tory begging to spend the summer running these fields, a border collie or two in tow. It sounded magical and like the type of summer I would have given almost anything for as a kid.

"I've talked your ear off enough. I'll let you get back to your yoga." Dot turned to me, laying her hand on my arm. "Just think about what I said. Not all romances have epic starts. You can't plan for everything, Audrey. Sometimes, when you let yourself get a little lost on your way, magic happens."

With that parting comment, Dot stood, looping her arm through Hank's and following him into the house. I barely registered the screen door closing behind them as I turned to stare across the fields, thinking on Dot's words.

There was safety in planning. It kept me from getting hurt again, safe from the Lyles of the world and their cheating ways. But in keeping myself safe, was I also shutting myself off from the Hanks of the world, good men with kind hearts who offered something even better than the life I'd planned? Was it possible Grey could even be one of those men?

I was scared to open my heart and find out. And yet, maybe I really would find magic if I tried. The question was, how did I start the process?

Chapter Nine

I CUT MY YOGA flow short, my mind wandering instead of focusing on the present as I continued mulling over Dot's story and observations. Instead, I rolled up my mat, promising myself I'd get in a good session once we reached the cabin.

I entered the kitchen to find Grey standing at the counter in a grey flannel shirt rolled up to his elbows, the same pink and yellow floral apron from the night before wrapped around his waist, and specks of flour dotting his beard. He was grinning at Dot, whisking batter in a bowl, and I had to fight the sudden urge to walk over to him and see if the flannel hugging his arms was as soft as it looked. There was something about watching a strong, manly man helping an elderly woman in the kitchen that had my heart skipping a beat.

"How was yoga?" Grey continued to work as he caught sight of me and pulled me into the conversation.

"Good," I stammered, rushing to tack on something to keep the conversation going, not wanting to draw attention to how I had been ogling him only moments before.

"I'm so glad!" Dot called from her place by the stove where she was stirring a pan of hashbrowns. Based on the amount of food already covering the table, she had to be expecting more guests. There was no way Grey and I could put a dent in the food in front of us, even if it smelled divine.

Dot and Grey continued to work, turning his bowl of batter into pancakes. I offered to help, but Dot waved me away, promising they had everything under control. I headed upstairs and showered while they worked. I returned my hair to its messy bun, not wanting to bother with washing, blow drying, and curling it when we were going to spend several more hours in the car. I did, however, take more time with my makeup, wanting to hide any traces of the long day of travel yesterday. I pulled out my favorite eyeshadow palette, a gift from my mom that she swore complimented my skin tone, and took extra care highlighting my green eyes. Once I was fully put together, I headed back downstairs, my stomach growling as I smelled all the wonderful food waiting for me.

"Take a seat and we'll dig in." Dot waved me over to the table, following behind with the pan of hashbrowns. The rest of the food already waited on the table. "Hank had to run a couple errands, but he said to tell you he'd pick you up later to drive you to the tire shop."

"This looks delicious," Grey observed as he settled into the same seat as last night, the chair creaking slightly.

I nodded and sat down next to him, fighting the urge to lean into his warmth at the small table. "You didn't have to go to all this trouble."

Dot waved away my concerns, settling the pan she was carrying onto a hot pad and taking the seat across from me. "It's no trouble at all. It's nice to have someone to cook for besides Hank."

We filled our plates and dug in, savoring the food as Dot rambled on about her kids and grandkids.

"Now, if I can just convince Tory to visit. Ever since she started dating that Travis, she hasn't had time to come up."

"You mean Trent?" I asked as I took a bite of pancake drenched in syrup. I hadn't made pancakes at home in far too long, and Dot's cooking had me committing to making them more often. A decision that had nothing to do with my discussion about hobbies from the day before, or at least that's what I told myself. I didn't want to examine too closely my sudden desire to revisit some pastimes I'd let fade into the background.

"Travis, Trent, Tyler...it's hard to keep track of all their names. The only one that stays consistent is Brad, and Tory promises me they're just friends. Which is silly. If you find a guy who looks that nice and wants to spend time with you, I say snap him up! Don't leave him in the friendzone." Dot waved her fork at me as she spoke, and I bit back a snort, having had the same conversation with Tory on multiple occasions. Also, Dot was more up on current slang than I gave her credit for if she was familiar with the "friendzone."

"Yes, ma'am," I said solemnly, refusing to say anything that would anger the woman responsible for the delicious breakfast in front of me.

"And you"—Dot turned her fork on Grey—"show some backbone. Don't let a girl force you into the friendzone if you want something more. Show her how you feel."

Grey took a giant bite of eggs and simply nodded. Smart man.

"I don't want to hear any of this 'I don't want to ruin the relationship' nonsense either. In the end, most of those relationships fade anyway. But your relationship with your spouse, that's something special that should last."

I used my food as an excuse to keep from answering. What Dot said made sense, but relationships in my life had a tendency not to last, regardless of if they were romantic or more platonic. Lyle was the perfect example, though he wasn't the first and likely wouldn't be the last man to skip out of my life. My dad was top of the list. I couldn't even remember the last time we had talked, and even that was likely to have been stilted and forced, all about his amazing career success and new family.

My mom was the only one who stuck around, and that relationship was constantly evolving and changing, especially now that she'd remarried and was raising the twins.

Grey and I said little the rest of the meal, Dot's words echoing in my mind with each bite until, finally, I couldn't eat any more. I excused myself to finish packing, the what-ifs of a relationship with Grey chasing me every step of the way.

If I didn't get out of here soon, Dot would have me accepting a first date with Grey without him even asking.

Chapter Ten

AN HOUR LATER, GREY and I hit the road. We'd helped Dot clean up breakfast, with Hank showing up partway through to eat leftovers and chat with us while we worked. When the tire shop called, Hank gave us a ride to the store. As we gave Dot hugs, she insisted on sending us with a giant tub of cookies, claiming she and Hank couldn't possibly eat them.

Hank groaned at the gesture, complaining he hadn't gotten to eat nearly enough of them. But Dot promised to make more when she saw me hesitate to accept the container.

When it was my turn to tell Dot goodbye, she pulled me in tight for one more hug and whispered in my ear, "Don't forget what we talked about. Don't let a good one like that slip through your fingers."

She nodded at Grey, the gesture far from subtle as she released me and waved us on our way.

As if I could possibly forget about Grey and how just looking at him sent my pulse pounding. I told myself the pounding was from nerves or anxiety, but I wasn't fooling myself. After our conversation in the dark of night, I'd found it increasingly difficult to force Grey back into the safe, platonic box I'd stuck him in when he'd picked me up yesterday. A box that didn't risk heartbreak.

When I finally climbed into Grey's car and kicked off my shoes, scuffed tennis shoes this time, I breathed an audible sigh of relief. While I adored Dot and Hank, their questions and pointed looks were getting to be a lot. I could only dodge Dot's raised eyebrows for so long. I had never been so grateful for stale, fast food-scented air and the blast of a car AC, knowing the escape it promised.

I settled into my seat, connecting my phone to the speaker and fiddling with the music to give my hands and brain something to think about besides Dot's commentary and sharing a bed with Grey. I finally landed on some Loverboy, the familiar melody easing the tension in my shoulders.

"If I'm going to survive this drive, I'm going to need caffeine," I said, scanning the street for the closest gas station.

"We can make that happen," Grey said.

A few minutes later, he pulled into the drive through of a local soda shop, and I could have cheered as I looked over the menu with its variety of drinks and syrup flavors.

"What's your poison?" Grey asked, turning to me with a quirked eyebrow.

"Pepsi with green apple, strawberry, and raspberry." I rattled off my order without hesitation, already anticipating the burn of soda that would come with my first sip.

"Definitely not a combination I would have pegged you for. I figured you would want something less fussy." Grey looked at me, pondering for a moment before giving a decisive nod. "Maybe something with lime and a hint of cream."

"Don't let appearances deceive you. I'm very particular about my flavored sodas," I said, pulling my wallet out of the front pocket of my backpack. "Because I asked you to stop, I've got this. It's the least I can do, since you're driving."

Grey waved away the offer. "I'm not worried about it. Just know I may have to try your drink. It sounds weird, but maybe it's as delicious as you claim."

I wasn't big on sharing drinks, but I'd make an exception if it meant I could have caffeine running through my veins for the rest of the drive.

"Deal," I said, slipping my wallet back into my backpack.

Grey placed the order, and we pulled forward with me only half listening to what was going on around me. The three and a half hours ahead seemed daunting, especially with our day-long delay. We should be able to reach the cabin before nightfall, but knowing Grey, we were likely to take a few more detours that would postpone our arrival time. Maybe if I knew to anticipate the delays, they wouldn't bug me quite as much.

"Hope you're thirsty."

I turned to find Grey offering me a 44-ounce Styrofoam cup, a giant grin splitting his face like he was a kid showing off his newest toy. I could feel the ice shifting in the cup as I accepted the offering with a thank you and smile of my own.

"You didn't tell me a size, so I guessed bigger was better, in this case," Grey said as he pulled back onto the road, his car spouting out directions to help us get back on track.

"Bless you," I said. I took a big swallow, the sugar and caffeine hitting my system and causing the tension to ease from my shoulders. I took another long pull before placing the cup in the cupholder next to Grey's equally large cup.

"What's your drink of choice?" I asked, turning slightly to face Grey.

"I'm a Mountain Dew guy. I switch up the mix-ins, but it's always Mountain Dew." He shrugged, as if his drink choice was a given.

"I've never really gotten into Mountain Dew. It tastes like caffeinated Sprite," I said, leaning back into my seat and watching Cache Valley pass by outside my window.

Grey scoffed. "This coming from a woman who drinks Pepsi."

"What's wrong with Pepsi?" I sat up, ready to defend my favorite drink to the end. "Also, if you're going to mock my drink, you don't get to try any."

I picked up my cup, jokingly moving it out of Grey's reach.

"I can live with that. Nothing's wrong with Pepsi if you don't have any taste buds."

"Drinking Pepsi was my mom's thing," I said, opting to give him a glimpse into my life that I rarely shared with others. Grey's vulnerability the night before and easy conversation had me wanting to be brave. "She told me it was her sanity juice when I was a kid. I was always stealing sips from her drinks until, finally, in junior high she'd let me get my own bottle when we stopped at the grocery store or gas station. We'd talk about our days while sipping on a Pepsi. So really, I guess no other soda stood a chance for me."

I tried to look nonchalant as I waited for Grey's response.

"I guess if you're going to pull the mom card, I can't tease you too much about your drink choice." He gave me a wink over his shoulder before a mischievous grin stretched across his face. "Though, I don't know if I can trust someone who drinks Pepsi."

I laughed, playfully smacking his arm and embracing the lighter direction of our conversation. "I could say the same thing about Mountain Dew drinkers."

"Then we're in for an interesting car ride."

"I've already slept with you. What else could possibly happen?" I quipped. My face immediately heated as the words registered.

Grey snorted, though I could have sworn I saw the slightest hint of pink under his beard. "I get how it is. You just wanted me for my pillow wall skills."

I took the out. It was safer than talking about last night and revisiting our late-night conversation. He'd opened up to me about his family, and it wouldn't take much for him to convince me to do the same, a reality that left me equal parts thrilled and terrified.

"It's hard to find a good pillow wall builder these days," I said with mock seriousness, returning my drink to the cupholder. Our fingers brushed as he reached for his own cup. "But I'm curious. How are you at couch forts?"

Grey schooled his features, appearing to give the question great thought. "You know, it's been a long time since I've had to use those skills, but I think I could pull together something decent. How big of a fort are we talking here?"

Chapter Eleven

It took until the Idaho border for the caffeine to fully kick in and my anxiety to completely dissipate. While my improving relationship with Grey had worked wonders for my stress, I still felt some lingering nervousness about the trip and stepping so far outside of my comfort zone. Just as I was relaxing and appreciating the fields passing outside my window, my phone rang.

I answered without looking at the screen, assuming it would be Tory wanting an update on our drive. Instead, an all-too familiar nasally male voice greeted me.

"Audrey, where do I find the most up-to-date trainings for new products?" My supervisor's tone was gruff and clipped, hinting at building frustration.

I sat up with a jolt, causing my seatbelt to lock and dig into my shoulder. Once the locking mechanism released, I shifted my feet from where they were resting on the dashboard back to the floor, as if my boss could see me.

Grey hit a button to disconnect my phone from the speakers, and I shot him a grateful look.

"Why are you calling me, Drew?" I asked, confusion filling my tone as I tried to ignore the jolt of anxiety that always accompanied an unexpected work call. He'd approved my time off—there was no reason to worry. My job, for better or worse, was secure.

"Because I can't find the trainings," he said with a huff.

I shook my head, trying to process his request and why he'd felt the need to call me. It was a simple enough question, something anyone on the team could help him locate. "They're with all the other trainings on the knowledge base."

"I know, but what do I search?"

"Drew, how would I know off the top of my head what to search? I'm not in charge of trainings." I did my best to keep the frustration out of my tone. My confusion was gone, completely replaced by anger as I was once again presented with my supervisor's incompetence.

"Because you know how to find everything, and Angela needs a refresher—"

"Talk to the training team. They can help you find it." I pinched the bridge of my nose, doing my best to sound polite and professional. I wished I could hang up and replace this conversation with the girl-power music of Pat Benatar.

Did people in other jobs have to deal with the same number of inane questions I navigated on a daily basis?

"Why didn't I think of that?" He muttered into the phone. I could hear some shuffling on his end like he was walking somewhere in a hurry.

I remained silent, waiting to see if Drew had any other unnecessary questions for me. Instead, he mumbled something that vaguely resembled goodbye and hung up.

I dropped my phone into my lap and slouched in my seat, returning my feet to the dashboard. How Drew managed to stay a supervisor, I would never know.

Because you do everything for him. I silenced the nagging voice in my head, telling myself Drew would find someone to do his job even if I wasn't there. Maybe someday I'd find a job that actually felt fulfilling instead of one that just paid the bills. My recent internet search history, which included bookmarking several yoga certification courses, came to mind. But it was a fun, escapist dream, nothing more.

But did it have to be? It was a question I didn't want to examine too closely. Dreams led to uncertain futures and constantly changing jobs—like my mom. I refused to repeat her mistakes, no matter how appealing the alternatives looked after a phone call with Drew.

I reconnected my phone to the car speakers, scrolling through my music options, looking for something with a good beat. I landed on "I Love Rock 'N Roll" by Joan Jett & The Blackhearts.

Needing a distraction, I turned to Grey, who had spent the duration of my phone call studying the road and pretending not to hear every word I spoke.

"We've been on this road trip together for"—I glanced at the dashboard and flinched at the time—"way too long, and after spending the night together, I feel like we need a redo. Tell me about yourself."

Grey laughed and raised an eyebrow, glancing at me. "Seriously? Beyond the soul-baring I did last night?"

I flinched a little, realizing Grey had already shared much of his story the night before. If I'd been a better conversationalist, I would have remembered. My mom, Lyle, Emily. They all would have remembered.

"I can start, if that would make you more comfortable." The words came out in a rush. I attempted nonchalance, ignoring the worry clawing at my throat. This was probably a terrible idea, but I had to try something. He'd shown me a glimpse into his life last night. It was my turn to do the same. Not to mention if we were talking, I wouldn't open my work messaging app to pass the time. I doubted Drew's ability to handle things while I was away, but knew if I cracked that door open, there was no closing it again on this trip.

I took a deep breath before jumping in, figuring there was no time like the present to give Grey a quick peek into my life.

"My mom raised me on her own after my dad walked out when I was three. They'd married straight out of high school after going a bit too far on a date. Neither was ready for parenthood, but my mom refused to consider any alternative besides raising me when she found out she was pregnant. It was us against the world until my sophomore year of high school." My fingers clenched into fists in my lap as I thought about those years, worrying about my mom and if we'd have enough money to get us through the week. Trying to roll with her spontaneity but worrying it would come at the cost of dinner that night. I tried not to think about how it felt to go to bed hungry, knowing my mom was doing her best, and yet it still hadn't been enough. I forced myself to relax and unclench my fists. That was the past. My life was safe and settled now. "Mom decided to give online dating a try, and after a slew of terrible dates, she met Dave and promptly fell in love. They married my senior year of high school and were surprised by fraternal twin girls about a year later."

Silence followed my declarations, the only sounds the chorus of a Queen song as Grey processed my words.

"Did I say too much? Sorry, my life's a lot." I stammered, attempting to backtrack and recall the words. Maybe I'd shared too much. There was a difference between sharing secrets in the dark of night and blasting them out in the middle of the day.

"No, I'm just...processing. It's a lot to unpack." Grey rushed to reassure me, glancing between me and the road a few times. It was as if he wanted to watch my face, but also recognized the need for safety while driving. I was grateful he couldn't fully read the emotions I was sure were written across my face.

"How do you feel about all of that?" He gestured vaguely, attempting to encapsulate all my words.

A small smile teased my lips as I chose to focus on the positive, ignoring the moments of stress and 'not enough' that had defined my childhood.

"I'm happy for Mom. Dave makes enough money that she gets to stay home and be the cool mom she never had the time to be when I was growing up. I'm grateful she found her happy ending. It's just..." I hesitated, knowing I could leave it there and Grey would be none the wiser. For all anyone knew, the emotional trauma of my childhood was healed, and I had no secret hard feelings at my mom's second chance at a happy, perfect family.

If I was anywhere else, not trapped in a car for several hours unable to escape, I wouldn't hesitate to end the conversation and run away. Instead, Dot's words encouraging me to be brave filled my mind.

I took a deep breath, deciding to give Grey the vulnerability and honesty he deserved after opening up to me last night.

"It's hard not to worry about it falling apart...or about how I fit into it."

The truth tasted bitter on my tongue. These were thoughts I usually kept to myself, safely bottled up where no one else could or would learn about just how much of a mess I truly was. I hadn't even expressed these thoughts and fears to Lyle. Apparently, hours trapped in the car with Grey had broken my filter. Just more evidence I was no good at socializing. I went straight from small talk to the hard things, with little warning.

"I imagine that would be difficult." Grey's voice was soft, like he was trying not to spook a deer. I stared straight ahead, not wanting to see concern, or worse, pity written on his face. These conversations were much easier in the dark of night, where reactions could be hidden.

"Don't get me wrong. I'm grateful she found Dave, and I love the girls. They feel more like nieces or little cousins than sisters. I mean, it's hard to connect on a sisterly level when you're in your third year of college and they're learning to walk. But we have our fun. They come out to visit about once a year, and I go out to California to see them over the holidays. Dave usually foots the bill for me to take them to Disneyland, so there are worse family situations." I shrugged, rattling off the many perks of being a big sister after having spent most of my life as an only child. If I focused on the positive, brushed away the hard, maybe this conversation could be salvaged and Grey would have no idea how messed up I truly was.

"Tell me about them," Grey said, giving me full permission to return to safer topics.

"They're seven, almost eight. Lily is the oldest, but Poppy will be the first to inform you it was only by two minutes," I said with a smile. Their slight age difference was a major sore spot for Poppy.

"Wait." Grey held up a hand to stop me, his forehead scrunched. "Their names are Lily and Poppy? As in, both of your sisters are named after plants?"

I laughed. "Mom went through a gardening phase right after she married Dave. Mom's always starting new hobbies and swearing this will be the one that lasts. Currently, she's into sourdough and talks about opening a bakery. Next month it'll probably be crocheting book covers and opening an online shop." My lips tipped into a smile, thinking about Mom's many hobbies over the years. "The hobbies never stick, which is why we tried to convince her to name them something a little less floral. But Mom wouldn't hear of it."

"Makes sense. I don't know that I'd name my children after plants, but you do you." Grey's smile widened, his teeth a flash of white against his beard.

"At least the names are cute and easy to spell. For a minute she was talking about naming the girls Amaryllis and Chrysanthemum." I gave a mock shudder. "It was a rough week before we convinced her Lily and Poppy were better. She said they were going to be her garden babies. I'm still not sure what that means."

Humor laced my voice as I thought back to those conversations before the girls had been born. Dave and I had tried repeatedly to brainstorm ways to get her to choose new names. I couldn't count the number of texts I'd sent Mom my first year of college with baby name suggestions. No matter what I'd come up with, Mom had been set on something floral.

"If your sisters were named after a hobby, where did your name come from?"

"Believe it or not, it came from a hobby too," I said, a hint of pride in my voice. I loved my name and the story behind it. It felt like my own special piece of my mom, just for me to hold onto. "Mom went through an Audrey Hepburn phase when she was pregnant with me. We used to watch a different Audrey Hepburn movie on my birthday every year to celebrate where my name came from."

"Sounds like I should have been asking your mom for hobby suggestions at the beginning of this trip." Grey threw me a wink, taking out any potential sting that could have come from his words.

He had no way of knowing that Mom's ever-changing hobbies were the ultimate sign of her inability to settle down. Now that she was married to Dave, it wasn't an issue. But my childhood had been a different story, each hobby leading to a different dream job with the associated costs and potential moves. After all, you can't be a surfer if you don't live near the ocean.

I'd always taken pride in my hobbies and how they symbolized a settled life of sorts. After all, I picked hobbies and stuck to them. Now I was realizing Lyle had stolen that from me, and it was long past time I stopped giving him that power. I needed to rediscover what it meant to be Audrey Byrd, hobbies and all.

"I'm just grateful she was into Audrey Hepburn when I was born. Shortly after I was born, she got really into rock collecting." I playfully shuddered, letting the humor chase any heaviness that could accompany the conversation.

"Sounds like a missed opportunity! You could have been named Amethyst," Grey said, clear enjoyment in his tone as he considered the possibilities. I decided to play along.

"Or Geode." I nodded sagely, biting back a smile.

"Granite."

"Schist," I said, picking the worst rock-related name I could possibly think of, courtesy of a geology class I'd taken my first year of college.

Grey burst out laughing. "I'll have to keep that name in mind for my future children. Schist sounds like a good strong character-building name."

My laughter joined his as the music changed to "Carry On My Wayward Son" by Kansas. I bobbed my head to the music, lost in thoughts about my family.

"What are Lily and Poppy like?" Grey asked, pulling me back into the conversation.

"They look nothing alike. They think it's hilarious to tell people they're twins and watch the confusion." I reached for my phone to pull up a picture but realized I would have to show Grey later, when he wasn't driving. "Lily has blonde hair, blue eyes, and skin so fair she burns if she even thinks about going outside. Poppy has brown hair like mine, though hers has a bit of curl to it. She's got green eyes and the biggest smile. Lily is all things tomboy and Poppy is definitely the princess. The two are inseparable most of the time."

"It sounds like you're close," Grey observed.

My cheeks were starting to hurt from the constant smiling that always accompanied conversations about my sisters. "I've lived in a different state their entire lives, but I do my best to be present in their lives. Lots of video calls and trips to California make a huge difference."

"They sound like a lot of fun," Grey said.

"They definitely keep Mom and Dave on their toes." Affection filled my tone. It had been far too long since I'd seen my sisters. I'd have to do a video call when I got home.

The conversation petered out, and I racked my brain for something else to say. The music changed to another song, the beat and growling guitar of Joan Jett's "I Hate Myself for Loving You" filling the silence.

"What about you? I mean, your family." I stumbled on the words as I tried to transition the conversation away from me. I took a deep breath and tried again. "Your turn. Tell me about your family."

I dropped my feet to the floor and shifted in my seat to better face Grey, the faux leather sticking slightly to my legs. Grey took a moment to gather his thoughts, and I watched him as he stared out the windshield, trees flying past on both sides of the road.

"Up until about three years ago, I would have told you we were a normal, average Utah family. My dad worked an office job. My mom was a teacher so she could have summers off with me and my brother. Mason is two years younger than me, so we fought like siblings do. But we also protected and watched out for each other. Mason was finishing college, and I was bouncing between jobs, trying to find the right fit. And then, it all changed. Dad died from a heart attack, and Mom...Mom's been lost ever since."

Grey paused for a moment, taking a few deep breaths before continuing. I sat still, not sure what to say and afraid to break the moment with the wrong movement or comment. The moment felt like the night before, heavy and filled with vulnerability.

"Mom still works, still goes through the motions, but her anxiety runs rampant, and she tends to panic over the slightest change. Mason couldn't handle her constant hovering and phone calls, so he took the first out-of-state job he could get and only comes home when he absolutely has to, which doesn't include major holidays." Grey's voice had grown small and quiet. "Though he's recently become convinced all our problems would be fixed if Mom got a change of scenery and we all moved to Oregon with him."

My heart ached at the sadness and strain written on Grey's face. Worry lines appeared at the corners of his eyes as he white-knuckled the steering wheel.

"I'm so sorry."

He blew out a breath, his cheeks puffing out with the motion. "Me too. It's hard." He paused, swallowing and working to gather his emotions. "Most people don't know what to say, so it's not exactly something I broadcast to the world. I'm just doing my best to keep my family from falling apart."

"And trying not to fall apart yourself." Sympathy filled my voice, and I gave his shoulder a squeeze. His hand came up, resting on mine for just a moment before releasing it. He seemed to appreciate and accept my meager attempt at comfort. If the struggles of my childhood followed by Mom's accident and Lyle dumping me had taught me anything, it was how to appear fine while secretly falling apart inside.

"I think you're the first person I've told who actually understands." He gave a dry, humorless laugh. "Everyone else just tells me to stick Mom in therapy and do what's best for me. But it's not that simple."

"There are no easy fixes," I said, nodding my understanding. I'd received similar advice after Mom's accident, being told to let Dave handle it even though Mom's recovery was long and she had two young children to care for.

"Losing Dad was just so unexpected, and we each handled it differently. Mason ran away. Mom tries to control everything."

"And how do you handle it?" I winced as soon as the question was out, knowing it was probably the wrong thing to ask. Yet, I didn't want the moment to fade, becoming just another awkward conversation I wasn't sure how to navigate.

"I try to live everyday like it could be my last. I don't want to look back on life with regret. Because…" He hesitated, unable to finish the thought.

"Because 'not all who wander are lost'?" I quipped back, knowing it didn't make any sense but certain it was somehow the right thing to say.

Grey gave a small laugh, the color returning to his knuckles as he loosened his grip on the steering wheel.

"Exactly. I want to wander and get lost and experience the world. My dad actually introduced me to that quote. He was obsessed with *The Lord of the Rings*. He talked about going on epic adventures all the time. How someday, when he had more money, more time, we'd visit all the national parks, fly to various countries, see everything the world had to offer."

He grew quiet, as if processing all the things his dad would have never done. The atmosphere in the car was heavy and thick, filled with loss and regret.

"I'm just doing my best to do right by him." This last sentence was spoken so quietly, I wasn't sure I was meant to hear.

We sat in silence, small towns slipping by out the window as we got closer to the cabin. I attempted to think of a question or comment, something to change topics and get the conversation back to safer ground.

Grey gave a stiff shake of his head and reached over to fiddle with the music volume for a moment before speaking.

"Now that we're both thoroughly depressed," Grey said, his tone full of forced cheer. "I vote for a change of topic."

"What do you have in mind?" I asked, more than happy to let him take control of the conversation. Just about anything he suggested would be lighter than loss and family drama.

"What is your favorite kind of ice cream? There are no wrong answers, unless you say vanilla." Grey pursed his lips, waiting for my response.

I hesitated for only a moment before deciding to lean into humor, trying to bring back our banter.

"What about bubble gum? I feel like bubble gum is definitely a wrong answer."

By the time we reached the cabin, my sides ached from laughter. Grey and I had bantered and discussed favorites, careful to avoid the deeper, more sensitive topics from earlier in our drive. Our delay in Logan had come with one huge advantage: we arrived at the cabin in the afternoon. Which meant, while we'd still had to watch for wildlife, it was easier to see.

We parked next to Tory's SUV in a clearing in front of the cabin. Trees surrounded us, and a firepit sat a few paces to our left flanked by camp chairs. A hammock hung from two trees beyond the firepit, and I could already picture myself curling up in it with a book.

The cabin was a log structure, with a large porch occupied by two wooden rocking chairs. From my previous visit, I knew inside would be welcoming, with worn sofas, the faint smell of moth balls, and décor reminiscent of my mom's kitchen growing up: large vinyl sayings on the walls, pops of red for color, and animal figurines for decoration. Why Tory's parents thought chickens and roosters made sense as cabin décor, I'd never know, but I loved it all the same.

"This place is nice." Grey whistled as he climbed out of the car, slipping a flannel shirt around his shoulders.

I shivered as I slipped on my shoes and stepped out of the car, a burst of cool air greeting me and bringing goose bumps to my legs and arms. While summer was in full swing in Utah, I'd forgotten that this far into Idaho, the temperatures tended to be cooler. I immediately wished my jacket wasn't packed away in my duffle in the trunk. Outside was quiet, the distant mooing of cows the only sound to break the silence, and I took a moment to breathe in as the faint scent of pine trees reminded me why I loved the mountains.

The sound of the cabin door closing brought my attention to the porch, where Tory and her boyfriend, Trent, stood. Tory waved, fairly bouncing on her toes with excitement. Her black curls were pulled up into a ponytail, and she wore a well-loved Yellowstone National Park sweatshirt. Trent stood, stoic as always, his lips pressed in a straight line.

His buzz cut and muscled build reminded me of a military man, an impression furthered by his no-nonsense personality. How such a quiet, straightlaced guy had ended up with my overexuberant friend, I'd never know. But they seemed happy, or at least Tory did. I had seen very little emotion from Trent.

"I'm so glad you guys made it," Tory said, joy lacing her tone.

I grinned and rushed up the stairs, happy to see my friend even if she'd had to force me on this trip. While nothing had gone to plan so far, I could already tell I was making memories I'd laugh about for years to come.

I dropped my backpack on the porch and gave Tory a hug.

"Happy birthday, a day late!" I held on an extra moment to whisper in her ear. "Next time you want to play matchmaker and strand me alone with a guy for several hours, just don't."

She gave me a wicked smile and shrugged, whispering back, "How was I supposed to know y'all would get to spend extra...quality time together? Besides, the alternative was you staying home, which is the last thing you need right now."

"Or I could have waited and come up with Brad, Alex, and Kylie," I said, referencing the rest of the group who would join the trip tomorrow after Kylie got off work. I stepped back and slung my backpack over my shoulder once more.

"Which would have increased the chances of you backing out. This way I get extra time with you in my favorite place in the world, even if car trouble cut into that a bit," Tory said, not even looking the slightest bit contrite about how everything turned out.

Grey bounded up the steps behind me, both of our bags slung over his shoulder. "Where should I stash these?"

"I'll show you and then give you the grand tour. Grey, you'll be sleeping downstairs with Trent in The Cave." She gestured to her boyfriend who stood off to the side, looking like a statue and not bothering to greet us.

After we took off our shoes, Tory showed us around the cabin. It hadn't changed much since I'd visited a couple of years ago. The same well-worn, comfy couches graced the living room, and the same log-framed beds waited in each of the bedrooms. There were even the same roosters and chickens watching us from on top of the kitchen cabinets, though they did look a bit more faded with age. The cabin was comfortable, with its open concept kitchen and living room and enough space to sleep 15 people—or more, depending on people's willingness to share beds or sleep on the couch. Tory's family frequently used it as a reunion space during the summer.

When we reached the room affectionately termed The Cave, Grey deposited his bag and settled on one of the beds. "I could get used to this."

"This is my favorite room," Tory said, gesturing to the dark space filled with several bunkbeds. "When we were kids, my siblings and I would drape blankets from all the beds and make forts."

I glanced at Grey, catching his smirk as we both remembered our discussion about pillow walls and couch forts.

Oblivious, Tory continued. "It's the coldest, darkest room in the cabin. Perfect for sleeping with a mountain of blankets."

I shivered as the cold seeped from the cement floor, regretting having removed my socks along with my shoes when I'd come inside. "If we stay down here much longer, I'm going to need slippers and a jacket."

Tory shrugged. "Just remember those things when we come down later for a movie."

"How late are we talking? You know I turn into a pumpkin after 10:00," I said. I did not do late nights well. My anxiety had a tendency to wake me up early, no matter when I went to bed.

"It wouldn't be a trip to the cabin without late night movies and treats," Tory insisted, leading the way back upstairs. "I didn't even bring any chick flicks this time. It's going to be all action and comedy this weekend. No hints of romance allowed, as promised."

One of Tory's arguments for getting me on the trip had been that it would just be a bunch of friends hanging out without dating or romantic pressures. She knew how much I resisted setups after things had fallen apart with Lyle. I decided to ignore Tory and Trent's current hand-holding and the fact that they would spend the entirety of any movie snuggling—or more.

I avoided committing to the movie for the moment as I deposited my bag in one of the rooms upstairs and changed into sweats and a hoodie. Trying to chase away the cold of the basement, I pulled on my thickest socks and walked into the kitchen for food, curious to see what else the day would hold.

Chapter Twelve

BETWEEN A LATE LUNCH, unpacking, and a hike to a nearby pond, the day passed quickly. After dinner, we'd all gone our separate ways for a bit, and I took the opportunity to do some simple stretches in my room. While not a full-on yoga flow, it was enough to relieve stiff muscles and let go of some lingering stress. Since arriving at the cabin, I'd received no less than twenty work messages. I'd ignored them so far but knowing the notifications waited put me on edge.

I'm allowed to take PTO, I reminded myself with every movement, trying to push the notification bubble from my work messaging app from my mind. It was moments like these that left me wishing my internet searches on becoming a yoga instructor were more than idle curiosity and an actual career plan I could pursue.

When I finished stretching, I found everyone sitting at the dining room table, a stack of games and junk food surrounding them.

"I thought we were watching a movie." I stifled a yawn as I sat at the table, trying to join in the fun but also wishing I could go to bed without being the resident party pooper.

"We are, but that's not until later. It's only 9:30." Tory gave me a smile and wink before gesturing to the games in front of her, a mix of decades-old board games and card games. "What should we play?"

We settled on a card game, and I finally felt the knot in my stomach unwind as we teased and trash-talked our way through the familiar games. By the time we finished and Tory was ready to start the movie, I decided it was late enough that no one could fault me for bowing out.

"Are you sure?" Tory asked as the guys went downstairs to get the movie setup. "It'll be fun. Promise!"

"I believe you, but I'm beat." I stretched, my back popping as I arched into the movement, my body clearly agreeing with my need for rest.

Tory pleaded with me a little longer before finally giving in.

"Fine, but you're watching the movie tomorrow night. I brought superhero movies, and you know I didn't bring those for myself." She shook a finger at me, emphasizing her point.

"We both know you didn't bring superhero movies for me," I said with a laugh. "Trent would probably hitchhike home if we didn't watch at least one superhero movie during this trip."

"True." She acquiesced, giving me a hug and disappearing downstairs with the guys, leaving me alone to get ready for bed.

I stood at the top of the stairs for a moment, soaking in the quiet before heading to my bedroom. I hated being the first one to call it a night. And yet, I was fully aware this was my identity. I was the stable person who went to bed at a reasonable hour. Why should I change that now?

I washed my face, surprised as always at how different I looked without my makeup. Mom had gone through a makeup artist phase, teaching me how to contour and use a variety of products. I hadn't really gotten into it until I dated Lyle—he valued having a woman who always looked her best. What had once been a fun, occasional hobby had transformed into my armor and identity. Now I refused to be seen without my perfectly applied eyeliner and foundation, even when staying at a cabin in the woods.

I brushed my hair out, noting that it was time for a hair appointment. When my hair got long, it struggled to hold curl, becoming flat and straight, not the flattering waves I'd learned to style each morning. Grateful no one could see me in my undone appearance, I walked out of the bathroom and headed to the kitchen for a glass of water.

I turned the corner from the hallway into the kitchen and ran into something warm and solid that made an "oof" sound when I collided with it. I stumbled back, shocked to find I wasn't alone in the dimness of the cabin.

Grey's hands gripped my arms, steadying me as his ever-present grin filled his face. "Careful! Don't want any injuries, especially this early in the trip."

Warmth traveled up my arms at the contact, and I stepped away. Hopefully the dim lighting hid the blush suffusing my cheeks.

"Sorry. I thought I was alone upstairs. I wanted to grab a drink of water before bed." I babbled, my hand reaching up to run self-consciously through my hair. I realized the gesture drew attention to my undone appearance and forced my hand back down to my side. Maybe he wouldn't notice.

"Good news, the sink works great and the water's refreshing. I just checked." Grey walked over to a nearby cupboard, pulling out a blue plastic cup and offering it to me.

I accepted the cup with a thank you, not sure what to do next with Grey blocking the sink.

Grey watched me for a moment, his head tilted to the side. "You know, I hadn't realized your hair was straight. You've had it pulled up most of the trip. I like it this way."

My hand shot up to my hair, and I wished I hadn't completed my bedtime routine. He'd caught glimpses of me the night before in the dark of the room we shared, but this felt different, more exposed. I turned away, hoping he didn't notice how much of a mess I looked without my makeup. "I know it's a disaster. That's why I try to keep it styled."

Grey studied me, his lips pursed. "It doesn't look like a mess. It looks nice."

"That's because it's dark. Trust me, if you saw it—"

Grey stepped past me and flipped the switch, filling the kitchen with light before I could finish my sentence. I blinked at the sudden brightness, taking a step back as if distance could hide my lack of makeup and messy hair. Instead, the kitchen lights seemed to serve as a spotlight, dispelling any anonymity afforded by the darkness.

Grey moved to stand in front of me, arms crossed over his chest, his head nodding as he looked me over. "I was right. It doesn't look like a disaster. It looks nice." His eyes burned with something I didn't recognize, but it made my stomach clench with an energy I'd never felt before, not even when dating Lyle.

It was almost like he found me attractive. Which was ridiculous. After all, this was Grey, a guy I hardly knew. Yet, his gaze made me feel seen and, somehow, beautiful despite the fact that I was wearing pajamas and no makeup.

With that simple statement, Grey grabbed his cup and headed towards the stairs.

"You coming?" He paused at the top of the stairs, the shadows cast by the kitchen light hiding his expression as he turned back towards me.

I shook my head, hair brushing my shoulders with the motion. "I need sleep."

"But it's one of the best action movies of the year." Excitement filled his voice, reminding me of a little kid.

"That's what I've heard, but—"

"You haven't seen it yet?" Grey walked over to me, his expression incredulous, though a hint of mischievousness lurked in his eyes.

As he approached, I caught a hint of his scent, something woodsy and manly that made me want to lean in and take a big whiff. I must be more tired than I realized.

"But it's incredible," Grey continued, pulling me back to the conversation at hand. The corners of his mouth twitched, and I found myself biting my lip. He was teasing me.

"The film to define our generation. A pure master—" Grey broke off, a laugh escaping. He leaned forward, resting his hands on his knees as the laugh took over. "Sorry, I can't keep a straight face."

I shook my head, trying to keep my lips from tilting up in an answering grin.

He straightened, the remnants of laughter still written in the curves of his face. "It's a good movie, though I think it's been hyped up. But don't let Trent know I said that. When Trent finds out you haven't seen his favorite movie, he is going to lose his mind. He'll probably come drag you from your bed and force you to watch."

"Trent? Mr. I-Only-Smile-When-No-One's-Looking?" I asked, incredulous. Trent had maybe said three sentences to me the entire day, and that included while we had been playing board games earlier.

Grey crossed his arms over his chest and shrugged, making the muscles in his arms flex. "Well, probably not. I'm Tory's neighbor and have only heard the man speak when absolutely necessary. But learning you haven't watched his favorite movie could change the man! This could be the thing that transforms him into a chatterbox, obsessed with ensuring the whole world gets to see this epic masterpiece. Save us all the headache and come watch with us."

"Given that Trent talks a grand total of five times a day, that's a risk I'm willing to take." I stepped farther into the kitchen, opening cupboard doors and searching aimlessly to give my hands something to do. If I looked into Grey's eyes for too long, he'd convince me to join, and I needed sleep. At least, that's what the reasonable, predictable part of me said. It was the side that had guided my life and kept me safe through the ups and downs of life, including my mom's spontaneity and Lyle's betrayal.

Grey followed me, and I jumped from his sudden closeness. For a full-grown man, he had an uncanny ability to move quietly. I tried to unsuccessfully ignore his presence as I closed another cupboard and picked up my cup from the counter, fiddling with the plastic and doing my best not to look at him.

"Or," Grey said, "you come down, act as if you're going to watch, and sleep through the movie on the couch."

"Why would I do that when I could sleep in a nice, comfy bed all night without being woken up by random fight scenes?" A bed that wasn't covered in lacy pink pillows and did not include a bearded man who smelled amazing and made me want to reevaluate my stance on dating.

I turned on the sink, filling my cup with water and drinking the contents before refilling it. I would probably have to pee in the middle of the night, but I needed to distract myself from this man and his skills of persuasion. Nothing good came from losing sleep.

"Because then I won't tease you all day tomorrow about how I can't believe you went to bed first. If this was a sleepover, that would be an invitation for pranking. You'd probably wake up with a permanent marker mustache." Grey's tone was serious, his expression earnest.

"Good thing everyone here is an adult and not a twelve-year-old boy on his first overnighter." I stepped around Grey, heading towards my bedroom and the promise of a quiet night.

"I just want to note that no good story starts with, 'Once upon a time our heroine got a good night's sleep,'" he called after me, causing me to pause in my doorway.

He made a good point. In that moment I could hear all the voices that had called me a party pooper and encouraged me to step out of my routines. But routines meant safety and control, and I wasn't about to change that now.

"Maybe not, but they also don't start with, 'Once upon a time a sleep-deprived heroine sluggishly went about her day because she had a headache and no energy after staying up late watching a mediocre movie.'" I quirked an eyebrow at him, waiting for his comeback. Who even wanted to be a heroine after all? Going on adventures and being the center of a story sounded exhausting.

"Fair enough. Though who knows what you could find by losing a little sleep?" Grey said, heading down the stairs.

I ignored the comment, walking down the hall to bed and pretending like his words hadn't hit their mark, leaving me questioning my decision.

Chapter Thirteen

I CLIMBED INTO BED, fluffing my pillow and settling under the cool sheets. Grey's pleading expression filled my thoughts as I closed my eyes, trying to push his words from my mind. I needed sleep. I didn't need to stay up until the wee hours of the morning watching a movie I didn't really care about.

Another voice joined Grey's logic, this one with Lyle's distinct deep timbre.

"Stay a little longer. You're no fun. I know it's late, but what's a few more hours? You never stay late."

My breath hitched as I thought about those distant conversations. They had usually happened on a weeknight when I needed to be up early for work, something Lyle ignored anytime I brought it up. If he had an early meeting, I was out of his apartment by 9:00 p.m. so he would have time to prep and get to bed. When the shoe was on the other foot, I felt like I was waging a war, trying to justify my need to do well at work, climb the corporate ladder, prove to everyone I had what it took to live a stable, successful life. A safe life. A life where I could work nine to five instead of being at the beck and call of a store, restaurant, or cafe manager.

I rolled over, trying to silence my thoughts. There was nothing wrong with getting a good night's sleep. And yet, my thoughts continued to churn, arguing the pros and cons of a late night.

I didn't have work tomorrow. In fact, I didn't need to be anywhere in the morning except right here. What would it be like not to be the party pooper, for once? Not to be the responsible one? What if the movie really was good? I'd been meaning to watch it but hadn't made the time when it was in theaters. Why not join in, be social?

After a few more minutes of tossing and turning, I sat up with a groan, realizing that once again, Grey had won. His gentle teasing and persistence had convinced me to leave my comfort zone behind, listening to my inner voice of fun that I so often ignored. Grabbing my blanket and pillow, I stomped downstairs. Just because I was going to have fun didn't mean I had to be happy about it. Or maybe, more precisely, I didn't have to let Grey know I was happy about it.

The lights were off, the TV providing the only source of light in the dark space. The opening scenes filled the TV screen, casting a blue/green glow over everything. Tory and Trent sat on the loveseat, not seeming to mind the smaller seating area as they cuddled. Grey lay sprawled on the large couch, an American flag blanket draped over him, one arm flung above his head.

"Move." I nudged him with my leg.

Grey sat up, a huge grin splitting his face. "Couldn't stay away from me?"

"Hardly. I didn't trust you not to stick my hand in warm water if I didn't come down," I grumbled, putting on a front. Grey didn't need to know he'd given me the permission I hadn't realized I needed to let loose and enjoy the moment. I could always go to bed early tomorrow.

I sat on the end of the couch opposite Grey, laying my head on the armrest and curling my legs into the middle cushion. The couch dipped in odd places, testifying to its many years of use. Yet, it was oddly comfortable as I settled in, draping my blanket over me in an effort to stay warm in the frigid basement. I'd forgotten socks and was careful to keep my feet covered as I settled in.

The motion on the screen held my attention for a moment as I tried to follow the storyline. But it wasn't long before the last few days caught up with me, dragging my eyelids down as I drifted off to sleep to the sound of gunfire on the TV.

I woke to shuffling sounds and whispered voices, music playing faintly in the background. I tried to roll over, snuggle back down into my cozy cocoon of sleep, but a warm hand on my calf stopped me.

"Careful there. I was happy to let you stretch out a bit, but I draw the line at getting kicked." The voice was deep and amused.

With a start, I sat up, drawing my legs out of Grey's lap. My cheeks heated with embarrassment as I looked around the room.

"How did...what...?" I stuttered, my thoughts scattered and lost in the lingering fog of sleep.

"You stretched out about halfway through the movie. I didn't have the heart to wake you up and make you curl back into your tight ball from earlier." Grey spoke softly, his hands outstretched as if trying not to spook a wild animal.

"What time is it?" I rubbed my forehead, still processing what had happened.

I was guaranteed to look a mess: my hair a tangle of bedhead, my cheek covered in crease lines from the couch. Thankfully, I could hide most of that in the dim light of the basement.

Grey looked at his phone. "Just after one in the morning. The movie just ended."

I flinched at the late hour. The last time I'd been awake this late, I'd been helping my mom manage the pain from a broken collarbone and other injuries following her car accident. I looked around, noticing Tory and Trent had disappeared at some point, leaving me alone with Grey in front of the TV. It emitted a faint glow as the end credits scrolled across the screen.

"Trent was a bit bugged you didn't even make it through the first fight scene. But after two days trapped in the car with me, no one could really blame you." Grey winked at me and then pushed up from the couch, stretching as he stood. "I'm calling it a night. There are rumors of a video game tournament tomorrow night, and I want to be well-rested."

"Goodnight," I said, trying to wake myself up enough to make the trek upstairs.

"Goodnight," Grey said over his shoulder as he disappeared down the hall into the room he was sharing with Trent.

I stayed on the couch, shaking my head as I tried to make sense of the night. I hadn't intended to sleep through the entire movie. I'd planned to watch a few minutes and then bow out again if I started to get tired, proving to Grey I wasn't a stick in the mud and getting to bed before the wee hours of the morning. How I'd ended up with my feet in Grey's lap, comfortable enough to sleep through the entire three-hour movie was beyond me.

I was making a habit of sleeping with Grey, and I didn't know how I felt about it.

Pushing up from the couch, I gathered my blanket and pillow. My gaze snagged on the spot Grey had occupied, my cheeks heating as I thought about how I'd sprawled across him as if he was more than the friend of a friend. Any other guy, and I would have been too tense to relax enough to enjoy the movie, let alone fall asleep. But there was something about Grey. His presence was somehow simultaneously stressful and soothing. Like he knew how to push my buttons, but just enough to get me out of my shell, convincing me to stay up for a movie or visit a cheese outlet.

"'Not all who wander are lost,'" I muttered with a shake of my head, the barest hint of a smile tilting my lips. In fact, wandering downstairs to watch the movie had been a good thing. I'd spent time with people and watched the beginning of a movie. The detours on this trip had proved enjoyable so far, getting me to try new foods and spend time with Dot and Hank. Maybe I'd find the courage to do a bit more wandering on this trip, particularly if Grey led the way.

Chapter Fourteen

I WOKE TO SUNLIGHT streaming through the blinds in my room, the exhaustion in my bones telling me I hadn't slept nearly enough. I stretched and rolled over, surprised I'd managed to sleep until almost seven. While this constituted sleeping in for me, I had a feeling I'd be the only one awake for at least another hour.

I rolled out of bed and slipped into leggings and a tank top, piling my hair into a messy bun. The internet at the cabin was spotty, just enough to get the constant barrage of work messages but not steady enough to stream a yoga video. However, I felt confident enough in my yoga abilities to at least throw together a simple flow to start my day, though I'd avoid any headstands just to be safe. Not to mention if I didn't do a full yoga flow soon, I was going to lose my mind. I had way too many questions circling through my head, most of them to do with a certain bearded man who made an excellent sleeping companion.

Wishing I hadn't left my yoga mat in Grey's car, I sat cross-legged on the living room floor and took a few deep breaths. I was grateful for the open, airy space of the living room. Even with two couches and a recliner, it had enough room for me to spread out and stretch.

I let myself get lost in a simple vinyasa, moving through the various poses to work the kinks of travel and sleeping on the couch out of my muscles, my body stretching and flexing with each movement. Doing yoga was one of the few moments when I felt fully at peace, letting go of self-consciousness and doubt. In a perfect world, I would be a yoga instructor, embracing this peace and confidence full-time.

The carpet scratched my skin as I spread out in savasana, lying flat on my back with my arms down at my sides. The sun streaming through the windows warmed my skin. I concentrated on the support of the floor beneath me as I finished my practice, breathing deep and letting all my worries melt away.

"Are you dead?"

I jerked up, startled to find I wasn't alone. Grey sat on the loveseat behind me in a red flannel shirt, his hair tousled.

"What...? When...?" I stammered, my heart pounding in my chest. Any peace I'd found from my practice fled with the surprise.

"I couldn't sleep, and thought I'd watch for wildlife while I waited for everyone to wake up." Grey settled back into the couch, his face filled with mischief.

"How did that turn into watching me do yoga?" I stood and walked to the couch, settling onto the opposite end from Grey, moving closer but not too close. My cheeks flamed as I thought about what he might have seen.

"You were already done when I got here. At least, I'm assuming you lying flat on the floor with your eyes closed means you were done. I honestly thought you'd fallen asleep." He shrugged, and I breathed a sigh of relief that he hadn't been up earlier to watch me with my butt in the air doing downward dog.

"I guess I won't call you a complete creeper, then," I said, shaking my head and pretending I wasn't sans makeup in full daylight. Maybe if I pretended comfort in my casual attire, I'd actually feel it. It was worth testing. After all, who cared if I was wearing makeup this early when vacationing in the mountains?

"Just a partial creeper?"

"You did sneak up on me while I was doing yoga and scared the living daylights out of me." I snagged the blanket off the back of the couch and draped it over my legs, cold now that I was sitting still. Grey had the right idea with his flannel. Idaho summers still carried a chill in the mornings and evenings.

"Next time I'm trying not to wake the whole cabin, I'll make sure to stomp up the stairs and slam a few doors so as not to startle anyone." He rolled his eyes as he spoke, humor filling his tone.

"Seems reasonable to me. You could probably throw in some bear growls for good measure. Make people think a grizzly broke into the cabin," I said, deciding to play along. I peeked up at him through my lashes as I toyed with the ends of my blanket.

"Bear growls? I could make that work. I've got the hair to help me get into character." He stroked his beard as if seriously considering playing the role of a grizzly bear wandering a mountain cabin.

"I've heard that's really the reason men grow beards, to get in touch with their animal side," I said, doing my best to ignore how said beard added definition to his jaw and made his smile pop.

"Are you saying my animal persona is hairy, eats all the time, and spends several months of the year sleeping? If so, I'm not mad about that at all." He nodded with mock seriousness, though his lips still twitched with humor.

"When you put it that way, I think I might declare my animal persona to be a bear too. Though if the majority of my diet has to be fish, I'm out."

We drifted into silence, my brain scrambling to come up with something else to talk about. Instead, my mind went blank as I stared at the blanket in my lap, searching the quilt for answers it refused to provide. The only topics I could think of were ones I wanted to avoid, like asking if he'd been as comfortable watching the movie as I had been or if he found me attractive with my hair a mess.

Mumbling something about needing to get ready, I slipped out of the room and into my bedroom, wanting to escape the awkward conversation I could feel waiting in the wings. Something about the way he looked at me, taking me in without styled hair or makeup, left me feeling vulnerable. Not to mention the two unintentional cuddle sessions we'd engaged in since this trip started. I might be a coward, but there were some things better left unsaid, especially when Grey's gaze warmed me in ways I didn't want to think about.

I needed someone to talk to, but Tory was sound asleep. I wished Chloe and Mallory were here so I could hash out my emotions with my roommates. Unfortunately, they were hours away in Utah, and I doubted I could fully encapsulate my emotions in a text. Not to mention it felt too early for a phone call.

I pulled on some leggings and one of my favorite t-shirts, a blue shirt that read "Real girls like the classics" with an image of a rock-on hand signal. A college friend had designed it for me as a birthday gift, and I wore it every chance I got, despite repeated protests from Lyle that it was ratty and outdated.

Once I was dressed, I pulled my hair into a new bun and added some subtle eyeshadow and mascara. I grabbed a book and a hoody, slipping past Grey where he dozed on the couch wrapped in the quilt I'd left behind. I settled outside on a wooden porch chair, enjoying the quiet morning. The only sounds that greeted me were the conversations of birds and squirrels. The stillness spoke to my soul, the cool air surrounding me like a familiar blanket as I breathed in the mountain air heavy with dew. I'd forgotten the peace and stillness of the mountains first thing in the morning. Maybe tomorrow I would move my yoga practice outside, really soak in the moment.

I sat and read for about an hour before the sounds of creaking floorboards and closing doors alerted me to movement in the cabin. I pushed up from the rocking chair and headed inside, noticing that Grey no longer dozed on the couch, though he'd left the blanket behind. I wondered if it would smell like him or if it would need more contact with his skin first.

Tory stood in the kitchen wearing a deep blue lounge set, the fridge door open, as she rummaged around.

"Need any help?" I asked, and she jumped before straightening and turning to look at me.

"I thought everyone was asleep. I guess I shouldn't be surprised you're the first one awake. You never could sleep in. Though the late-night party animal is a new side," she said with a wink. "What did you think of the movie?" Tory asked, amusement coloring her tone. She pulled a carton of eggs and a jug of milk from the fridge and set them on the counter before closing the door.

"It was fascinating," I said, not missing a beat. I didn't bother mentioning that Grey was awake too. For all I knew, he had gone back to bed after creeping on my yoga practice and snuggling in my blanket. "Even after a late night, mornings are the best time to get things done."

"This is way too early for me. I think Trent picked the longest super-hero movie on the planet. I'm not completely sure what happened beyond things blowing up, though don't think I didn't notice the snuggle session going on between you and Grey." Tory waggled her eyebrows, her lips tilted in a teasing grin.

"I fell asleep and unconsciously stretched out. And you're one to talk. If you and Trent sat any closer, you would have fused together." I did my best to keep defensiveness from my tone, averting my gaze from Tory and focusing on pouring myself a glass of milk. What I needed after so little sleep was Pepsi, but that meant maneuvering around Tory to get to the fridge and potentially making eye contact.

I lifted the glass to my lips, grimacing at the taste and texture, but committing to the drink and the distraction it provided. If I closed my eyes and pretended hard enough, maybe I could convince myself two percent tasted just as good as the flavored milks Grey and I had purchased the day before. I'd have to stick a couple in the fridge to go with breakfast tomorrow.

"Why are you awake?" I glanced at the clock, opting for a change of topic. It was barely after nine, and while Tory had beat me to bed, I was guessing she hadn't slept through most of the movie.

"Because I don't want to sleep away the day. We're at the cabin! While I'm a fan of taking it easy, I'm also a fan of exploring and doing fun things before the day gets away from us." Tory waved around a whisk she'd grabbed, and I was grateful she hadn't started stirring the eggs quite yet. I didn't need scrambled eggs splattered all over my clothes.

"What are we doing today? Floating the river?" While I'd only been to the cabin once, I knew Tory's favorite activities all involved water.

"That's a possibility, though Grey's never been up here before. I was thinking it would be better to spend the day in Yellowstone. We could hit the Grand Prismatic and, if we're feeling extra brave, we could battle the Old Faithful crowds and see if the geyser is still on schedule."

"You are feeling brave. I don't know if I've ever attempted Old Faithful this time of year. I'm guessing just getting into the park will be a struggle." I pictured the entrance to Yellowstone, with its line of ranger-containing booths, anticipating the long line of cars that would await us once we reached West Yellowstone.

"I have a good feeling about today, especially if we can get out the door before lunch."

"I thought the entrance was busiest in the morning." Her logic confused me, but I would roll with it if it meant a distraction from my thoughts of Grey and whatever was building between us.

"It is, but the sooner we get in line, the sooner we get into the park, and the sooner we can start our epic adventure." She stood with her hands on her hips, looking like an exuberant cartoon character ready to tackle the day. I couldn't help but love her for it.

I helped Tory fix breakfast: scrambled eggs, hashbrowns, and a towering mountain of toast. When it was ready, Tory disappeared downstairs to get the guys while I washed dishes, the smell of breakfast causing my stomach to growl. One downside to life in the woods—there wasn't a dishwasher. But somehow the view of aspen trees outside the kitchen window with mountains in the distance made up for the lack of modern conveniences as I scrubbed pans and utensils.

I turned off the water as I heard footsteps coming up the stairs. I settled at the table and was shortly joined by Tory. A few minutes later, the guys surfaced. Trent was groggy, still wearing green superhero pajamas and only mumbling a greeting before flopping into a chair. Grey had taken the time since I'd seen him to comb his hair and get ready, though he still wore the same flannel shirt from earlier. I hadn't realized how much

I liked a man in flannel until this trip. Now, the pattern would forever remind me of muscled arms and long car rides.

We fixed our plates and dug into the food, Tory and Grey providing most of the conversation as they discussed the potential plans for the week. Once we had eaten, Tory explained the plan for the day.

"Sounds great," Grey said, leaning back into his chair and stretching his arms above his head.

Trent nodded his head, blinking like he wasn't sure if he was dreaming, his expression remaining stoic.

"Let's get ready and try to be out the door in 20 minutes." Tory stood and moved towards her room. "And pack your swimsuit. If it's warm enough, we can swim in the Firehole."

I froze. "I thought we'd just drive around the park, maybe do some simple hikes."

"Where's the fun in that?" Tory closed her bedroom door, and the guys disappeared downstairs.

I hesitated, biting my lip and debating my options. While I had planned on wearing my swimsuit to float the river one day while we were here, I hadn't planned on anything more involved. Floating the river meant maybe getting my torso wet. Swimming was a whole other story that would likely mean messy hair and smudged makeup. Not to mention, I knew from Tory's stories that swimming at the Firehole meant jumping into the water and riding the rapids, something far more adventurous than I cared to experience.

I shook my head, dislodging my fears. Just because the others went swimming didn't mean I had to. I could pack a book, sit in the sun, and enjoy time outside, working on my tan. It would be fine.

I forced myself down the hall, grabbing my swimsuit and towel along with a book. I could participate, just on my terms.

Yet, despite my logic, my heart wouldn't stop pounding at the thought of swimming in the rapids and the loss of control it promised.

Chapter Fifteen

THE WAIT TO ENTER the park took forever, something that felt even longer since I was wearing hiking shoes and hadn't wanted to deal with the hassle of putting them back on. I deeply regretted leaving my shoes on as my toes itched to be free. Add to that a massive traffic jam a few miles into the park, and I was quickly regretting our decision to visit Yellowstone.

"There had better be a bear at the end of this line," I muttered as I shifted uncomfortably in my seat, ready to hit the trailhead and start exploring the park. At the rate we were going, we would be lucky if we made it to Old Faithful before lunch.

We continued to crawl forward inches at a time. I sat in the back next to Grey, listening to his running commentary about the national parks he hoped to visit someday. His constant dialogue was giving me flashbacks to the start of our trip, and I struggled to think of questions or comments to break up his monologue. Tory and Trent were no help, with Tory focused on the road and Trent being his usual stoic self.

Just as I was about to give up all hope of conversation between the four of us, Trent spoke up.

"Ten bucks says it's a bison," Trent said from the front passenger seat, his monotone matching his lack of expression as he glanced over his shoulder at me.

"It's either that or an elk." Tory tapped her fingers on the steering wheel, her voice upbeat, if strained.

One of Tory's music mixes, a combination of current and early 2000 hits, played quietly in the background, providing a soundtrack to our snail's-paced trek into the park. I itched to switch it to Journey or Bon Jovi, something to cut through the frustration in the car. After waiting over a half-hour to get into the park, the slow traffic just past the entrance felt like a personal insult. Especially when there was no end in sight.

"Am I missing something? Seeing an elk or bison sounds cool to me." Grey looked back and forth between us, his brow furrowed in confusion. He shifted in his seat, looking out the windshield as if watching for an animal to come trotting down the road straight for us.

"Sure, they're cool, but not when they're causing this big of a traffic jam. Besides, we'll probably see herds of both deeper into the park," Tory said, frustration tinging her tone as she leaned forward as if silently willing the cars in front of her to move faster.

Trent and I nodded in agreement.

"Makes sense." Grey looked out the window, scanning the trees, before turning back to me with a goofy grin. "I can't believe I'm finally getting to see Yellowstone. How busy do you think it'll be at Old Faithful?"

"If we ever get there, insanely busy," Tory said, her tone flat. Tory hated crowds in nature, making me wonder if we'd stick to the plan and visit the iconic geyser, or if Tory would take us off the beaten path to some secret corner of the park that wasn't as popular.

We continued to battle traffic, which had been caused by an elk, for a few miles before things cleared up. Grey snapped several photos of the animal, taking advantage of the forced slow down to observe the elk and exclaim over its size. I bit back a smile at his clear enthusiasm, his reaction making the traffic jam worth the delay.

We finally reached the fork in the road where we turned towards Old Faithful. The drive, which was still crowded but moving, passed quickly thanks to Grey's excitement and questions about everything we passed. If we hadn't been headed to a clear destination, he probably would have begged to stop at every pullout, soaking in the magic of Yellowstone with its mix of fields, forests, mountains, and geologic features.

We made it to Old Faithful and found a spot on the worn, weathered boardwalk near the back of the crowd. I watched Tory's shoulders bunch towards her ears as she took in the people, knowing it was taking all her self-control not to bolt to the car and wait for us there. While she'd chosen our destination, I knew she'd done it for Grey. Tory, who loved people, also loved the quiet and calm of the mountains, something that was counteracted by the bustling crowds at tourist attractions like Old Faithful.

Despite the crowds, the sunshine was pleasant and helped erase my tension from the earlier traffic jam. Excitement built in the crowd the closer we got to eruption time. Grey fairly bounced on his toes, his enthusiasm palpable.

I wanted to reach over and grab his hand, feed off his energy and excitement. Instead, I slipped out my phone, capturing his expression as the geyser went off. The pure wonder on his face would live in my memory for a long time, encapsulating a moment of magic.

We watched, along with hundreds of other tourists, as Old Faithful launched thousands of gallons of water skyward. Grey's expression of amazement made me imagine what he had been like as a young child, and for a moment I got lost in the wonder of watching frothy white water explode from the earth, wind heavy with steam blowing in our faces.

"Are we sure it isn't manmade? Or magic? The fact nature can just launch water into the air like that...Wow!" Grey rambled as we climbed back into the car.

"Just wait until you see the Grand Prismatic. It's indescribable," I said as I buckled my seatbelt, his excitement reminding me of my first visits to the area as a kid.

Back then, everything about Yellowstone had felt otherworldly, and I had impatiently anticipated what waited around the next corner as my mom and I had driven from one end of the park to the other. Not all of her adventures had ended in disaster. Some had given me memories of just the two of us that I would treasure forever.

"I don't know. It's going to be hard to beat boiling water shooting into the sky. How high do you think it went?" Grey asked, settling into his seat. His golden-brown eyes shone, and he fairly vibrated with residual enthusiasm, causing the seats in the back of Tory's car to move slightly.

"I've been thinking. What if we save the Grand Prismatic for after everyone gets here?" Tory called from the front seat as we waited for an opening to pull out of our parking spot. "I don't think Kylie's been to the park either, and I'm sure she'll want to see it too."

"That, and you're dying to get into the water," I teased, reading the tension in Tory's shoulders as she dealt with the crowds. If there was one thing guaranteed to alleviate Tory's stress, it was spending quality time outside in a body of water.

Tory shrugged, her black curls dancing with the movement. "Guilty as charged."

We all agreed to the change of plans, and Tory drove to the Firehole. It was still fairly busy, making it difficult to find a parking spot, but Tory was able to squeeze into a spot after waiting for a family in a minivan to pull out. We each took turns in the nearby bathroom to change. I did my best to ignore the smell as I changed into my one-piece blue floral swimsuit and water shoes. I wiggled my toes in relief now that I was wearing sandals as opposed to the stiff, restrictive hiking shoes.

I stashed my clothes in the back of the car and reached for a camp chair to set up along the riverbank. The sun felt wonderful on my skin, and I welcomed its warmth.

"What do you need that for?" Grey asked, pointing to the chair. He had joined me at the back of the car wearing green swim trunks, a life jacket slung over one shoulder. I did my best to ignore his bare chest. While he didn't have a six pack and bulging muscles, it was clear Grey took care of himself and wasn't a stranger to exercise or the sun.

"I'm not swimming. I figured I'd read a book on my phone and enjoy nature." I waved my phone to prove my point.

Tory joined the conversation with a shake of her head, her curls pulled up into a bun on top of her head. Her black and white polka dot swimsuit had a vintage feel that made me wish I had more polka dots in my wardrobe. "But you have to swim! This is one of the best things to do in the park."

"I'm not a big swimmer," I protested. Though perhaps the more accurate way to explain my swimming ability was that I *could* swim, I just chose not to. Swimming involved a whole lot of hassle that, since I'd become an adult, rarely seemed worth it.

Trent didn't comment, simply joined our circle in blue swim trunks, his arms crossed over his bare chest, muscles bulging. He clearly spent multiple hours a week working out.

Grey watched me quietly, reading my hesitation.

"Are you afraid of the water?" he asked softly, trying to get at the root of my hesitation.

I shook my head. "I can swim."

"Is it the rapids?" Concern pinched his brows, and I wanted to reach over and smooth out the crease.

"No, I can handle them."

"Then what are you afraid of?" Grey continued to watch me, and my fingers lifted self-consciously to my bun, playing with a strand of hair that had escaped its confines.

"I'm not afraid. I just don't want to swim." More accurately, I didn't want to take the risk. While it appeared safe enough on the surface, something could go wrong. Somehow, I got the feeling that Grey could see right through my excuse. He watched me a moment more, taking in my every gesture, and I shifted awkwardly under his scrutiny. He seemed to find what he was looking for before giving a decisive nod.

"Chicken," Grey said, looking straight at me, his brow quirked, issuing the same kind of challenge he'd used at the cheese outlet to get me to step outside my comfort zone. It was the same expression that had convinced me to try root beer milk—and was absolutely not what I had been expecting. I'd thought he would back down. Maybe try one more half-hearted attempt to get me to join in before following Tory and Trent to the river without a backward glance. Instead, he'd thrown out the challenge, pushing my buttons once more.

"Excuse me?" I glared at Grey, determined not to let his tactics work on me again. It was one thing to try a new flavor of milk. It was something else entirely to jump into a flowing river so deep I couldn't touch the bottom.

"You heard me. What happened to the brave Audrey who tried cheese curds without flinching?"

I threw my hands in the air, exasperated. "There's a big difference between trying new foods and swimming in a river."

"You said you can swim, right?" Grey raised one finger.

"Yes, but—"

"You have a lifejacket?" A second finger joined the first.

I gestured at a red vest in the trunk of the car. "I do—"

"And you trust us to protect you and help you?" He raised a third finger, challenge written in every ridge of his body.

"Yes," I said in exasperation. "Skills and support aren't the problem. What if I genuinely don't want to?"

Even as I shot the question back at him, it rang false. A part of me, a long dormant part of myself that I'd stopped listening to around the time I'd started dating Lyle, wanted to jump into the river. But what if that part of myself was wrong? What if there was a valid reason for ignoring it and sticking with the safe, steady option of reading on the shore?

Grey crossed his arms over his chest, watching me. "I don't think that's it. I think you're scared."

I hadn't grown up with siblings, but something about the way Grey quirked his eyebrow made me think this was how it felt to have an overbearing older brother. Though, the feelings I was developing for Grey felt far from brotherly.

"I'm not scared," I shot back, rising to the bait, knowing I didn't have to argue with him, but unable to resist.

"That's the only reason I can think of for why you won't. Because I highly doubt your book is interesting enough to beat swimming in a river warmed by one of the world's largest volcanoes." Grey gestured to the river behind us as it flowed and churned over rocks, the shrieks of other swimmers enjoying themselves underscoring his every word.

I bit my lip, waffling. Seeming to sense my weakening, Grey stepped closer to me, his expression softening.

"If you're genuinely afraid and don't want to do this, I'll stop pushing. But I don't want you living with the regret of not experiencing something so unique. How many chances will you have to swim in Yellowstone?"

"When Tory's your friend, more often than you'd think." My quip was half-hearted, and he knew it. The fact that he cared enough about me to stop pushing if I needed him to warmed me in unexpected ways.

I could do this. I could be brave enough to jump into the river, risk the loss of control. Trade safety and perfect makeup for memories and an adventure.

"Not all who wander..." Grey trailed off, and I bit back a laugh at the completely out-of-context quote, and yet, it was the perfect thing to say.

"Fine." I shoved the chair back into the car, trading it for the lifejacket. "But if I drown or have a terrible time, I'm blaming you." I poked a finger into Grey's chest, ignoring the warmth that spread up my arm at the contact.

He just grinned, covering my hand with his and giving it a squeeze before breaking contact and heading towards to the river. Had his pulse also jumped at the contact?

We followed Tory over some rocks, down to a spot in the river where people were jumping in.

"Everyone have their lifejackets?" Tory called over the sounds of laughter and splashing water. "We're not cliff jumping. There's a rock in the river that, once you reach it, you can jump from into the current. It takes some maneuvering to get to, but it's the best way to experience the Firehole."

We all nodded, tugging at buckles and straps to ensure our lifejackets were secure. Tory stepped into the water first, Trent close behind her. I went to follow but hesitated. While I'd claimed not to be afraid up by the car, the nerves I'd been fighting through my entire exchange with Grey chose that exact moment to rear their ugly head.

I looked at the river in front of me and attempted to swallow down my misgivings. Instead, they lodged in my throat, making it hard to breathe. *It's just swimming, Audrey. You've been swimming before.* I'd been swimming in lakes and rivers, even the ocean, before. While the current was strong enough to create a few rapids in this stretch of the river, it wasn't anything I couldn't handle.

The arguments against getting in continued to stack up, eclipsing my confidence and making it impossible for me to take another step towards the water. *You can't do this. It's a terrible idea.* Each word rang with an odd sense of familiarity, spoken in a deep man's voice that I refused to examine too closely.

As I watched, a guy jumped off a rock in the river into the current with a yell, disappearing below the water. A few moments later he popped up down river, punching a fist into the air with a whoop of victory.

"I don't think I can do this." I gasped out, my heart racing at the thought of jumping into the water and the resulting loss of control. It was the kind of thing my mom would do without hesitation, without thinking about the repercussions if something went wrong. The kind of thing I'd learned to avoid—because one of us had to be responsible.

"I'm right here with you. You got this." Grey gave gentle encouragement, moving to stand next to me.

"I don't." I said, shaking my head vehemently and inching my way back towards the car.

"Take a breath. You've got a lifejacket and friends to watch out for you. Nothing's going to happen." He put his hand on my arm, giving a gentle squeeze of encouragement.

I breathed in through my nose, counting to four, before releasing my breath through my mouth.

"That's it." Grey nodded, moving his hand to rub comfortingly up and down my arm. I wanted to lean into the touch, letting it ground me. "Show me your best yoga breath."

I took another deep breath before taking a hesitant step forward, breaking the contact. I immediately missed his warmth, but if I didn't move soon, I wouldn't go. I wouldn't step into the river, let alone jump in.

"You'll be with me the whole time?" My voice shook slightly as I waited for his response.

"Yep. Every step of the way. I won't let you wander off and get lost." He gave me a wink, and I bit back a groan as he butchered the familiar saying.

I took one more deep breath and stepped into the water, grateful for Grey's reassuring presence behind me. I was tempted to entwine my fingers with his, but I resisted the urge, knowing I likely wouldn't let go once I latched on.

With each step, the water became deeper, the cool temperature making me flinch.

"I thought you said this water was warm." I pushed the words through clenched teeth, looking over at Tory, who had paused when she'd noticed Grey and I weren't directly behind her.

She shrugged and continued making her way into the water, crouching down so that most of her body was in the river. "I said it was *warmer* than most rivers. It's not a hot spring. It's still a river out in the woods."

Promising myself that I only had to ride the rapids once and then this "fun" adventure would be over, I continued following the group until we reached a massive crevasse between two rocks. The water was clear enough that I could see the rocks I walked on, sharp, dark stones that spoke of a volcanic history. About halfway to the cliff on the other side of the river, a large gap appeared between the two rocks. No matter how hard I looked, I couldn't see the bottom.

"Here's the deal. You want to jump across the gap to that rock shelf over there." Tory gestured to the rock floor next to the cliff. "If you don't jump far enough, you'll have to swim hard and quick to get over before the current drags you away. From there, make your way to the head of the rapids where you saw that other group jumping. Once you reach it, jump in and pull your legs in tight. You don't want to knock up against these rocks if you can avoid it."

"What happens after you jump?" I knew it was a stupid question, but I couldn't help the voice of fear sitting in the back of my mind, taunting me. *You can't do this. This is insane. Why jump into the current of a fast-flowing river when you could be reading on the shore?*

Grey took pity on me, giving my hand a squeeze. "You ride the current and have fun. Just follow my lead." With those parting words, he jumped into the river and swam across to the shelf.

"You're next," Tory said, blocking Trent who had moved to follow Grey.

My gut clenched. "Are you sure this is safe?"

"I've been doing this for years. As long as you can swim and you've got a lifejacket, you'll be fine." Tory kept her tone light and reassuring.

I hesitated a moment more before looking over to where Grey stood, watching me from the rock shelf. He tucked his thumbs into his armpits, making fake chicken wings. I could almost hear the accompanying clucking sounds over the rushing water. I bit back a snort, grateful for the mix of goading and kind encouragement my friends were using to help me in this moment. Steeling myself, I dove towards the shelf.

I didn't make it quite far enough and had to swim to beat the current. When I got close enough to the shelf, Grey reached out and pulled me up. My fingers laced with his and didn't let go, needing the contact as I processed what I'd done.

I was drenched, hair falling out of its bun, heart pounding as I stood on a narrow rock shelf. Not only had I jumped across a bottomless pit, now I would willingly climb over rocky terrain to jump into rapids. Mild as they were, I was still choosing adventure in this moment, and I kind of wished my mom was here to see me be brave like her.

Once Tory and Trent joined us, I released Grey's hand and hoped Tory didn't notice. I had no idea what was going on between me and Grey and didn't want her questions complicating things. Our group climbed the short distance to the rapids. Despite Tory's reassurance that they weren't bad, my stomach clenched at the sight.

"Who's jumping first?" Grey called over his shoulder, gesturing towards the spot where we'd watched others jump in.

"Dibs not!" I called, wrapping my arms around my midsection as a breeze kicked up and goose bumps rose on my arms. I wanted to watch at least one, maybe two people do this before I took the plunge.

"Go, Grey! We'll just jump in order," Tory said, waving him forward.

Grey gave me a toothy grin.

"I dare you," he said.

The three words were barely audible over the rushing water, but I heard them, feeling them race down my spine and sink into my toes, grounding me in this moment. I wasn't about to let Grey show me up.

Grey jumped off the rock into the rapids with a yell, the current sucking him down into the river and away from us. He rode the water, dodging rocks, laughing and hollering until he was out of sight. Grey survived, and he even made it look fun.

I gave myself two deep breaths, just enough to calm my nerves but not enough to back out, before I jumped, praying I wouldn't regret this.

Chapter Sixteen

THE COLD WATER GREETED me, stealing my breath for a moment as the current transported me downstream. I allowed my lifejacket to pull me to the surface and sucked in a giant gulp of air once my head broke through the water. Adrenaline coursed through my veins, my heart pounding as the river pulled me away from the rock where I jumped.

"You did it!" Tory yelled, cheering behind me. Her voice rang with excitement.

I focused on the sharp rocks around me and the pull of the river. I kicked my feet, testing my control. The current was strong, but not impossible to navigate. I did my best to tuck my legs in, seeing the rocky edges beneath the water's surface. I allowed the current to pull me past people cooling off in the river and around a bend until I came out in an open area where Grey stood waist-deep in the water, grinning.

"How was it?" he asked, extending a hand.

I grabbed it, allowing him to help me to my feet. I misjudged the strength of his grip, stumbling into him as I worked to find my balance on the rocks of the riverbed. My hand came to rest on his chest, his arms wrapping around my waist to steady me. His enveloping warmth contrasted with the chill of the breeze on my wet skin, and I found myself wanting to lean into him more and accept more of his help than was strictly necessary.

Startled at my thoughts, I took a step back, breaking his hold and instantly regretting the lost contact. I wasn't sure what to do with the emotions and desires filling me.

"I survived." I tried to hide my enjoyment, wanting to tease him and maybe even pull out his laugh, a sound I found myself craving in this moment.

Grey saw through my efforts, his grin stretching even farther. Water clung to his beard and hair, his eyes sparking with excitement.

"You loved it, didn't you? Better than root beer milk, right?" He nudged me with his elbow, nearly throwing off my balance with his enthusiasm.

I couldn't contain my smile anymore, a giant grin filling my face as I shook my head, water droplets scattering from my hair. "It was amazing!"

And the thing that made it even more amazing was the man standing next to me, cheering me on for my bravery. Bravery that, if I was being honest, had been minimal. Yet, Grey had a special ability to make me feel seen. Like he recognized just how difficult each step outside my comfort zone was and wanted to celebrate every single one with me.

A girl could get addicted to the energy and magnetism that was Grey.

"Makes you wonder what else you've been missing out on, doesn't it?" Grey's quiet comment, so similar to my own thoughts, gave me pause as, together, we stood on the banks of the river watching for Trent and Tory.

"Maybe." I conceded. Anxiety still curled in my belly, but there was also a fire there. Like something had awakened, and I wasn't sure I wanted it to go back to sleep.

Tory appeared around the bend, followed shortly by Trent. She fairly glowed with happiness, in her element as she finished her float and stood from the river. Trent was stoic as ever, his face giving nothing away about his experience.

"Want to go again?" Grey asked, once our group reunited, Trent and Tory rounding out our circle.

I looked at the others for a moment, gauging their reactions. They looked at me, checking to make sure I was okay. I nodded, surprised at the excitement I felt at the prospect of jumping again. "Let's do it!"

The four of us climbed out of the water and made the trek back to the other section of the river near where we jumped. A few more people had joined in the fun and were riding the rapids. We climbed in, and I dove to the rock shelf, making my way to the rapids, leading our group. The rush I felt silenced the what-ifs in my head, and I let myself enjoy my new adventure.

More and more, I was starting to think wandering off the expected path could be fun.

Chapter Seventeen

I DIDN'T SAY MUCH as we drove back to the cabin, mountains and trees passing outside my window. Instead, I reveled in the memory, still amazed at myself for jumping into the river. The towel underneath me was wet, likely soaking into the car seat. I'd kicked off my water shoes, allowing my toes the freedom they'd been craving all day. My hair was a disaster. A few tangled strands had escaped from my bun, and I could guarantee I had mascara smudges giving me raccoon eyes. Yet, I felt happy—content, even. I had jumped, despite fear and anxiety and self-doubt. Not just that, I'd jumped multiple times, experiencing a level of fun and enjoyment I hadn't anticipated. Maybe there was something to be said for losing control every once in a while.

"They made it." Tory exclaimed, pulling me from my thoughts.

A silver car was parked in the clearing next to Grey's SUV. Tory parked on the other side of the silver car, and I quickly slipped my water shoes back on, following the others out of the car.

The cabin door opened, and a group of three familiar faces trekked out onto the porch, waving. The twin blond-haired guys in their late twenties were staples at almost all of Tory's social functions. While I knew there had to be other indicators, the only way I knew how to tell them apart was that Alex wore glasses and Brad didn't. A few steps behind them was Kylie, one of Tory's roommates. Her thick, auburn hair bounced in the wind, and her excitement was nearly tangible, coming off her in waves. She looked picture-perfect, with flawless makeup and hair, and I instantly felt self-conscious. I tightened my grip on the towel around my waist as I took in Kylie's appearance and remembered my own wet, makeup-smudged state.

I hung back, following behind everyone as Tory dashed up the porch steps to hug her friends.

"How was the drive?" She slung an arm around each of the twins, leaving wet marks on their shirts as she hugged them simultaneously. They laughed, slipping from her grip with pretend dismay. Tory then turned to Kylie, who held up a hand with a laugh to stop her approach.

"I'll wait on the hug until you're dry"—she waved vaguely at Tory while taking a step back—"but it's so good to see you."

"Oh, come on! It's not that different from the time at camp when we were kids," Tory protested, jokingly going in for another hug while Kylie ducked away, hiding behind Brad for protection.

"The difference is I'm an adult now who really doesn't want to have to change her clothes," Kylie said, gesturing to her pink top and leggings.

"I didn't realize opting out of wet hugs was an option," Brad joked as he pulled his shirt away from his skin, exposing a band of tan, muscled stomach.

"You love it, and you know it," Tory said, giving him another hug, making sure to soak even more of his shirt. "We've been friends for too long for you to worry about a wet shirt."

"True enough." Alex shrugged, pushing his glasses up his nose. "But he can be bugged by how cold you are. Where were you swimming? The

Antarctic?" He gave a mock shiver, emphasizing his point as he leaned against the porch railing.

"We hit the Firehole since we weren't sure when you'd get here. You made great time," Tory said.

"I got off work earlier than planned," Kylie said. "I didn't want to miss any more of your birthday trip!"

"Are you sure they won't fall apart without you?" Tory quirked an eyebrow. "You've been sprinting up the corporate ladder so fast, I'm not sure they'll know how to function without you."

Kylie gave a delicate shrug. "I might have to answer a few emails while I'm here, but I'll make it work. I've always loved a challenge."

Tory blocked the door, so Grey, Trent, and I hung back, watching the exchange. Trent's posture tensed as he watched his girlfriend catch up with her childhood friends. I didn't know Trent well, but his reaction was odd. For someone so stoic and not reactionary, his clear dislike of Brad and Alex seemed out of character.

"Can we pause the shoptalk to discuss the really important topic here? You went to the Firehole without us! Please tell me you saved floating the river for when we got here," Brad said, nudging Tory with his shoulder.

"Of course! I wouldn't dream of floating without you guys. You brought tubes, right?"

Tory and the twins became lost in conversation, talking about plans for the rest of our trip. I wrapped my arms around myself, pretending I wasn't eager to duck inside to shower and repair my appearance.

As a breeze rustled the trees around us, I shivered, goose bumps breaking out on my skin. If Alex thought a hug from Tory felt like the Antarctic, then I felt like I'd been vacationing on Pluto thanks to the combination of my wet swimsuit and where I was standing in the shade of the porch. I was well on my way to turning into a popsicle, the higher elevation of Idaho bringing with it an added chill.

"Hey, Tory. Do you mind letting the rest of us into the cabin? I'm glad you're reconnecting with friends, but I, for one, would really like to change before hypothermia sets in." Grey called from behind me where he stood on the stairs, watching the exchange.

I smiled at him in appreciation as I rubbed my arms, trying to get rid of my goose bumps.

Tory jumped as if she'd forgotten about us in her banter with the twins.

"Yes, of course," Tory said, stepping aside to let us pass and giving a welcoming sweep of her hand to wave us inside. "I just wanted to make sure you wouldn't get overheated in the cabin."

Her comment was completely ridiculous. The cabin was several degrees cooler than outside, and I did my best to fight down my grimace. I would likely have more of a sense of humor once I'd had a chance to stand in the warm shower spray for at least 20 minutes.

I hurried around Tory, eager for a shower and the chance to warm up. My toes were cold enough that I'd likely need fuzzy socks to feel warm again. I had nearly made it inside when Kylie snagged my arm.

"Audrey! I'm so glad Tory convinced you to come. I was worried you'd back out." Kylie reached to hug me but stopped short, noting my bedraggled state. "I owe you a hug too, once you're dry."

I gave an awkward laugh, not quite sure of the correct response. Kylie and I were friendly, but I hadn't realized we were on hugging terms. She'd always felt more like Tory's friend who was comfortable around me as opposed to someone I counted as a friend. Perhaps I needed to reevaluate that perspective. Maybe vacationing with someone changed those dynamics.

"Darn wet swimsuits, always getting in the way," I joked, wishing it wasn't rude to dash into the cabin and let the door slam behind me in my haste to get warm again. Could you get frostbite from swimming in a river in the middle of summer?

"Exactly! I wish we could have gotten here sooner. You guys look like you've had a blast. I hated missing the fun, but I couldn't escape work until today. You know how it is, being a career woman and all." She gave me a friendly nudge with her shoulder, careful to avoid my swimsuit.

While it was not fair, the comparison fairy in my head had convinced me to keep Kylie at arm's length despite her repeated attempts to get to know me better. Kylie had always been friendly, excited to see me whenever I visited Tory. Yet, she left me feeling self-conscious. She always looked picture-perfect, with subtle but striking makeup and clothes that cost more than I cared to think about. Her current ensemble of name-brand leggings and a flowy top hinted at money. She'd completed a business degree about the same time as me, and while mine did nothing but collect dust in a drawer somewhere in my bedroom, hers seemed to throw doors wide open. She'd recently started a job at a new company and was already climbing the ranks, going on regular business trips to exciting locations. She was nothing but nice to me, but that voice in my head loved nothing more than pointing out how much more successful Kylie was compared to me.

Kylie led the way into the cabin, chattering away about corporate life. It was a side of business I knew little about, thanks to being perpetually stuck in customer service. Kylie's stories about big projects and corporate meetings felt like a distant dream—a dream I wasn't sure I wanted any more, not if it came with the type of stress Kylie seemed to revel in. Though, the business trips and pay raise would be nice.

"Don't worry. Now that we're here, the real party can begin!" Kylie gave my arm a squeeze before turning to look at the rest of our friends who had followed us into the cabin.

"Grey!" If it was possible, Kylie's voice filled with even more excitement. "I'll also be taking a raincheck on a dry hug from you." She flipped her hair as she spoke, and I was grateful her back was to me so I couldn't see her expression. It was probably the perfect combination of interest and invitation.

Grey's face, on the other hand, was strained as he stepped around her and headed for the stairs, hinting at a history I'd have to ask Tory about later. "Good to see you, Kylie. Unfortunately, I don't raincheck hugs."

"In that case, I guess I'll take a wet hug instead." Her voice held a note of invitation, making my hackles rise. It was an unfamiliar sensation, which I tried to ignore.

I slipped down the hall towards my bedroom, not wanting to hear the rest of their exchange.

"Grey, you are so funny." Kylie's voice followed me down the hall as I ducked into my room to grab a change of clothes.

I bit back a grimace. Strengthening friendships with Tory's friends would be a good thing. It was part of why I'd come to the cabin. Also, sharing Grey meant I wouldn't have to listen to any more of his monologues. I might have enjoyed one or two of his nudges, but I reminded myself that there was value in predictability. Having Kylie, Brad, and Alex here was for the best. If I repeated the mantra enough times, I might even believe it.

I showered quickly but took my time styling my hair and applying makeup. Kylie's perfect hair had left me feeling dowdy, and I needed the protection of my makeup and curled hair to soothe the anxiety that had returned with her arrival. It roiled in my stomach, almost as if the fun, carefree day in Yellowstone had never happened.

Later, I joined Tory in the kitchen and helped pull together dinner while the others explored the surrounding area. After the meal, we played games until dark. The mood had shifted significantly with the arrival of more guests. Instead of the comfortable banter of the night before, the air was charged. The twins brought a competitive, teasing spirit that I appreciated, but Trent's jaw indicated he felt differently. I watched him flinch each time Brad or Alex brushed arms with Tory.

I was surprised to discover I understood his sentiment. Kylie, with her giggling and need for attention from Grey, set my teeth on edge. I couldn't tell if she really didn't know how to play the various games we chose or if she liked how asking questions gave her an excuse to lean into Grey and capture his attention when he explained a particular rule. These exchanges left me feeling unsettled for reasons I didn't want to examine too closely. I knew Kylie. She was a brilliant strategist, and yet, she played dumb with Grey, something he clearly noticed as he edged farther from her and frequently asked if she genuinely didn't understand the rules.

"I think that's enough games for tonight," Tory said after our third or fourth round of cards, and I almost sighed in relief. "It's supposed to be a clear night. Who's up for stargazing?"

The group mumbled their assent, and we broke apart, everyone going their separate ways to change into warmer clothes and gather blankets.

I was one of the first people outside. In the light from the porch, I could see a lone figure lying in the grass next to the firepit. Using my phone flashlight as a guide, I picked my way over to whoever was already outside, careful not to trip on a protruding rock or root.

"It's going to be difficult to see the stars with that thing on," Grey said, laughter clear in his voice as I drew closer.

"I'll turn it off once I'm safely lying down. The last thing I need is a twisted ankle." I spread out one of my blankets and settled next to Grey, pulling the other blanket over my legs. I was close enough to feel the heat from his body, but not close enough to touch, though a part of me wanted to roll over and snuggle into his warmth like I'd done the last two nights. Unintentionally sleeping with Grey was becoming a habit I needed to break.

Or did I? asked a mischievous voice in my head. It sounded very much like something my mom would ask, urging me to step outside of my comfort zone and chase something unexpected.

"That *would* make hiking tomorrow difficult," Grey mused. He was close enough that his breath tickled my ear, and I was tempted to scoot in even closer, soaking in his warmth and comforting scent.

We lay quiet for a minute, more stars appearing as my eyes adjusted to the dark.

"Where's everyone else?" I asked. "I figured everyone else would have already come out while I was changing."

"Kylie mentioned something about searching for bug spray. Tory and Trent disappeared for what looked like a pretty serious conversation. I'm not sure what happened to the Adonis twins."

"That's the perfect nickname for those two," I said, humor lacing my tone. Not sure what to say next, I opted for a change of topic, hoping humor would add to the moment. "My hair's going to be a mess after lying on the ground. Promise not to look too closely when we head inside?"

"Do you ever get tired of all that?" Grey's words gave me pause, and I sat up to look at him, dragging the blanket with me and hugging it close.

"What do you mean?"

"Tired of constantly worrying about your hair. Tired of being perfect all the time. Tired of trying too hard. Tired of not being yourself."

His words surprised me. He'd only interacted with me a handful of times. How did he know who my true self was? "How do you know I'm not being myself?"

"It's just...you look like you're always checking over your shoulder, watching and waiting for someone to call you out. Today at the Firehole..." He paused, and I felt him shake his head. "That's the most comfortable I've seen you on this trip. And I shared a bed with you."

I snorted a laugh.

"I was in a swimsuit about to jump into a rushing river. How does that constitute comfortable?" I folded my arms across my chest, trying to hold in the emotions his observations stirred.

"I'm not talking comfortable like sweatpants. I'm talking comfortable like you weren't trying to hide. You were just you, this amazing, kind woman who's braver than she thinks and willing to take my teasing and give it right back." He blew out a deep breath. "Of course, what do I know? I'm just a random guy who speaks without thinking."

I settled back onto the blanket letting the warmth of his words fill me as I stared up at the stars once more, taking in the specks of light framed by treetops. A breeze blew through the clearing, causing the windchimes on the porch to tinkle.

"I'm not sure what you want me to say." I finally spoke, my words filling the space between us as I focused on the first part of what he said. "I mean, after that first jump, I did feel comfortable. But that's just because I knew what I was doing. That first jump was a big unknown. Now, I know what I'm getting into when I jump."

"Do you always approach life so carefully, afraid to jump into the unknown? Afraid to wander off course?"

Before I could answer, the cabin door opened, followed by voices.

"Sorry it took us so long," Kylie chirped as she walked over and settled onto the blanket on Grey's other side. "I forgot my hoodie and we were scrambling to find enough layers to keep me warm. You might need to offer me your arm if it gets too cold, Grey."

I shifted away from Grey, grateful for the distraction while also missing his warmth.

"Or, if you get too cold, you can go inside. No one's making you stargaze," Tory pointed out as she settled on my other side, effectively sandwiching Grey and me in the middle of the group.

"Don't be silly. Of course, I want to be out here with you guys. Making memories with friends and all that," Kylie said.

We settled back into silence, and I gazed at the sky. Someone had turned off the cabin lights when they came out, making even more stars visible. Maybe if I wished on one of them hard enough, I could make sense of what was going on between me and Grey. His comments about my kindness and bravery replayed in my mind, making my toes curl with happiness.

As if reading my thoughts, I felt Grey's pinky brush mine, and I froze for a moment, my breath hitching in my lungs. We'd briefly held hands at the Firehole when he'd been helping me reach the rapids for my first jump. The sensation had been pleasant, and I found myself wanting a repeat of the contact. Mustering my courage, I nudged his pinky with mine and inched my hand closer. Following my lead, Grey interlaced his fingers with mine, and warmth traveled up my arm at the contact. I relaxed into the sensation, liking the way his fingers felt tangled up in mine. I liked holding Grey's hand and listening to him talk—not his monologues, but his actual conversations. Maybe knowing that much was enough for now.

Chapter Eighteen

THE NEXT MORNING, I was the first one awake again. We'd stargazed until well past midnight, counting shooting stars and telling stories. After one story when Tory recounted nearly being trampled by a moose in the very clearing where we were lying, we collectively decided to call it a night and head inside, carrying blankets and doing our best not to trip in the dark.

I quickly got ready, pulling my hair into a braid but pausing when I reached for my makeup. We would be hiking today, and the only guy who I might care to impress had made it clear last night that he didn't care about my makeup. Deciding to be brave, I skipped that step and headed into the living room, surprised to find Tory had woken up while I got ready. She sat on the couch, bundled in a blanket, her brows pinched as she stared out the windows to the trees beyond.

"What's the matter?" I asked, sitting next to her and stealing a corner of her blanket to snuggle under. The denim quilt was heavy and settled as a comforting weight on my legs.

"It's Trent. He gets weird when the twins are around, no matter how much I promise there's nothing to worry about. We've been friends since

I was seven. Their grandparents own the cabin next door." She nodded out the window towards a two-story log structure I could see just past the trees. "But it doesn't matter how many times I tell him we're just friends—Trent doesn't believe me. Last night he even accused me of secretly wishing I was dating Brad instead of him. Ridiculous, right?"

She threw up her hands in a huff, looking to me for confirmation of her thoughts.

I paused, biting my lip and thinking through my response before speaking.

"I can kind of see where Trent's coming from."

Tory sat up, twisting to face me more fully. "What do you mean?"

"Think about it. You're a bubbly, friendly person, and you're that way with everyone. But the twins—they seem to bring out an extra level of energy that I don't see in you around anyone else."

"That's not true. I'm the same level of bubbly with all my friends." Tory protested, her face pinched.

"You greet all your friends with overly enthusiastic hugs when you're wearing a wet swimsuit?" I asked, remembering the day before and the tic in Trent's jaw every time Tory was in Brad's vicinity.

Tory remained quiet for a moment, processing my words before collapsing back against the couch with a groan.

"I guess I can see that. We've been friends for so long. I forget that most people don't know how to react to our dynamic." The words were soft but loaded with memories and meaning.

"And you can't tell me you've never thought about dating either one of the twins. I mean, look at them! They're gorgeous."

Tory stayed oddly quiet, and I shifted to watch her face. She bit her lip and refused to make eye contact.

"I may have thought about it, once or twice," she said finally, her green eyes darting up to meet mine and then away.

"Tory!" I grabbed a throw pillow and gave her a gentle thwack. "And you never told me?"

"What was I supposed to tell you? 'Remember Brad, that guy I've told you repeatedly is just a good friend? I wouldn't mind if he was more than a friend.'" Her cheeks were bright pink, and I couldn't contain a grin.

"That would have done the trick. Do you still have feelings for him?"

She shook her head. "Absolutely not. I'm dating Trent, and he's the only person I have romantic feelings for. Now, if only I could get Trent to see that."

"Want my advice?" I hated the words I was about to speak, but I knew they needed to be said. Memories of walking in on Lyle and Emily kissing, after repeated assurances that they were only friends, played through my mind. Emily had been particularly adamant. She'd referenced our many years of friendship, asking me if I trusted her. Turns out I should have questioned her more, not less.

Tory closed her eyes and nodded.

"If you really care for Trent, don't give him any room for doubt. If that means putting distance between you and Brad, do it. You, Trent, and Brad all deserve at least that much."

Tory shifted, resting her head on my shoulder with a groan. "I know you're right, but that doesn't mean I have to like it. I don't know how to have less of Brad in my life."

We sat quietly for a moment, soaking in the stillness of the cabin before Tory broached the one topic I'd been avoiding.

"Now, tell me about your dating life. You and Grey looked awfully cozy when you got to the cabin, and I know I saw sparks flying yesterday at the Firehole."

I rested my head on the back of the couch and stared at the ceiling, not quite sure how to explain the feelings and emotions churning inside me. "Nothing's happening with my dating life. You know better than anyone that I'm not really on the dating market."

"Why? Did you get a boyfriend and I missed it?"

I shook my head, the couch cushion rubbing against my neck, its worn texture oddly grounding.

"After everything that happened with Lyle—"

"That happened over a year ago! I'm sorry, Audrey, I know Lyle and Emily hurt you. What they did was unforgivable, but it has nothing to do with your dating life now."

"Excuse me?" I sat up to glare at her.

Tory straightened too, turning so she could look me in the eye. "Hasn't Lyle stolen enough of your life without letting him have a minute more?"

"I'm not giving him more of my time. I'm giving myself time to heal." I scrambled to explain. It was the same reasoning I gave my mom, my roommates, and anyone else who asked about dating. It was safer that way. Though this weekend with Grey had me reevaluating that stance, a fact I found terrifying and exhilarating, liking jumping off the rock into the Firehole. I was right on the edge, and stepping forward could end in either joy or disaster.

"There's time to heal, and then there's running scared," Tory said, holding her hands out like she was trying to calm a cornered animal.

Her words stung, and I shifted away from her, scooting until my back hit the armrest. I curled my legs under me, trying to find comfort in the position.

"Who says I'm running?" My words were quiet, the conversation reminiscent of so many I'd had with my mom. I was fine. What Lyle and

Emily had done had left its mark, but I was healing, moving on with my life.

Are you really? This time the voice in my head sounded like me, and I didn't like what it was saying.

Relationships meant risk and vulnerability, two things that went against my natural tendency to seek security. I'd been burned so many times as a child with friends when a move had created just a little too much distance for me and someone I cared about to stay in contact. By the time I reached high school, I didn't date because it was easier. In college, Lyle had wormed his way under my armor, convincing me to take the risk and let him in. When that relationship had ended in the ultimate betrayal, I'd retreated back behind my armor, where it was safest. But was safety really worth living my life alone and scared?

Tory studied my face a moment longer before nodding, letting the conversation drop. "Just make sure you're not allowing that jerk to control your life a moment more. You deserve happiness. I hate watching you live on the fringes of life, afraid of being hurt again."

"That's why I love you. You're always watching out for me." I shifted closer and reached over giving her a one-armed hug, before settling back against the armrest. "Though it might be a moot point. Kylie looks pretty determined to catch Grey's attention."

Tory scoffed, shaking her head. "Kylie likes chasing what she can't have. She's the youngest of several sisters, each one more competitive than the last. If Grey had given her the time of day when she'd first flirted with him, she would have moved on by now. But because he doesn't want her, Kylie doesn't know how to handle it."

"That sounds like an exhausting way to live." My heart went out Kylie then, constantly chasing what she could never have.

"She'll get the message eventually. Don't let her scare you away from what you want."

I just nodded, not sure how to respond. Was Grey what I wanted? Every day I spent with him, it felt more and more like he was, a fact that terrified me.

We stayed there, each lost in our thoughts, until the guys and Kylie made their appearance.

Chapter Nineteen

AFTER BREAKFAST, EVERYONE GOT ready for hiking. I slipped a water bottle and snacks into a drawstring bag along with sunscreen before pulling on my hiking boots. I'd opted for comfy, worn workout clothes. Everyone else was similarly attired, though Kylie's workout gear was clearly name-brand and brought attention to curves I sadly lacked.

We piled into cars, with Kylie hesitating only slightly when Grey opted to ride with me, Trent, and Tory instead of joining her and the twins. Tory's explanation of their history had shed light on their dynamic, making me wonder how long before Kylie would finally either admit defeat or convince Grey to give her a chance.

The gravel parking lot for the trailhead boasted one other car as we pulled in. The drive to the trail had been a bumpy trek over a dirt road full of hills and the occasional pothole. I'd repeatedly looked behind us to make sure the twins' car was handling the road, though Brad had driven the road with skill.

After we parked, I scrambled from the car, eager to get moving and stretch my legs. The echoes of my conversation with Tory continued to play through my head, and I longed to move, to clear my head with much needed exercise. My drawstring bag knocked against my back as I walked, making me wish I'd traded it for a more stylish shoulder bag like the one I'd seen Kylie carrying on her way to the car.

I waited at the trailhead while everyone climbed out of the cars and gathered their supplies. The area was a mix of trees and rocks, with the river only a few feet away down a slight hill. A concrete dam with a walkway across the top was to the right, with the trail I assumed we would follow to the left. The wind teased the end of my braid, carrying with it the smell of pine and damp earth.

"This is gorgeous," Kylie said, stopping beside me and immediately bending down in a calf stretch that showed her legs off to advantage, though a petty part of me noticed she couldn't quite touch her toes. Maybe yoga had given me at least one advantage over this woman who seemed to have everything I could only dream of. "I can't believe I almost passed on the trip and missed the chance to see this."

I nodded. While I'd only visited Tory's family cabin once, my extended family loved the area, and I had many happy memories of time spent in Island Park, hiking, floating the river, forgetting the uncertainty that waited at home as Mom worked to make ends meet. No matter how crazy life got, Mom had somehow always found time for those trips.

"It's a beautiful area. If the winters weren't so cold, I'd move here in a heartbeat," I said, surprised at the truthfulness in the words. I wondered if Island Park could use a yoga studio.

The others joined us at the trailhead, everyone eager to start hiking in the mountain air.

"I vote we play a game as we hike," Brad called, starting the group down the trail. His voice carried with ease, his confidence that of a man used to being followed.

I hung back, uncertain of where I fit in the group. While I was friendly with everyone, Tory and Grey were the only ones I'd count as friends. And Grey's upgrade to that status was only a recent change. Though since we'd slept together twice and held hands the night before, calling him a friend seemed inadequate. Anxiety wound its way up my throat, and my mind drew a blank as I thought about trying to make conversation and contributing to a game the entire hike.

Alex groaned. "Is it the Brad is Quiet Game? You know, the one where you keep your mouth shut and let the rest of us enjoy a break from your voice?"

"Ha-ha, very funny." Brad grabbed his brother in a mock choke hold, and they wrestled, blocking the trail and forcing us to wait a moment for them to finish roughhousing. After a few moments of scuffling, they bumped into a tree and broke apart, grins splitting their faces and hinting that such behavior was normal for these brothers.

"I'm the worst at the Quiet Game," Grey said as we started moving again, our steps making a scuffing sound in the dirt. I bit back a laugh, imagining him remaining silent for an entire hike. I think the only time I'd experienced full quiet from Grey was when he slept.

"That surprises no one," Tory called. She was in the middle of the group next to Kylie, with Trent acting as a buffer between her and the twins. I assumed his position wasn't accidental. Apparently, the conversation between Trent and Tory the night before had done little to ease his worries and possessiveness.

Grey placed a hand on his chest, mock-offended, before breaking into a grin and dropping his hand back to his side. "Fair enough. Since we all know I'm going to lose, I vote for another game. Something that involves a *lot* of talking."

"I was thinking something along the lines of Top Five. I'll pick a category, and everyone shares their top five favorite things in that category. If I say restaurants, you list your top five restaurants, same with color, snack foods...you get the idea." Brad kept looking back at us as he spoke, making sure we understood the game. I was impressed he didn't get whacked in the face with a tree branch.

"Now, hold up, picking only five favorite restaurants is a tall order. I mean, are you talking fast food? Sit down? Chain? Locally owned?" Grey asked, ticking each option off on his fingers.

I snorted, realizing that picking only five favorite restaurants might actually cause Grey physical pain.

"You know Grey's top hobbies are eating food, talking about food, and talking while eating food," I said, the words slipping out before I could second-guess myself.

Tory barked a laugh as she stepped over a fallen tree. "Truer words have never been spoken."

We were passing through a forested area full of quaking aspens and the occasional pine tree. The gaps in the trees revealed glimpses of the river, which we could hear in the breaks in our conversation. Grasses and wildflowers carpeted the ground on either side of the dirt trail, adding pops of color to the scenery. I focused on our surroundings, trying to block out the heat filling my cheeks as everyone reacted to my comment.

Grey shot me a mock glare followed by a smile, white teeth contrasting with his beard. Even here in the woods, he kept it well-groomed, and I found myself wondering why I hadn't been interested in bearded men before now. "I'll have you know it takes time and skill to develop such a wide range of knowledge about eating. I bet I could come up with top five places just for tacos in Utah County."

"Spare us!" Kylie joined in the banter, throwing me a wink. I was still figuring out how to read her. At times she seemed friendly, and at others it felt like she saw me as competition for Grey's attention. "Brad, we'll play your game, but you can't pick any food categories. The last thing we need is Grey waxing poetic about a mediocre burger."

"I'll have you know I save my poetry for only the best burgers. They have to earn the poetry." Grey stopped and struck a dramatic pose, one hand on his hip, the other draped over his forehead.

Kylie shook her head, stepping around Grey with a pat on his arm. "As long as the poetry is earned..." She trailed off, not realizing what she had invited.

"In that case, let me share a little ditty I just composed called, 'Ode to a Mushroom Burger.'" Grey cleared his throat, and the group gave a collective moan.

"Boo! No poetry!" Tory said, covering her ears. "I refuse to listen to anything about ground beef and cheese."

"Did you miss the part about mushrooms?" Grey persisted as he followed behind Kylie. He was directly in front of me, and I found myself wanting to reach for his hand and twine my fingers with his. I fought the impulse, surprised I only felt a small amount of hesitation.

"No burger poetry. If you're going to recite food poetry, at least make it about something really epic, like cream puffs," Alex said.

"Cream puffs? What, dear brother, is epic about cream puffs?" Brad asked, humor in his voice.

"Have you ever tried to make cream puffs from scratch? They're not easy," Alex explained with a shrug, unembarrassed by the ridiculous turn in conversation.

"I feel like we've lost sight of our objective," Tory called, reining the group back in. "Brad, pick the first topic."

"I'm going with top five movies. Alex, kick us off!"

The game progressed from there as we continued along the trail, climbing over rocks and under tree branches. The group joked and laughed as we went. Brad's game turned out to be fun, and I felt the band of anxiety in my chest loosen with the light atmosphere—until Brad asked us to pick our top five songs.

"Only five?" The incredulity in my tone carried, and everyone turned to look at me in surprise, my cheeks flushing with the attention.

As we paused in a clearing, I could see surprise written on every face except Grey's. I considered laughing it off and pretending like I was joking but decided to hold my ground. If Grey could declare restaurants off limits because it was too hard, I could do the same with music. There was no way I could pick only five favorite songs. Five favorite songs by Earth, Wind, and Fire? Easy. Top five songs of all time? Impossible.

"It's not that hard," Kylie chimed in, quickly ticking off five popular songs on her fingers.

"We'll examine later why all of your favorite songs are by Taylor Swift," Grey joked, coming to my rescue. I breathed a silent sigh of relief at having someone else redirect the attention. "I agree with Audrey. That's no different than asking me to pick only five favorite fast food restaurants. Girl is a classic rock junkie!"

This caught Trent's interest, and he faced me fully, arms crossed over his chest in challenge. "Classic rock? Can you even name five classic rock artists?"

I could hear the disbelief in his tone, and my hackles rose. I'd heard this reaction many times, though it typically came from older men who couldn't believe a girl my age could possibly care about music beyond current hits.

I squared my shoulders, refusing to back down. "Do you want five artists from the 60s, 70s, or 80s?"

Trent smirked, clearly thinking he had me beat. "The 60s."

I pursed my lips and tapped my finger on my chin, pretending to think. "Let's see, the 60s would be the Beach Boys, The Rolling Stones, The Beatles, The Temptations, and Pink Floyd."

Trent's smug smile vanished, and he stepped back, pretending disinterest. "That was too easy. Everyone knows those groups."

"I didn't know all of them," Alex said, raising his hand and looking around the group. The others shook their heads, and I felt bolstered by their reaction.

"I can keep going," I said, giving a shrug while also refusing to back down. I could feel hints of anxiety at all the attention, but this was one of my passions, and I was going to make sure everyone here knew it. "Fleetwood Mac, the Bee Gees, Black Sabbath, though all of those groups sort of bridge the sixties and seventies—"

"Dang, girl! You really do know your stuff," Brad said, respect lighting his eyes as he stepped between me and Trent, putting an end to our exchange. "Next time I play music trivia, you're on my team."

Trent turned without a word, his posture stiff as he resumed hiking. I ignored him, blushing at the praise and appreciation from everyone else as we continued down the trail. My fears of feeling like an outsider with this group dissipated after that. While I remained quiet for most of the hike, I joined in the game and participated in conversation when I had something to add. Mostly I observed everyone, curious about this mix of humans I found myself sharing a cabin with.

Alex was the quiet, steady presence, though he also knew when to give the others, Brad especially, a hard time. Kylie was the follower, jumping into whatever the group did with enthusiasm and class. Tory was the ringleader and the connector, bringing the group together. Brad and Grey alternated between being the joker and butt of the jokes, but they both seemed to roll with the teasing, hamming it up for a good laugh. The only one who didn't seem to fit was Trent, and I couldn't figure out why. Tory clearly wanted him to be part of the group, but he seemed to hold himself back, unwilling to join in fully. He answered questions when asked directly, not volunteering more than the bare minimum. His challenge of my music expertise was the one exception, and he spent ten minutes after sulking and refusing to answer any questions. I didn't understand what Tory saw in him but wanted to trust my friend and her instincts.

We walked for about a mile and a half before turning back. The trail stretched for miles without a particular destination at the end. Instead, it gave us beautiful views of the river and the chance to exercise and soak in nature. When we weren't talking and comparing our favorite rom-coms or vacation spots, I could hear birds and squirrels chattering and the calming sound of rushing water.

If someone had asked for a definition of my perfect day, this would be close to my answer: enjoying the outdoors with a group of friends. No worries or stress about work or general life concerns. Maybe I could open my heart enough to claim this group as mine. Outside of my roommates and Tory, I didn't have many people I counted as friends. Funny what happened when your best friend and your boyfriend betrayed you. Although, neither Lyle nor Emily would have enjoyed this moment that was filling me with joy, seeing it as a waste of time or an inconvenience.

"You've been quiet," Grey said, hanging back to chat as we neared the parking lot.

When we'd started hiking, he'd been wearing another flannel, this one green. But over the course of the hike, he'd tied it around his waist, revealing a worn t-shirt that hugged his arms in wonderful ways.

"I answered my questions," I said, looping my fingers through my bag straps to give my hands something to do. "And I'm guessing Trent wished I'd been even quieter."

Grey snorted a laugh. "That was awesome. I'd pay good money for a repeat performance." He trailed off, thinking for a moment. "I guess I mean you didn't talk much outside of the expected moments." Grey held a branch out of my way, and I walked past, close enough to feel his warmth.

I shrugged. "I was listening, watching."

"And what did you see?" Grey's voice was inviting, reminding me of our conversations on the drive up.

"Alex is a lot more athletic than you'd think." I picked the least risky option. While he wasn't as muscular as his brother, Alex had spent most of the hike leading the group, setting a steady clip as we hiked. Part of why I'd hung back was because I wanted to soak in the scenery, not rush through it.

Grey nudged my shoulder. "Come on, anyone could tell you that. Despite the video game t-shirts and glasses, I think he might spend more time actually exercising than Brad. He doesn't do it in the gym, but dude loves his mountain bike. And I swear he's telling me about a new hike every time I see him."

"Fine. Tory insists that she and Brad are just friends, but I think Brad wouldn't mind something more." Tory had similar feelings, but I kept that thought to myself, recognizing the sensitivity of our conversation from that morning.

Grey nodded, surprise fliting across his face. "I could see that. Trent presents a bit of a problem with that possibility, though."

I ducked beneath another branch and kept my gaze focused on the trail, not wanting to twist an ankle on a protruding root. "If you watch Trent, he's aware of the threat. There's a reason why he pushed to the front of the group, and it's not because he enjoys hiking like Alex."

Throughout the hike, Trent had regularly stepped in front of Tory, working to create a buffer between her and Brad.

"You've got some solid observations there. Anything else you noticed?"

I paused mid-step, biting my lip.

"There is something. You have to tell me." Grey stopped too. The parking lot was in sight, but we stood several feet away, just outside of hearing range of the rest of the group.

As we'd hiked, I'd watched Kylie glue herself to Grey's side. She regularly used rocks, roots, and branches as excuses to touch Grey, grabbing his arm to keep from tripping, brushing his fingers when he'd held a branch back so it wouldn't hit her. I swallowed, remembering Tory's insights from this morning and not sure how much I should share.

I shook my head. "It's nothing."

"If it was nothing, you wouldn't have paused, not to mention you're going to nibble a hole in your lip," Grey persisted.

"Fine, but take it with a grain of salt. I was just people-watching, so it might mean nothing."

"Now you're making me nervous."

We started hiking again, not wanting to draw attention as everyone else waited for us in the parking lot.

"Kylie doesn't want to just be your friend." I said the words quickly, glancing at Grey's face while I spoke, watching his reaction.

His face tightened as he processed the words and then shook his head. "She and I have talked. She knows I don't feel that way about her. We're good friends. That's it."

I shrugged. "Friends or not, I don't think the two of you are on the same page with that assumption."

Grey shook his head, not commenting as we finished the hike.

I almost regretted sharing my observations, my anxiety from earlier starting to gnaw at my belly. Had I misspoken in telling Grey my thoughts? Yet, I knew he'd be the first one to tell me to speak my mind, which was exactly what I'd done.

I slipped into Tory's car, only half listening to the discussion around me as Tory rambled on about other hikes we could do. I was too busy thinking about what I had seen when we got to the parking lot. Trent and Tory had been standing next to Tory's car, Trent's arms wrapped around her from behind. Brad had been a few steps away, making Tory laugh with something he'd said, Trent glaring daggers at him from over Tory's shoulder. Alex had been leaning on the other side of Brad's car, head ducked down, looking at his phone. And separate from the group, watching the trail like a hawk, had been Kylie. I'd watched as instant relief, followed by concern, had flitted across her face before she'd sidled up to me, asking my thoughts on the hike and positioning herself between me and Grey.

Just friends. That might be what Grey wanted, but Kylie clearly had other plans.

Chapter Twenty

WHILE THE HIKE HAD been relatively level, my muscles smarted from my sudden increase in physical activity. I did yoga almost daily, but it worked my muscles differently than walking mountain trails and jumping into rivers, and my hips were making me well aware of that fact by the time we got back to the cabin.

As if reading my mind, Grey said, "Hey, Audrey, could you show me some yoga to help my back? As great as The Cave is, that mattress downstairs has seen better days." He rubbed his lower back with a wince as we entered the cabin.

I ducked my head, heat stealing into my cheeks as all eyes turned to me.

"I could use a bit of stretching too," Brad chimed in. "That's how I know I'm getting old. I used to have to do a crazy workout for my body to hurt. Now I just have to drive a car for several hours."

"I'm not a yoga instructor or anything," I stammered, surprised to find the entire group watching me and nodding with interest. While it was a dream of mine, I'd yet to take the plunge to start my certification.

"You might as well be," Tory said, giving me a hip bump as she walked past. "I think you spend more time in yoga classes than sleeping."

"I can pull up one of my favorite videos." I attempted to defer, waving my phone. Service was terrible, but maybe if I was lucky I would have just enough signal to get a video to play. I wasn't sure how I felt about teaching my first yoga class in front of this new group of friends.

"Come on, Audrey! Show us your moves." Grey gave me a gentle nudge of encouragement, waving me towards the living room.

I looked around the group of eager faces and nodded slowly. I could do this. I'd jumped into the Firehole and tried root beer milk. Teaching a yoga class, taking that first step towards my impractical dream, was nothing in comparison.

"Fine. I can show you some of my favorite poses, but remember, I'm not an instructor. This is just a hobby."

"For now," Tory said with a knowing smile. "I still think you should become a yoga instructor, make it a career. It would beat that stuffy office job."

I shook my head, ignoring her comments as I considered where our whole group could fit for a yoga session.

While the basement had more room for everyone to stretch out, the upstairs living room was where we landed. I worried the cement flooring of the basement would be too hard and uncomfortable to move on. The guys pushed the couches and recliner back into the dining area and hallway, giving us a bit more space to work in while I snagged my mat from Grey's car. Brad, Alex, Grey, and Tory spread out in the living room, leaving space for me at the front of the group.

Trent settled on one of the couches in the kitchen, phone in hand. He scowled when he noted Tory was settled next to Brad on the carpet.

Kylie came down the hall, pausing when she saw us scattered around the living room. "Looks like I'm missing the party."

"There's space for one more." Alex waved to a patch of carpet in front of him.

Kylie shook her head, waving her phone. "I need to work on some emails. Work doesn't wait, even when I'm on vacation. Am I right, Audrey?"

Her words made my stomach clench as I wondered what I was missing by not checking my work messages or emails. Refusing to give into the anxiety, I shook my head.

"I'm on vacation. They'll survive without me." If I said the words, maybe I'd believe them.

I took my place at the head of the group in front of the wall of windows, one of my favorite features of the cabin. I settled cross-legged on the floor, placing my hands on my knees, and encouraged the group to follow suit. They sat on spare towels we'd grabbed from the linen closet. While not as comfortable as yoga mats, I hoped the towels would at least be softer than the carpet.

I breathed in deeply through my nose, noting the subtle aroma of moth balls, and used the flow of air to anchor myself before jumping in. I encouraged everyone to breathe deep and clear their minds. I tried not to feel self-conscious as I started the group on a sun salutation, warming up our muscles before moving into some of the more intense poses.

"You're doing it wrong, Grey." Kylie's commentary, spoken with a laugh, pulled me from my flow.

I looked up from my downward dog to find Grey with his shoulders hunched towards his ears, instead of relaxing into the angled shape he needed. I pushed out of my pose and walked to Grey. I ignored Kylie, who sat with her phone in hand, the blank screen indicating she wasn't actively responding to work emails like she claimed.

"Do you mind if I move you into the pose?" I asked, remembering the many classes I had attended over the years in which instructors had asked me the same thing.

"Please." Grey's response came out in a huff of air, hinting at his discomfort in the inverted position.

"The goal is to form a triangle shape of sorts. You want to hinge from your hips, with a gentle curve in your spine. You don't want to rest all of your weight in your arms, but to distribute it equally between your feet and hands."

As I spoke, Grey straightened his arms, which relieved some of the hunch in his shoulders. However, he was still pitched too far forward. I moved behind him, grabbing his hips and giving them a gentle tug to fully shift his weight to where it needed to be.

"If you wanted to get handsy, all you had to do was ask," Grey said, laughter tinging his tone.

I blushed, but continued observing Grey's pose, making sure everything was aligned. I did my best to ignore his smell, something woodsy I could detect under the hint of sweat from our earlier hike.

"How does that feel?" I asked.

"Much better. Though if I forget, do you promise to help me again?" Grey's face was red, and his voice was more of a grunt.

Warmth settled in my chest at the flirty tone that had still managed to come through, even in his inverted position. Shaking my head, I turned back to the rest of the group who had been in downward dog far longer than I'd intended.

"Look forward, and on your next exhale, step or hop your feet towards your hands."

As I walked towards the front of the group, I caught Kylie's eye. She smiled, but it seemed forced. Something lurked in her gaze before she turned back to the phone in her hands, tapping to unlock the screen. I'd only caught a hint of something brewing in her eyes, but her message was clear: Kylie did not like me touching Grey.

As we kept working, I chose moves geared towards the hips and lower back, though I also made sure to stretch calves and hamstrings. I glanced up periodically, checking form and seeing if anyone needed help. As I moved, talking everyone through each pose and movement, I slowly stopped worrying about what everyone thought, Kylie included. Instead, I focused on the feel of my body and how I hoped the others also felt the relief and release I found in these movements.

My voice rang with confidence as I talked everyone through the final moments of our practice, the word "Namaste" tasting sweet on my tongue.

When we finished, everyone stood and scattered in different directions, but I stayed on my mat, trying to soak in one more moment of stillness. My anxieties had calmed, my breath coming easy. If only my job left me feeling this fulfilled.

"That felt amazing. Are you sure you're not an instructor?" Brad said as he walked into the kitchen for a glass of water.

"I had no idea yoga could feel so good," Alex added, following his brother.

"I keep telling her she should teach." Tory attempted to sit on the couch next to Trent, but when he didn't move to make room for her, she settled for the floor next to his feet.

"You would be an amazing instructor. You have the perfect personal touch," Grey said with a wink. "You can adjust my downward dog any time."

"Way to make it dirty, Grey!" Brad barked a laugh as a blush infused my cheeks.

Suddenly the calm I had found dissipated, replaced by a stampede of bison in my stomach.

"I don't know." I rolled up my mat, resting it against the wall, and walked into the kitchen, desperate for something to distract everyone's attention from me. "Yoga instructor isn't exactly a secure, nine-to-five career option."

"So what? Not everything is about security." Grey followed me into the kitchen and leaned against the counter next to me as I pulled a Pepsi from the fridge. "I kind of fell into my job. I don't think it's a forever career, but it pays the bills and is good enough for now. If I wasn't happy where I'm working now, I even have a job offer in Oregon that I could take."

I pushed aside his words—words that sounded oddly familiar, reminiscent of my childhood with a single mother who had always been chasing her next dream.

"Maybe not, but security is generally a good thing." The soda hissed as I twisted the bottle open and released some of the carbonation. I took a few good swallows, feeling the burn as it traveled down my throat.

"Not if it comes at the expense of your happiness." Grey's words sounded casual enough on the surface, but I could hear my mom saying the same thing repeatedly over the years.

"Who said I'm unhappy?" I turned to glare at Grey, who stood closer than I'd anticipated. The sudden stop required to keep from bumping into him caused my Pepsi to splash over the side of the bottle, puddling on the floor.

"Shoot." I deposited the bottle on the counter and snagged a kitchen towel to mop up the spill, biting my tongue as I worked.

"No one. I just—"

"You spent one car ride with me and listened to me take one frustrating work call and now you think you're an expert on my professional life?" I snapped, ignoring everyone else in the room, my attention focused on Grey and this loaded conversation.

Countless conversations with my mom rang through my ears as I spoke. Conversations about following dreams and finding fulfillment in work. But dreams and fulfillment didn't pay bills or buy food, something I wished she had realized when I was a kid and uncertain if there'd be dinner when I got home from school.

"I need a shower." I dropped the towel on the counter and skirted around Grey, afraid to see his face or hear his response to my question.

Chapter Twenty-One

I FINISHED SHOWERING, TAKING my time as I dried my hair and tried to ignore the emotions Tory's comments and Grey's questions had stirred. I hadn't been happy at work for a long time, but that didn't mean it wouldn't get better. I just needed time. At least, that's what I told myself every time dissatisfaction hit and I started dreaming crazy things, like quitting to become a yoga instructor. I'd envisioned it many times, quitting on the spot during a particularly frustrating day, walking out and leaving Drew to fend for himself.

It sounded exhilarating and exactly like something my mom would have done when I was a kid, before Dave had swooped in, making it so she didn't need to work anymore.

Any time those thoughts got to be too much, I reminded myself the years spent getting a business degree, working my way from a junior to a senior call center agent had to be worth something. Management kept promising me it would be.

But what if it wasn't?

I'd been promised a promotion for months now, if I could just "hold on a little longer." But the promises felt hollow, especially with Drew's recent promotion. Friends in other departments who had been hired after me were climbing the ladder faster. While I envied their progress, they also seemed more stressed and less fulfilled with the change. Whenever I thought about work and the years ahead, it was with a vague sense of panic that had me reaching for a yoga mat. Something I'd promised myself would fade with time as I grew into each new position.

My phone vibrated on the bathroom counter with a text from my mom. She always seemed to know when my anxiety was reaching peak levels.

MOM: *How's the cabin?*

ME: *Good so far. Lots of fresh air and socializing.*

MOM: *Sounds like the perfect weekend.*

ME: *To a degree. How are the girls?*

MOM: *Currently fighting over a stuffed animal.*

I bit back a smile, picturing the familiar scene.

ME: *If it's the pink unicorn, don't believe Lily when she says it's hers.*

We chatted for a moment, and a sense of longing and loneliness replaced the anxiety I'd been battling since my exchange with Grey. The picture Mom painted, one of bickering daughters and a loving home, was one I'd dreamed of my entire life. It was hard not to envy her, getting to live that dream, while I was a grown, twenty-six-year-old adult, too old to live at home and enjoy my mom's new reality.

Shaking off the melancholy, I stole one more glance in the mirror. My hair was curled to perfection, my makeup applied as if I was headed into the office instead of hanging out in the woods. I knew there were only a few hours left in the day. Yet, I needed my armor tonight. I needed something to hide behind if Grey or Tory started asking tough questions about my job again.

Chapter Twenty-One

I FINISHED SHOWERING, TAKING my time as I dried my hair and tried to ignore the emotions Tory's comments and Grey's questions had stirred. I hadn't been happy at work for a long time, but that didn't mean it wouldn't get better. I just needed time. At least, that's what I told myself every time dissatisfaction hit and I started dreaming crazy things, like quitting to become a yoga instructor. I'd envisioned it many times, quitting on the spot during a particularly frustrating day, walking out and leaving Drew to fend for himself.

It sounded exhilarating and exactly like something my mom would have done when I was a kid, before Dave had swooped in, making it so she didn't need to work anymore.

Any time those thoughts got to be too much, I reminded myself the years spent getting a business degree, working my way from a junior to a senior call center agent had to be worth something. Management kept promising me it would be.

But what if it wasn't?

I'd been promised a promotion for months now, if I could just "hold on a little longer." But the promises felt hollow, especially with Drew's recent promotion. Friends in other departments who had been hired after me were climbing the ladder faster. While I envied their progress, they also seemed more stressed and less fulfilled with the change. Whenever I thought about work and the years ahead, it was with a vague sense of panic that had me reaching for a yoga mat. Something I'd promised myself would fade with time as I grew into each new position.

My phone vibrated on the bathroom counter with a text from my mom. She always seemed to know when my anxiety was reaching peak levels.

MOM: *How's the cabin?*

ME: *Good so far. Lots of fresh air and socializing.*

MOM: *Sounds like the perfect weekend.*

ME: *To a degree. How are the girls?*

MOM: *Currently fighting over a stuffed animal.*

I bit back a smile, picturing the familiar scene.

ME: *If it's the pink unicorn, don't believe Lily when she says it's hers.*

We chatted for a moment, and a sense of longing and loneliness replaced the anxiety I'd been battling since my exchange with Grey. The picture Mom painted, one of bickering daughters and a loving home, was one I'd dreamed of my entire life. It was hard not to envy her, getting to live that dream, while I was a grown, twenty-six-year-old adult, too old to live at home and enjoy my mom's new reality.

Shaking off the melancholy, I stole one more glance in the mirror. My hair was curled to perfection, my makeup applied as if I was headed into the office instead of hanging out in the woods. I knew there were only a few hours left in the day. Yet, I needed my armor tonight. I needed something to hide behind if Grey or Tory started asking tough questions about my job again.

I stepped out of the bathroom to the sound of kitchen cupboards slamming and the smell of cooking meat filtering throughout the cabin. When I entered the kitchen, Tory stood at the stove, spatula in hand, as she talked to Alex, who had perched himself on a nearby barstool. Trent was lounging on the couch, typing on his phone. Someone had returned the furniture to the living room while I'd gotten ready.

"Where is everyone?" I asked, snagging an olive from a yellow bowl sitting on the counter next to Alex and doing my best to pretend I hadn't stormed out in frustration earlier. Maybe if I ignored my behavior, they would too.

"Dang girl, you clean up good! Got a hot date?" Tory's eyebrows danced, and she waved the spatula in my direction, dripping flecks of oil onto the floor.

I grabbed a paper towel and wiped up the mess, pretending like her comments hadn't made me blush.

"After a day in the woods, I wanted to feel human again." I shrugged off her words. My appearance had nothing to do with Kylie's name-brand clothes, Grey's cheeky smiles, or my echoes of self-doubt as I pondered my career, full of security but lacking enjoyment.

Thundering footsteps were the only warning before Grey and Brad appeared at the top of the stairs, roughhousing and laughing as they tried to beat each other to the top.

"She lives!" Brad called, when he spotted me. "We were worried you'd gotten lost when it took you so long to get ready."

"You guys didn't have to hold dinner for me," I said, looking at the platters of food Tory had laid out on the counter.

"Kylie also showered. I think she's still getting ready."

"You can't blame our delay solely on the ladies, Grey," Brad chimed in, peeking over Tory's shoulder to see what she was cooking. "Those phone calls with your brother and mom took a good chunk of time too."

"True," Grey said, refusing to elaborate. I watched his face, trying to read from his expression if everything was okay at home. Instead, he smiled and came to stand beside me, reaching for an olive and bumping my shoulder in the process.

He quirked an eyebrow, as if asking if I was okay, but instead saying, "You look nice. Though I also liked the no-makeup-braid look from earlier."

I ducked my head. "Sweaty and covered in hiking dust is hardly my best look."

"Could have fooled me. Though this outfit brings back memories of a certain bed." Grey's eyebrows danced, and I gave him a playful shove. His gaze captured mine, and I became lost in the chocolate depths of his eyes as I soaked in his sincerity and a promise of something more filling their depths.

"Great minds think alike. You look good, Audrey." Kylie's words broke into the moment.

Kylie stood in the kitchen, wearing a near identical teal lounge set to mine. But while mine was clearly well loved, the fabric worn and pilling in spots, Kylie's looked brand-new.

"If I'd known, I would have brought my matching pajamas too," Grey said as he stepped away from me and settled at the table.

Kylie was quick to join him, and I ignored the jealousy curling in my stomach. Instead, I helped Tory put the finishing touches on dinner, pulling out plates and utensils. When all was ready, we served ourselves and dug into the food, conversation flowing around me as I did my best to focus on my tacos and ignore how Kylie scooted her chair closer to Grey.

"What are we doing tonight? More stargazing? Movie marathon? Night games?" Alex asked around a mouthful of beans.

"I vote video game tournament. Y'all were trash talking on the hike. It's time to see those car racing skills," Tory said, serving herself a second helping of corn. "And since it's my birthday trip, I think my vote wins regardless of what anyone else says."

"You're on!" Brad said. "Be warned, I was the champion race car driver in my home for over a decade."

"Just because you cheat," Alex shot back.

Brad flicked a black bean at Alex, nailing him in the forehead.

"Sensitive, are we?" Alex asked with a laugh, picking up an olive to launch back.

"No food fights at the cabin!" Tory cut in, holding up her hands in a stop gesture. "My mom would kill me if she found out."

"Fine, though she wouldn't have to find out. I know a guy who can make all food fight evidence disappear," Brad said, arching an eyebrow.

"What are you, the food fight mafia?" Grey laughed, pointing at the bowl of olives with his fork. "Do you know a place where you can bury those olives where they'll never be found?"

I snorted, picturing Brad wearing a dark suit, his hair slicked back, as he buried the unsuspecting olives in a shallow grave behind the cabin.

"If you start a food fight at the cabin, it's your bodies that will never be found. Don't underestimate my mama." Tory reached for the bowl of olives, placing a few on her plate.

"Your mom? Isn't she like five feet tall?" Trent asked.

"And scary as all get out if you cross her," Brad said, his lips tipping up in a slight smile as he got lost in memories. "I remember when we were kids, Tory convinced Alex and I to let her try our bow and arrow—"

"Not that story!" Tory groaned, slumping back into her chair, the frame protesting at the sudden movement. "I was ten, and I'd never shot anything before."

"More accurately, you'd never *aimed* at anything before." Alex nudged Tory with his shoulder, joining in the banter.

"How was I supposed to know that little bow and arrow would have enough strength to break a window?"

"That was the day I gained a healthy...respect for Mrs. Allen," Brad said with a shudder.

The teasing and laughter continued as we finished the meal and Tory, Brad, and Alex regaled us with cabin stories from their childhoods. Trent's stony silence was a clear sign that not everyone enjoyed the jaunt down memory lane.

Following the meal, the guys ushered Tory, Kylie, and me out of the kitchen, promising to clean up from dinner. I settled on the couch, book in hand, only processing half of what I read as I tried to ignore Grey and Brad splashing each other while they did the dishes.

"What are you reading? Anything good?" Kylie settled on the couch next to me, phone in hand.

"Oh...uh..." I glanced at the cover. I'd grabbed the book from the bookcase in the hallway, not paying attention to what I'd picked. A vector cover with two characters locked in an embrace greeted me. "I'm not actually sure."

I held the book up for Kylie's inspection.

"I've heard good things about that one. I don't really have much time for reading, though. TV either. Or most hobbies." Kylie turned back to her phone, waving her hand towards me and my book. "You know how it is, being a career woman. Free time kind of evaporates. Got to keep climbing that corporate ladder."

I tried to push down the immediate feelings of inadequacy triggered by her words. I could only imagine Kylie's reaction if she learned how many hours I spent a week unplugged from work, doing yoga. Maybe that's why I wasn't a manager yet. I hadn't traded my hours of mindful movement and meditation for high-powered spin classes filled with multitasking and networking.

"Who's ready for an epic racing showdown?" Brad called, launching himself over the back of the couch and settling next to Tory. "We just need a couple of minutes to write up the bracket, and then we can head downstairs to the TV and gaming console."

Trent walked into the room and scowled at the pair. Tory scooted to the side of the couch, creating room for him, but Trent ignored the gesture, settling in the armchair across the room instead.

"You seem awfully eager to lose." Grey joined us in the living room, sitting next to me on the loveseat. Instead of waiting for me to move my feet, he picked them up and settled them in his lap, his hand resting on my ankle. Heat suffused my cheeks as I flashed back to our movie night.

"Not me." I waved my book as if it excused me from the video game shenanigans. "I'm no good at video games."

"Come on, Audrey! A tournament's only fun if everyone plays," Tory begged, her eyes wide and pleading.

"She's just afraid of losing," Grey commented.

"I'm no good, but I'm game," Kylie chimed in, her gaze lingering a beat too long on Grey's hand on my leg, my bare feet in his lap.

"I already know I'm going to lose, so how can I be afraid of it?" I shot back at Grey, moving my legs from his lap and placing my book on the floor.

He quirked a brow and shrugged, leaning back on the couch. "Why else would you back down from a video game tournament? Either you're a party pooper, or you're afraid."

I bit my lip, considering my options. Either I backed out and proved him right, or I took the bait and joined in the games. Giving into Grey's gentle teasing and nudging was becoming a habit I wasn't sure I wanted to break, even if it meant losing more sleep.

"Fine, but don't say I didn't warn you about my lacking skills." I pushed up from the couch and sauntered downstairs, faking all the confidence I didn't feel, hoping Grey would follow.

Chapter Twenty-Two

THE SECOND MY TOES hit the cold floor, I knew I'd made a mistake. My pride was not worth the hypothermia I'd suffer if I stayed down here and played without additional clothing. I turned to head back upstairs for my socks, but Grey stood in the doorway, blocking my exit.

"Where do you think you're going?" He crossed his arms over his chest, drawing attention to his muscles. I'd had no idea arm muscles could be so sexy, but Grey's physique regularly reminded me they were. Cover those arms in flannel, and I was a goner every time he flexed in my vicinity.

"I need socks." I gestured to my toes, bright pink toenails contrasting with the concrete floor. And if I got socks, maybe I'd conveniently forget to come back downstairs.

"How do I know this isn't an elaborate ploy to get out of the tournament?" he asked, eyebrows raised and a smirk teasing his lips.

"Why would I commit to play and immediately back out?" I reasoned, grateful Grey couldn't read my mind. Staying up late and waking up early the last several days was catching up to me, and I would not mind an early bedtime.

"You could just use a blanket." He motioned to the stack of blankets piled on the couch from movie night a few days before.

"That only works if I'm not moving. If I have to get up at all, my toes will freeze again." I tried my best to look pathetic and in desperate need of socks. I wasn't quite sure what the expression was, but surely I could pull it off. If I didn't end up coming back downstairs, it would only be because the siren call of my bed had become too loud. Everyone would understand.

Grey shook his head, seeming to read the intent on my face. "If you go upstairs now, how can I guarantee you'll come back for the tournament?"

"You're going to hold me hostage down here to play video games? What if my toes freeze off?" I crossed my arms over my chest, mimicking Grey's stance.

"That's a risk I'm willing to take." Grey shrugged, as if losing one's toes was a regular occurrence. "You'll still be beautiful, even without toes."

"Thank you? I think that's genuinely the weirdest compliment I've ever received," I said, not really sure how to react to someone talking about the loss of body parts I was very much attached to.

Grey grinned mischievously. "But you admit it was a compliment! I have better ones if you stay downstairs."

"If that's your bar for compliment excellence, I understand why online dating hasn't worked out for you yet." I laughed, imagining Grey messaging that same line to an unsuspecting stranger on the internet.

"Surprisingly, I haven't used that one. I'll have to keep it in mind for the future."

My stomach clenched at that. I did not like the idea of Grey on dating apps, using cheesy lines and impressive arms to woo other women.

Pushing aside the unexpected spike of jealousy, I considered my options. Grey completely blocked the door. But if I pushed, there was no way he'd continue blocking me, right?

I made a run for it, trying to duck under Grey's arm. He reacted, dropping his arm down to block my escape.

"No fair!" I said, dodging around him and attempting a similar move on his other side. Instead of letting me past, Grey looped his arm around my waist and pulled me away from the door.

I couldn't help but laugh at the ridiculousness of the situation. Thinking quickly, I threw my weight back against Grey, hoping to surprise him and escape his hold. Instead, he absorbed my weight and pulled me in tighter.

I looked into his face, laughter crinkling his eyes, and froze. His lips were only a few inches away and, for the briefest moment, I considered pushing up on tiptoes and finding out what it felt like to kiss a man with a beard.

The sound of footsteps on the stairs was the only warning before Alex appeared behind Grey. We quickly broke apart, but Alex's lips pursed as he took in the scene.

"Do I want to know?" Alex asked, stepping around Grey into the basement.

"Audrey's trying to chicken out of our contest. She claims she's just getting socks, but I know better," Grey said, regaining his composure quickly, though his lips still ticked up at the corners.

"You're being ridiculous," I said, proud I didn't sound more breathless. "Just let me upstairs. I'll be back in two minutes, tops. You can even time me."

"Why don't you just lend her some of yours? That way she doesn't have to go upstairs." Alex stretched out on one of the worn couches, his frame tall enough that his feet dangled off one end.

Grey glanced from me to Alex and back, considering.

"You'll also have to lend me a sweatshirt. I'm not dressed for arctic temperatures." I gestured to my short sleeves, grateful my pants were at least warm. Goose bumps were starting to pebble on my arms. I told myself it was from the cold and had nothing to do with having nearly kissed Grey.

"Fine, but if I come back to find you've gone upstairs, I'll take it as proof that you're the ultimate chicken and unleash the full fury of my pranking ability."

I nodded, accepting Grey's terms while also wondering if those pranks could possibly lead to other wrestling matches and near kisses.

Grey disappeared down the hall to The Cave, looking over his shoulder once to make sure I was still there.

"Now's your chance to escape. Hurry, run!" Alex said, laughter tinging his voice.

"If you think he's joking about the pranks, he's not," I responded, sitting on one of the many couches in the basement, this one a faded green and blue stripe.

"I know he's not. I was hoping I'd get to witness an epic prank war." Alex sat up but kept his legs on the couch, and sent me a wink. "Maybe we can try some of those pranks on Trent, help him find his sense of humor. Or he'll freak out enough that Tory will finally dump him. I'm good with either option."

I snorted, picturing stoic Trent and his lack of response to literally everything. "I think he'd just glare at you and go back to whatever's so important on his phone. Or he'd go for a run. All those muscles have to come from somewhere."

"Got them!" Grey raced back into the main area of the basement, triumphantly holding a pair of socks and a red flannel shirt above his head.

He threw the socks at me, and I caught them, surprised at the pattern.

"I didn't know they made flannel socks," I said as I pulled them on, my toes experiencing instant relief as the fabric chased away the cold that had all but seeped into my bones.

Grey shrugged, draping the flannel shirt around my shoulders. "I have a signature pattern. If it doesn't apply to even my socks and underwear, then who am I?"

I tried to push the image of flannel underwear from my mind as I slipped on his shirt, resisting the urge to bury my face in the collar and soak in his familiar scent. Needing a distraction, I turned to the TV and gaming console that would be my purgatory for the next several hours.

"Are we ready to start this tournament or what?" I asked, reaching for a controller.

Grey grabbed my hand, stopping me. "Not yet. Brad's making the bracket, and then we'll start."

"Bracket? I thought we'd just face off. Then I'd lose and get to call it a night."

"What do you think this is? Amateur hour?" Brad called from the doorway, holding a notebook above his head. "This is a double elimination tournament of epic-ness guaranteed to fill your evening with hours of entertainment as we determine racing superiority."

Brad walked to the couch, shoved Alex's legs out of the way, and sat. He then held up the notebook, showing me a complicated graph that was barely legible.

"Everyone races at least twice. That way we won't have any whiners blaming bad luck or a difficult course." He looked pointedly at his brother before continuing. "This is a battle to the end. Winner takes all: bragging rights until the next cabin trip."

"Great. Can I compete in the first two races?" I asked, covering a yawn. Now that I was warm, exhaustion was settling into my bones, and the siren call of my bed grew louder.

"Sorry, but race order has already been determined based on random selection. Don't want anyone crying foul." Brad handed me the notebook but refused to make eye contact. Something felt fishy about the whole setup.

I glanced at the sheet, and in bold strokes, everyone's names were written, with my brackets both conveniently listed last.

"How are both of my races at the end?" I directed the question at Brad but glanced up to find Tory entering the basement, a guilty expression on her face that she quickly hid with a yawn and a stretch.

"Just lucky! It means you have time to brainstorm your strategy before your races." Brad took the notebook, turning away from me and rambling about the first bracket.

If I was a betting woman, I'd bet there was nothing random about this bracket. However, since I'd been downstairs waging a sock war, I had no way to prove it. It had seemed odd that Grey was so insistent I stay downstairs. Was it just because he thought I'd bail on the tournament? Or was something else at play?

I looked between Grey and Tory, trying to find evidence of their plotting but coming up empty. I wouldn't put it past the two of them to conspire against me, but without proof, my options were to either back out or pray the races ended quickly. Deciding all I had to lose was a bit more sleep, I settled into my seat and prepared to watch the races.

"First up, Tory and Trent. Let's test this relationship and see who's the better driver," Brad said in his best announcer voice, eyebrows waggling in invitation.

Tory turned on the TV and started the gaming console, familiar cartoon racing characters filling the screen. Trent and Tory selected their avatars and settled on the floor, shoulders bumping.

"I hope you're ready to eat my dust," Tory said sweetly.

Trent just snorted.

The race began, and the two were off. Trent kept quiet, intensity radiating off him as he drove, wheeling around corners and using every advantage he could to slow Tory. Tory, on the other hand, was loud. Trash-talking as she passed Trent, bumping his shoulder when she happened to fall behind. The race quickly finished with a triumphant shout from Tory and a groan from Trent.

"Victory!" Tory stood, shaking her hips in victory as she handed the controller to Brad for the next race.

Trent shook his head, grumbling something about Tory having an unfair advantage before he walked to the bean bag in the corner and pulled out his phone.

The tournament continued, the racers sitting on the floor while the rest of us watched from the couches and bean bag. Trash-talking and friendly jostling filled each race. When it was finally my turn, I was pitted against Tory for the first race.

I quickly proved my ineptitude, struggling to turn corners and hit the correct buttons.

"I know wandering does not equate to being lost, but to win the race you have to go forward," Grey teased as I got spun around and drove in the wrong direction for a moment before finally getting turned back around.

"Watch it," I gritted back, attempting to stay on the racetrack and not fall off into a pool of water.

My struggle did not stop Tory from egging me on, talking about how I was going down. Even though her victory had been guaranteed, she still cheered when she crossed the finish line for the third and final time, beating me by more than a lap.

"That's right! Who's the champion? Oh, that would be me." Tory pointed to herself with both thumbs and did a shimmy dance as she strutted to the couch and sat down.

"All right, that was...entertaining," Brad said, recording the results of the latest match in his notebook.

"I think the word you're looking for is painful," I said, trying not to let my frustration show. I didn't play video games because, to put it gently, I sucked. Growing up, I hadn't had access to a console—we definitely couldn't have afforded one. Instead, I'd spent hours listening to my mom's old tapes and CDs or playing outside. If this was classic rock trivia, I'd be dominating.

"Get ready for the final match! We're almost ready for the next round." Brad waved the notebook with enthusiasm.

So far, only Trent had been eliminated from racing in round two. He'd gone up against Brad in his second race and lost by a hair. His reaction had been to throw down the controller and stalk off into The Cave. He'd yet to come back. I was slightly envious of his chance to go to bed.

"I can save you the trouble of watching another race. I guarantee I'll lose this round too," I said on a yawn. A look at my phone made me flinch as I realized it was well after midnight. The lack of sleep on this trip was going to kill me.

"And deprive me of going up against your impressive skills? I don't think so!" Grey stretched out on the floor next to me, holding the controller Tory had been using.

"We both know how this is going to end," I persisted.

"Come on, it'll be fun." Grey bumped me with his shoulder before selecting the next race and pressing start. "Who knows? You may even surprise yourself."

No words could describe the chaos that followed. I continued to struggle driving, and yet somehow, Grey managed to stay behind me. He ran over every trap and repeatedly fell off the track. At one point, I was certain he'd taken his finger off the gas button, though I couldn't see his controller well enough to be sure.

Far longer than it should have taken, I drove across the finish line for the third time, finishing the race. Grey followed right behind me, ending the torture, much to everyone's relief.

"You let me win!" I turned to face Grey, watching as he schooled his features into a neutral expression.

"No, I didn't," he said, shaking his head.

"Really? Because I watched you decimate Brad." I stood, hands on my hips, looking at Grey, who sat cross-legged on the floor pretending all was right with the world.

Brad spoke up in outrage. "Decimated is a strong word. I—"

Grey cut Brad off with a chuckle, pushing to his feet to stand toe to toe with me, hands in his pockets, a grin peeking through his beard. "Maybe beating Brad was a lucky fluke. Or maybe you're better than you give yourself credit for." He flashed me a wink before settling on one of the couches and patting the cushion next to him. "Either way, you're still in the game. Might as well get comfortable."

"I know you cheated," I muttered under my breath as I settled next to him, choosing to ignore how much I enjoyed his closeness and woodsy aroma.

"Maybe, but you'll never prove it." Grey slung his arm around my shoulders and pulled me in close to his side. "Might as well enjoy the show. Cheer me on to victory, and all that."

I crossed my arms over my chest and grumbled under my breath about cheating, self-satisfied men. But I didn't push away from Grey's side. I told myself it was because he was warm and the basement was frigid, but the way I leaned in to catch hints of his familiar smell said otherwise.

We continued playing into the wee hours of the morning. I was immediately eliminated with my next race, this one against Kylie, who showed no mercy. But at that point, I was too comfortable sitting next to Grey. Not to mention, I wanted Grey to win, if for no other reason than to prove that he'd cheated by letting me win our match. Or at least, that's what I told myself.

Chapter Twenty-Three

THE NEXT MORNING CAME too early. Despite going to bed hours later than normal, I was still the first one awake. Someday, I'd let go of anxiety and sleep past 7:30. Then again, maybe sleep deprivation would do me in, and I could sleep when I was dead. I lay in bed a few moments longer, attempting to doze off, but eventually accepted that I was awake and stumbled out to the living room.

I picked up the book I'd attempted to start the night before and settled in to read until everyone else woke up. My head pounded too much from the late night to attempt yoga.

The book was just starting to hold my interest when my phone buzzed and kept buzzing in my pocket. I pulled it out, the pressure behind my eyes intensifying as I registered who was calling: Drew. I rubbed my forehead, trying to relieve the tension, and accepted the call. The sooner I answered, the sooner I could get this over with. Maybe if I was lucky, my cell coverage would fail and the call would drop.

"Hi, Drew. What's up?" I didn't bother hiding my exhaustion, hoping he would hear it and cut our conversation short. Then again, I was more likely to discover unicorns in Island Park than for Drew to take interest in someone other than himself.

"Where are you?" Drew's words were clipped and rushed.

I glanced at a rooster-themed clock on the wall, noting that my work shift would have started only a few minutes ago.

"I'm on vacation, remember? It's been on the calendar for weeks." I pinched the bridge of my nose, trying to relieve the pounding in my head.

"I thought you were going for a couple of days. I'm certain—"

I cut in. "I'm *certain* my PTO request was for a week—and that you signed off on it. I can forward you the email approval, if you like."

Now his voice was breathier, each word coming out faster than the last. "What I meant to say was, I didn't expect you to take the whole time. You don't go on long vacations. At most you only ever take off a day or two at a time."

He hadn't been on the team when I'd taken my leave of absence last summer to help my mom after the accident. Helping with the girls while Dave worked and Mom healed had taken weeks. Otherwise, he wasn't wrong. Me and vacations weren't often on speaking terms. The missed work and prep to leave were rarely worth the hassle of taking time off. Or at least, that's what I told myself. This trip was making me reevaluate that assessment.

"This time, I am going to be gone the whole time. What do you need?" It wasn't the most professional way to speak to my supervisor, but the pounding in my head meant I had little patience for Drew and his mind games. I was going to need a Pepsi sooner rather than later.

"The system update rolled out last night, and we could really use more people on the phones. Do you think you could come in for a couple of hours?" Over the course of the conversation, Drew's voice had transformed from clipped and forceful to a nasally whine that would have done Lily and Poppy proud.

"No, I can't."

"We'll pay time and a half. We really need you!" His voice was panicked and desperate, and I felt an odd sense of satisfaction.

"Then you should have thought of that before approving my time off during the system rollout. If you need people so much, *you* can hop on the phones." Drew avoided working the phones like a hiker avoiding a bear fresh out of hibernation.

"I would, but I have meetings I really shouldn't reschedule."

"And I'm on a vacation that I really can't leave. Good luck!" I hung up before Drew could say another word. Normally, I would stress about my reaction, worried that I had jeopardized my job. But they needed me too much. If Drew fired me, he'd have to actually do his job, and we both knew he'd do anything in his power to avoid that.

I settled back to read, my heart pounding an odd rhythm of excitement and anticipation. I'd stood up for myself, and the world hadn't ended. It made me wonder what else would happen if I continued to stick up for myself, instead of just doing what everyone expected. I might wind up surprising everyone, including myself.

Hours later, after everyone had gotten up and eaten breakfast, Tory declared we would float the river today. Personally, I was shocked she had waited this long to go. Tory would live in the water if she could, embracing life as a freshwater mermaid. We all changed into swimsuits and grabbed inner tubes before driving to the river. We left Brad's car in a pull off next to the river and then all crammed into Tory's car to drive to the boat launch. Using a car pump that sounded like it was on its last leg and a couple of manual pumps Tory had found at the cabin, we got to work blowing up tubes for everyone.

With everyone else pumping up tubes, I put on sunscreen. I made quick work of my arms, legs, chest, and face, but struggled with my back. The sun, warm on my skin, made it clear I'd want the protection if I didn't want to turn into a lobster later.

"Tory, when you're done with that tube, do you mind getting my back?" I held up my spray tube of sunscreen and waved it at Tory, who sat sideways in the driver's seat, using the car pump to inflate one of the brightly colored tubes.

"Of course," she called over the buzz of the pump.

"I can do it," Grey offered from where he stood behind me.

"Thanks," I stammered, surrendering the sunscreen and turning to give him access to my back.

I braced for the cold contact of sunscreen on my skin but was surprised when his warm hands touched my back, rubbing the lotion into place instead of spraying it directly onto my back.

"Did you get your shoulders already?"

I nodded, the words stuck in my throat.

"What about your neck?" He was close enough that his breath tickled my skin, causing goose bumps to break out across my arms despite the warmth.

"Yep." I managed to squeak out.

What was wrong with me? A few days ago, I would have done anything to avoid getting this close to Grey. But now? Something had shifted, and I was terrified to see where it led. Yet, another part of me, that same part that dreamed of teaching yoga and celebrated sticking up to Drew, felt exhilarated at the possibilities.

"Sunscreen! Good idea. Grey, will you do my back next?"

Kylie's voice broke through our moment as she walked over to join us, her bright pink swimsuit drawing attention to her curves. I ducked away from Grey, my cheeks flaming as I moved to help Tory with the blue inner tube she was working on.

"What was that?" Tory asked, keeping her voice low so that only I could hear.

"Nothing," I mumbled, reaching to close the valve on the tube and lifting it onto my shoulder.

"How do I sign up for some of that nothing time with Trent? Dang, girl. That was hot."

"Stop it. It was nothing. See, he's doing the same thing for Kylie." I waved to where Grey helped Kylie with her sunscreen, but it clearly wasn't the same. He sprayed the sunscreen directly on her skin causing her to squeal at the cold, not bothering to rub it in before handing the can to her.

"All done," he said, moving to help Brad with another inner tube.

Kylie stood, looking lost, sunscreen in hand. I almost felt bad for the girl as she gave him a smile and batted her eyelashes at him. "Thanks, Grey. You're a lifesaver. Want me to do yours?"

Grey shook his head, and it was one of the few times I hadn't seen a smile hiding beneath his beard. "I'm going to keep my shirt on." He waved towards his t-shirt. It had a picture of bigfoot and the words "Hide and Seek Champion." It wasn't his typical flannel, but the green color did wonderful things for his eyes.

We finished blowing up tubes and slipped on our lifejackets before everyone made their way to the water. There was a family already at the boat launch, but they waved us ahead as they dealt with a stubborn toddler who didn't want to wear a lifejacket.

The water was cold, making me gasp with each step as I found my footing and navigated the river's rocky bed.

"This makes the Firehole feel like a sauna," I joked, looking around to see how everyone else was faring.

Tory and Trent were at the back, waiting for their turn to step into the water. Brad and Alex slipped around me to get into their tubes. I moved farther into the water, making room for Kylie and Grey near the boat launch before jumping up into my tube.

The inner tube was large, designed for a leisurely float on a river, with cup holders, a mesh bottom, and handles. I scootched around in my tube for a moment, getting comfortable as the current pulled me down river.

Brad and Alex were a few yards ahead of me, splashing and hollering at each other. If I hadn't known better, I would have thought the attractive twins were fifteen instead of in their late twenties. Behind me, Grey held Kylie's tube as she repeatedly attempted and failed to climb in. I had to give her credit—the woman was determined and used every situation to her advantage. She finally got into the tube and immediately began calling for Grey to join her. Tory and Trent were both on their tubes, hands linked, as they began their float. Apparently, they had worked out their frustrations from yesterday, though there were still hints of tension in Trent's shoulders and the corners of Tory's eyes.

Resting fully on my tube, I watched the scenery drift by, my legs and back growing accustomed to the cold water while the sun warmed my face. The river was lined with trees, an occasional cabin breaking up the forest. The sounds of people talking, birds chirping, and the river's gentle gurgle filled the air. Up ahead, I could see purple mountains. The river flowed gently, and while there were a handful of families who'd had the same idea, it wasn't nearly as crowded as I'd anticipated. I let the peace sink into my bones, attempting to close my eyes and doze.

The sound of splashing drew my attention, and I found Grey making his way over to me, his hands acting as paddles. Kylie trailed a few feet behind, her shorter arms making it harder to follow.

"What do you think?" he asked, snagging one of my handles and linking our tubes together.

"It's beautiful. If I lived here, I'd be tempted to float the river every day." Contentment filled my voice as I pictured living in Island Park. The summers would be glorious, though I wasn't sure I could handle the winters.

"Not me," Kylie said.

She'd given up on rowing to catch up with Grey, instead walking over to us, splashing water our direction with every step. The water hit around her knees, and when she reached us, she managed to climb into her tube without any extra help from Grey. She grabbed onto Grey's tube, making us a chain of three. She was determined, I'd give her that much. Even if the competitive nature Tory had mentioned meant Kylie couldn't accept Grey's clear disinterest.

"I hate getting my hair wet," Kylie said, taking control of the conversation. "I feel naked without my makeup, but it's much better than getting racoon eyes. Am I right?"

I nodded, not sure what to say in response. I thought I'd feel the same way, but I hated the thought of missing out on something so soothing because of the risk of racoon eyes.

"Racoon eyes are the worst. It takes hours to get my eyeliner just right, and this beard doesn't paint itself on," Grey said, causing a surprised giggle to burst from my lips. I could just picture Grey in front of a mirror, painstakingly painting on the beard that had occupied far too many of my thoughts this trip.

"You're such a joker, Grey! That beard is all you, and it is all man," Kylie said.

I bit down a gag, cringing at the terrible line. If Grey wasn't holding onto my tube, I would have done everything in my power to escape this interaction. I eyed his hold on my tube and watched his fingers tighten, as if he could sense my desire for escape.

I scrambled for something to say, desperate to rediscover the calm of only moments before.

"Kylie," I paused, still unsure what to ask. The words slowly spilled out of my mouth, hesitation evident in every syllable. "I feel like I barely know you. Remind me, how do you know Tory?" Maybe if I could steer the conversation away from anything remotely flirty, I would survive this river float.

"That's actually a great story. Tory and I met at summer camp when we were kids and stayed in touch. When she moved to her new apartment, she knew I was looking for a place to live and invited me to be her roommate. I'm lucky she thought to ask me. We spend so much time together, and she's introduced me to so many great friends...like Grey." She looked over at Grey with a wide smile, while Grey refused to make eye contact, staring determinedly at the reeds lining the riverbank. "What about you, Audrey? How do you know Tory? I don't think I've ever heard the story."

At least her question was easy to answer.

"We were college roommates and have been friends ever since." It wasn't the full story, but was the simplest way to explain our connection. It was hard to sum up the chaos that had been our college apartment, how Tory and I had banded together to help each other survive the difficult dynamics that had existed between our other roommates. Emily had been a part of that effort too, acting as a sounding board when our roommates got to be too much. It still stung to think about her betrayal and how I would never be able to turn to her for advice or help again. As ridiculous as it sounded, a small part of me wanted to talk to her about Grey, get her thoughts about this man who was slowly infiltrating my heart. Yet, she and I had discussed my feelings for Lyle on many occasions, feelings she had disregarded.

"That's so sweet. Aren't college friends the best?" The way she said "college friends" implied a certain level of childishness to our friendship that I chose to ignore.

I struggled to think of another question to ask when the river intervened. We'd drifted too close to the side, and I found myself headed for a patch of reeds.

"Oh no!" Kylie shrieked, kicking away from the plants.

"Hang on." Grey began kicking too, but even with the three of us working against it, the current continued pulling us closer until my rump got stuck on some rocks.

"Let go of my tube," I said, already pushing to stand up. "I'll walk back towards the center of the river and catch up with you guys."

"Are you sure?" Grey asked, leaning forward to stand as well. I couldn't tell if it was out of concern for me or because he didn't want to be left alone with Kylie.

I wasn't sure. I hated the thought of Kylie getting alone time with Grey, but I also recognized I wouldn't be able to escape the reeds without standing. Additionally, I didn't want to make them have to stand too, reforming our chain, with all its third wheel awkwardness.

"Of course. You guys go ahead," I said through a tight smile, wishing there was a way to send Kylie ahead and get Grey to myself. Before I could second-guess my decision, I shooed them away before marching back to the center of the river with my tube, the river coming up to my calves, the current making my steps feel unsteady. It took a couple of awkward hops, but I was able to climb back on my tube and resume drifting with the current.

Up ahead, Grey and Kylie continued on their way. Kylie grasping Grey's tube with one hand while the other waved animatedly in the air with whatever story she was telling.

"Are you sure that was a wise idea?" Tory called, floating up next to me and grabbing one of my tube handles. I looked around but didn't see Trent. Maybe they hadn't worked everything out after all.

"Grey's a big boy. He can handle himself. Not to mention I don't have a claim on him." I tried for nonchalance, but I could feel the anxiety just under the surface. If I didn't care for Grey, it would make things easier, safer. If I didn't risk my heart, I couldn't get hurt. Though I had a sinking suspicion it was too late for that. "Where's Trent?"

Tory shrugged. "We got stuck on a bank a little while ago and had to let go. He floated ahead."

I really hadn't been paying attention to my surroundings if Trent had floated past and I hadn't noticed.

"You didn't want to stay with him?"

"I wanted to keep my view of the Audrey, Grey, and Kylie show," Tory said with a smirk. "It's almost as good as a TV dating show."

"You're terrible!" I flicked water at her, and she shrieked at the cold.

"Okay, okay," she said, leaning away from me as I reached forward, ready to splash her more. "But you can't tell me nothing's happening there." She quirked an eyebrow, and I leaned over my tube, ready to splash her again, needing a change of topic.

"Fine." She held up the hand that wasn't grasping my tube in a placating gesture. "I can take a hint. New topic. I feel like we haven't had much time to talk since you got here. How's work? How's your mom?"

"Mom is great. She, Dave, and the girls are coming to visit in a couple of weeks, so that'll be chaos." Happiness filled my voice as I thought about the upcoming visit.

"I love your family. That'll be so fun to have them visit. How old are the girls now?"

"Seven, though they'll be eight in a couple weeks. They're starting third grade this fall, and Mom says they're already outgrowing their back-to-school outfits." I shook my head, trailing my fingers in the water. Thoughts of my family were a mix of bitter and sweet that left me longing for a childhood so different from the one I had experienced. "If they grow too much more, they'll be taller than me."

"How can they possibly be almost eight? That makes me feel old." Tory laughed, and we continued floating down the river, playing catch up on each other's lives.

Tory shared about her work frustrations and how she wished to quit her job and live in the cabin full-time as a recluse.

"You wouldn't survive a week. You're too much of an extrovert," I said, though the idea did hold a certain appeal.

I reciprocated, sharing about how I worried I'd be forever trapped in customer service.

"I got a business degree so that they'd see me as leadership material. But they just see me as a lackey who can fill in whenever leadership is gone, but not skilled enough to promote into an actual leadership role." I kicked my feet in frustration, my conversation with Drew from earlier echoing in my mind.

"I don't know why you stay there. They don't appreciate you." Tory leaned back into her tube.

"Where would I go? Most likely I'd have to start entry-level, and I don't know if I can handle that type of hoop-jumping again. At least I'm on the email team." Though Drew had a tendency to stick me on phones whenever the fancy suited him.

"You know, I never pictured you in some boring office job."

"Really?" I leaned forward to see her better. A boring office job was all I'd ever pictured, with its security and health insurance benefits.

Not true, a quiet voice whispered in my thoughts. It was the same voice, growing louder every day, that dreamed of teaching yoga and embracing a life of more calm and flexibility.

Tory shook her head. "Nope. I always thought you'd be a yoga instructor or something involving the outdoors. Maybe a park ranger."

I laughed, ignoring the first suggestion that had struck too close to home. "Can you picture me as a park ranger? I don't think I have the right bone structure for the hat."

"To be fair, I don't think anyone does."

We were the last ones to finish the float. By the time we got to the bank where we needed to climb out, everyone else was wrapped in the towels we'd left in Brad's car, their tubes already deflated.

"Where are Brad and Trent?" Tory asked, looking around for the missing group members as we navigated the muddy shore.

"Since Trent had your keys, Brad drove him to get your car. We weren't sure how far back the two of you were and wanted to save time getting back for lunch," Alex said as he took my tube. I gratefully accepted the help as I snagged my own towel, the breeze causing goose bumps to pebble on my skin now that I was out of the river.

"That was very...considerate and efficient of everyone." Tory sounded happy about the turn of events, but her face pinched in concern.

"I'm starving. What's for lunch?" I asked.

I hoped the change of topic would ease the tension around Tory's eyes, but I knew it wouldn't fully disappear until the guys returned without issue. She may have talked to Trent, but that didn't mean he'd let the tension between himself and Brad drop. I'd only known Trent a couple of months, and while his competitive nature was one thing that had attracted Tory to him, I had also seen it turn into ugly obsession. Hopefully, this time he really would let it go.

Glancing over, I noticed Kylie and Grey standing close together. Kylie's smile beamed as they talked, a private conversation for just the two of them. Grey, while not smiling, didn't look nearly as bothered by Kylie's chatter and proximity as he had earlier in our float.

I shrugged it off, telling myself I was happy for the two of them. If they'd found a way to get along better, it was a good thing. Unfortunately, that did not stop me from wishing I was the one standing next to Grey, sharing in a private conversation. Especially when he looked up, his brown eyes snagging on mine for a moment, his lips tipping up into a smile just for me. It made me miss our time in the car on the drive up, even the night in Hank and Dot's guestroom. Two experiences I'd never thought I would enjoy.

Chapter Twenty-Four

THE GUYS RETURNED INTACT, if slightly subdued. Brad, in particular, seemed abnormally quiet, and the tension that had been Trent's constant companion since Brad's arrival was still present. I had a feeling he wouldn't be happy until he was the only guy in Tory's life.

After lunch, everyone claimed exhaustion and scattered to different parts of the cabin to either nap or read, with Trent and Tory slipping out to take a walk. I sat on the front porch, settling into one of the wooden rocking chairs with the book I'd been attempting to read earlier. While I normally loved a good romance, I had a hard time focusing on the storyline, my thoughts bouncing between my conversation with Tory on the river and my attraction to Grey.

What did Tory mean when she said she'd never pictured me in an office job? I'd spent five years getting a business degree. What else did she think I'd do with it? Yet, hadn't I been having similar thoughts? Especially now that Drew was my supervisor.

What did I want out of this *thing* with Grey? I claimed not to be interested in dating him, but then I became frustrated when Kylie monopolized his time.

Topping the list of questions was simply the word: why? Why did I care what Tory thought about my career choice? Why did I care if Grey talked to Kylie and not me? Why was I letting any of this bother me and take over my mental space?

Frustrated, I slammed the book closed and went into the cabin, tossing the book onto my bed. I changed into leggings and a tank top, pulling my hair into a high ponytail. There wasn't really room in my bedroom to do yoga, but I'd make it work. No one was currently in the living room, but I didn't want to risk anyone sneaking up on me again. I'd had more than my fill of Grey seeing me in awkward positions.

The first part of my flow went smoothly enough as I focused on my breathing and did a few cat/cows, arching and curving my back to warm up my muscles. I selected poses I knew wouldn't take up much room, forcing my mind to stay in the moment. Unfortunately, the limited movement didn't do the trick. With each pose, I found my frustration growing, until finally, I threw my arms out in anger. Instead of relieving my pent-up emotions, I whacked my elbow on the bed post.

"Dang it!" I yelled, bringing my arm close to my chest and rubbing the tender spot. I sank onto the floor cross-legged, trying to breathe through the pain. I'd have a bruise tomorrow.

A knock sounded on my door before it cracked open slightly.

"Everything okay in here?" Grey poked his head into the room. "I was on the phone with my brother and mom in the living room and heard a shout."

I groaned, rolling onto my back and staring up at the ceiling. Of course it would be him.

"That doesn't sound encouraging." Grey came the rest of the way into the room, closing the door behind him and settling onto my bed. "Want to talk about it?"

"No." I threw my non-injured arm over my face, trying to block out the world.

"Are you sure? Because the sound I heard earlier makes me think you could use someone to talk to." Grey's tone was gentle, encouraging me to speak.

I hesitated, studying his face and reading the genuine concern furrowing his brow. It would be nice to talk to someone about my jumbled thoughts. Unable to discuss one of my issues with the source of the struggle, I decided instead to bring up my career woes. I leaned onto my uninjured elbow so I could see him better.

"Just pondering the meaning of life and wondering if I'm living mine to the fullest."

"Deep." Grey bobbed his head. "In any area in particular? Or are you talking about life in general?"

I quirked a smile. "I should probably examine all areas, but today I'm focusing on career choices."

"I see. I also find vacation, when I'm far from all responsibilities, the best time to ponder my career trajectory." He stroked his beard, a faux serious expression on his face. "Tell me more."

I snorted, dropping back onto the ground. "Why do I feel like I've just signed up for the most unorthodox therapy session in the history of the world?"

"Tell Dr. Grey your problems. I'm here to help."

"Fine," I sighed. "Also, wouldn't it be Dr. Whatever-your-last-name-is? What is your last name?"

"Nice! I'm here, ready to provide sage wisdom, and you don't even know my last name." Grey's face pinched into an expression of mock hurt, but the twinkle in his eye hinted at mischief lurking beneath the surface.

"Do you know my last name?" I asked.

"Of course."

"What is it?"

"It's a secret," Grey said, his cheek twitching as he attempted to keep a serious expression.

"Why would my last name be a secret?" I swallowed down a laugh and raised an eyebrow, waiting to hear his logic.

"Because," he stammered, "I don't want to make you feel bad for not knowing my last name."

"That's sweet, but I promise I'll survive. What's my last name?" I pushed to my feet and stood in front of Grey, hands on hips. I could feel my hair falling out of its ponytail, likely giving me a crazy halo, but I refused to be distracted.

Instead of responding, Grey snatched a pillow from the bed and threw it behind me. "What was that?"

"Not gonna work." I moved closer until our knees almost touched, staring him down.

"How do you know there's nothing behind you?" he asked, pushing to stand and mimic my pose.

"Educated guess."

Grey standing had robbed me of any height advantage, so I leaned forward, hoping that getting into his personal space would convince him to answer.

Instead, Grey leaned in closer, and my eyes snagged on his lips. I'd never kissed a man with a beard, and I'd always wondered how it would feel. Would it be scratchy and off-putting? Soft and tantalizing?

Grey must have noticed my eyes dropping to his lips because he grew still, watching me. Heat filled his gaze, making me want to lean in, remove the last few inches between us.

What was I thinking? As I'd told Tory, I wasn't looking to date, and I was not the kind of person who kissed guys casually. My mom's dating life before Dave had taught me that lesson many times over.

I swallowed, stepping back and putting needed space between us.

"My last name is Byrd." My voice came out breathless, and I turned to hide the flush in my cheeks.

I pulled open a drawer in the dresser and rummaged inside, not processing what I was looking at but needing to keep my hands busy. "I need to change, so if you wouldn't mind..." I gestured towards the door, keeping my back to him.

Grey touched my shoulder, and I turned to look at him. A small smile teased his lips as he extended a hand. "Hi, Audrey Byrd. I'm Greyson Stuart."

I hesitated before accepting his handshake, letting my hand linger in his. "Nice to meet you."

The electricity crackled between us as Grey held my hand, his rough calluses pressing into my smooth palm. How a handshake could hold so much emotion, I had no idea. I'd shared a bed with the man! Yet, the simple contact sent my pulse dancing.

His gaze dipped down to my mouth. I bit my bottom lip and watched as desire flashed in his golden-brown eyes. Giving my hand a gentle tug, he pulled me closer. My hand came to rest against his chest, his heart pounding a hurried beat beneath my fingers.

He leaned down, and I tilted my head up, my lips parting slightly as I anticipated the contact. Our breaths mingled. All it would take was one simple motion and—

The slamming of the front door reverberated through the cabin followed by Tory's call. "Where is everybody?"

I jumped back from Grey with a gasp, hands dropping down to my sides as my back bumped into the dresser.

"I...we..." I stammered, not sure how to react to what had almost happened. A part of me was mortified, but an even bigger part was disappointed not to know what Grey's lips felt like pressed to mine.

Grey ran a hand down his face, shaking his head before backing out of the room, mumbling something about helping with dinner. He slipped out of my room and closed the door behind him. Needing to clear my head, I turned back to the dresser. But I couldn't concentrate on the task at hand. Instead, I kept thinking of Grey's lips, just inches from mine, and how badly I wished I'd taken that final step to press my lips to his.

Chapter Twenty-Five

THE NEXT DAY WE drove back into Yellowstone. Tory wanted to hike more, and I couldn't sit around the cabin another minute. We'd spent yesterday evening watching movies, and I'd had to actively avoid sitting next to Grey for fear of picking up where we'd left off in my bedroom. I wasn't sure I'd be able to keep my hands to myself if I sat next to him. Instead, I waited until everyone else was settled on the couches before claiming my spot next to Alex, a nice neutral third party in whom I had no interest and whom I didn't have a history of falling asleep with. Kylie was more than happy to take my place, attempting to turn her close seat next to Grey into a snuggle session that he quickly shutdown, shoving several pillows between them.

I'd spent the duration of the superhero movie pretending not to look at Grey, watching his every move, though I was sure to look away quickly every time he caught me staring. I couldn't repeat a single detail about the movie, but I noticed every time Grey shifted in his seat or looked my way.

I'd claimed a headache and gone to bed early, but that hadn't turned off my churning thoughts. Instead, I'd found myself staring at the ceiling.

Normally, I would have used yoga to calm my mind, but after my struggle earlier in the day, I'd known better than to attempt a yoga flow in such close quarters. Not to mention it would have likely led to more thoughts about a bearded-man who smelled like comfort and the kiss we'd almost shared. Instead, I'd tried turning on a meditation app, but the soothing voice of the narrator had done little to quiet my thoughts.

For once, I hadn't been the first one awake, and yet I was still tired, as evidenced by the bags under my eyes, which I hadn't bothered to conceal. No amount of makeup could hide my exhaustion.

Adding to my mood was an odd phone conversation I'd overheard Grey having with his brother as I'd grabbed my drawstring bag for the hike.

I'd been in my room, making sure I had everything I needed, when Grey's quiet words outside my cracked door had caught my attention.

"I told you, Mason, now's not a good time." He'd paused, presumably waiting for Mason's response. "I need to look into the offer further. I'm not moving to Oregon on a whim."

My gut clenched at his words. Grey, moving? He hadn't mentioned it as a possibility when explaining his family situation, but maybe something had changed. Though surely he would have told me if it had.

A shuffling sound indicated he had begun to pace. I knew I was intruding, but there was no way to make my presence known without interrupting the conversation and making it clear I'd overheard him. So instead of leaving my room, I settled on the bed, scrolling through vacation photos on my phone while I waited for Grey to finish his phone call.

"It's a great offer, but I can't do that to Mom." Pause. "Do you really think she'd want to relocate? Leave Dad's grave and all the places connected to his memory?" Pause. "A fresh start could be good for her."

Pause. "Yes, having you there to help with the meltdowns would be nice, but what happens when you get overwhelmed again?" Pause. "I'm not having this conversation right now. I'll think about it, but that's all I can promise."

The sound of retreating footsteps followed this declaration, leaving me alone in the bedroom to process what I'd heard.

My brain was already swirling too much without the added anxiety of wondering if Grey would be sticking around. But I couldn't forget what I'd heard. Was Grey leaving? If so, how soon? Knowing there might be a time limit on whatever *this* was between us made my stomach clench and led to worries I couldn't ignore.

The car ride into the park was quiet, with Tory and Trent in the front and Grey and me in the back. Brad, Alex, and Kylie had piled into Brad's car, Kylie hinting that she wouldn't mind switching vehicles. I spent the drive staring out my window and soaking in the terrain we passed. I refused to look away from the window, telling myself I didn't want to miss any wildlife. In reality, I didn't want to look at Grey and see his expression after the tension and emotion in my room the day before.

The line to get into Yellowstone was shorter today, though it still took some time for us to enter the park. This time, it was a bison causing the traffic jam. He stood next to the road, unbothered by the vehicles passing within inches of him.

We parked a short distance away from the Grand Prismatic Overlook trailhead and I climbed out of the car, stretching as I did.

"Are we okay?" Grey asked, making me jump. I'd been so busy soaking in the scenery that I forgot to keep my distance.

"Of course. Why wouldn't we be?" My voice came out strangely high-pitched. I worried he would read in my face the conversation I'd overheard, a conversation I wasn't sure how to ask about.

"Things felt weird yesterday after—" He broke off, ducking his head. "I just wanted to check."

"I promise we're fine." I had spent the last several hours thinking about what his lips would have felt like, but he didn't need to know that.

"Good, good." He nodded a couple of times, looking like a flannel-wearing bearded-bobblehead, and I bit back a smile. That was one bobblehead I'd want in my car. "I don't want things to be weird between us. I want—" He broke off, looking uncertain, and in that moment I decided to forget about the conversation I'd overheard. It was probably nothing, just more drama connected to his brother and mom. If it was something I needed to know about, he'd tell me. I was going to enjoy this moment and embrace whatever adventure lay ahead.

"We're good." I gave his hand a squeeze, trying to communicate my emotions with the simple gesture.

We joined the rest of our group and made our way to the trail. We made up a motley crew, our manners of dress ranging from high-end outdoor gear to gym shorts. I'd opted for leggings, a tank top, and hiking boots with my jacket tied around my waist in case of a chill at the higher elevation, my drawstring bag over my shoulders. I looped my thumbs in the straps as I followed the group up the trail, hanging towards the back to soak in the moment.

Outside of our hike earlier on the trip, I hadn't spent much time on the trails this summer. I'd gone on one hike with my roommate, Mallory, and her boyfriend, Ridge, before they'd started dating but I really hadn't made time for the mountains, something this trip reminded me of at every turn. I'd forgotten how nature settled my anxiety, pushing it from the forefront to the background and allowing me to breathe deep. It was almost as effective as yoga in helping me settle my thoughts. Maybe I really should consider Tory's park ranger career suggestion. At least it would come with health insurance.

We walked up a slight incline, and my calves strained with each step. While not an overly difficult trail, my lungs still burned with effort, the summer air warm on my skin.

"This view is a bit more baren than I anticipated," Grey said from my right. He'd hung back with me, and I was shocked at how long he'd remained quiet.

I looked around at the handful of trees and the mineral-encrusted plains surrounding us. "It might not look like much now, but the view at the top is stunning. Probably one of my favorite views in Yellowstone. Trust me, the effort is worth it."

"I've found the best things in life often require a bit of effort."

I was startled to find Grey looking at me as he spoke, not the gravel trail we were walking. His golden-brown eyes sparked with an intensity that sent my pulse racing.

I cleared my throat, turning back to the trail. "How was the rest of the movie last night?"

"I'd seen the movie before, so I went to bed shortly after you did."

"Not worth a rewatch?"

"Not if you weren't there to enjoy it with me."

I tripped on a rock but managed to catch myself before face planting on the trail. Who said things like that? And why did I love it so much when Grey used his pick-up lines on me?

"That's too bad. We'll have to watch it another time then." My voice sounded weird to my ears, breathy and intense.

"I'll hold you to that."

We continued talking about innocuous subjects until we reached the turnoff for the Grand Prismatic Overlook. The steeper hill stole our breaths, and we fell into companionable quiet as our leg muscles worked to carry us to the view point. At the top, we found our group leaning on the weather-worn wooden railing, gazing over the plain. I waited for an opening at the railing and then pushed my way forward, eager to soak in the familiar view.

A rainbow of color exploded in front of me, the spring a vibrant blue in the middle and ringed with green, yellow, and orange. Steam drifted up into the summer air. From this distance I could see the boardwalk ringing the spring, filled with tiny people walking around. No matter how many times I saw the Grand Prismatic, it never ceased to amaze me.

The first time I'd done this hike, it had been just me and Mom. She'd quit yet another waitressing job, and I'd spent the entire trip fighting back worry over how we'd survive this latest setback. There was something about the spring and this view and the time spent with my mom that had made those worries disappear. I'd known in that moment that we'd make it work, even if I hadn't known how yet.

I pulled out my phone, capturing a quick selfie to send my mom, before Grey grabbed it from my hands.

"Smile big." He trained the camera on me, a giant grin splitting his face.

"I already got one of me," I protested, knowing it would be futile but trying all the same.

"Everyone deserves at least one good picture of themselves on vacation. One that isn't a selfie," Grey insisted, taking a step back for a better angle.

"I've never heard that rule before," I muttered, noticing that our group had vacated the railing and was making their way back to the trail.

"You can use it for a dating profile picture. It'll help you snag your unicorn. Show off how beautiful and well-traveled you are."

I snorted. "Trust me, no one would want to see this." I gestured at my dust covered leggings, messy bun, and makeup-free face.

"I would," Grey said, the words so quiet I wasn't sure I was meant to hear them.

I gave in, leaning against the fence and giving Grey my biggest smile. He moved back, taking picture after picture, coaching and teasing me into different poses until a laugh burst from my lips and the people around us were watching with curiosity.

"Enough," I finally said, my smile splitting my face as I pushed away from the railing.

"One more, I promise!" Grey said, stepping up to me and wrapping his arm around my shoulder, the camera flipped to take a selfie. "Say 'bison'!"

"Bison," I echoed, the largest, cheesiest grin stretching across my face as I looked into the camera and Grey captured the two of us standing in perhaps my favorite moment of the trip, the view behind me only a small piece of the reason why.

Chapter Twenty-Six

"THAT WAS GORGEOUS!" KYLIE gushed as we regrouped on the trail.

"Crazy to see what nature can do," I said, nodding in agreement and pretending like I wasn't dying to sneak a peak of the selfie Grey had captured.

Tory, Alex, and Brad stood a little apart from us, talking. Trent glared in their direction, a scowl filling his face. Curious about what was going on, I waited, letting those around me carry the conversation until Tory rejoined the group.

"How would you guys feel about making this a longer hike?" Tory had looped her arm through Trent's, though I couldn't decide if she was oblivious to the tension radiating off him in waves or if she was simply choosing to ignore it.

Brad stayed in his spot a little farther down the trail, watching the group. Since his one-on-one time with Trent, Brad only came near Tory when another person could act as buffer, not that Trent seemed to notice or appreciate the gesture.

"I'm game. What did you have in mind?" Grey asked from behind me, and a tiny voice in my head wondered what it would feel like to lean back into his solidness and warmth.

"There's a waterfall a few miles down the trail that's one of my favorites. It's a long hike, but not hard. Probably about five miles round trip from the car."

Now that I was on the hike, I wasn't ready for it to end. The combination of sun, exercise, and fresh air was intoxicating. Add in the gorgeous views, and I was happy to hike some more, especially if Grey continued to hang back with me. I might even find the courage to lace my fingers with his while we walked.

"I'm down to keep going," Grey said.

The others nodded their agreement, all except Trent, who remained silent next to Tory. We took his lack of response as agreement and continued down the trail. My stomach seemed to be hiking its own trail of excitement as Grey stayed by my side.

We once again found ourselves towards the back of the group. I wasn't sure how Tory was keeping Kylie up front with her, but I wasn't mad about it. I couldn't get enough time alone with Grey, a thought I wasn't going to examine too closely. Instead, I enjoyed the quiet between us, for once not desperately trying to think of ways to make conversation.

"I love hiking," Grey said as we followed the dirt path.

"I do too, though I don't go often enough."

"I'm the same way. Why do you think that is? We live in Utah. Some of the best hiking in the world is just minutes away, and yet, I barely leave my house on weekends."

I paused, trying to decide how vulnerable I wanted to be. I'd already told Grey so much. What was a little more? "I used to hike all the time with my friend, Emily. But then I started dating this guy who...who didn't appreciate nature unless it was on a golf course. And, well, I kind of stopped trying to get him to go with me. It was just easier to do what he wanted."

Grey stayed quiet, processing my words before speaking. "I know nothing about this guy except he's no longer dating you, and I can already tell he's an idiot."

I barked a surprised laugh. "You know, that is the best description of him I've ever heard. After all, how could you not love this?" I struck a pose, hip cocked, hands thrown in the air, sweat trickling down my back.

"Beats me," Grey said, his face serious and warm as he drank me in. It was the kind of look a girl could get lost in.

Clearing my throat, I started rambling while leading Grey down the trail, not quite sure what to do with the nervous energy building in my chest. "Of course, I can't blame him entirely for me forgetting nature exists. I've kind of been avoiding it."

I trailed off, my next words even harder to speak than sharing Lyle's betrayal. I swallowed, determined to press forward, show him all my hidden places.

"My mom was in a car accident involving a deer at night driving down a canyon. It messed her up pretty bad." My words were quiet. Even now I could remember that night, Dave's desperate phone call, me frantically booking a flight and packing, trying to get to Mom and the girls as fast as I could. It wasn't until after I'd landed that we'd known how bad she really was, those hours on the plane the longest of my life.

Grey stopped, snagging my arm and turning me to look at him.

"Was that why you were so determined to stay on schedule when we were driving to the cabin?"

I bit my lip and gave a small nod.

"Now I'm the idiot. I'm sorry, Audrey! If I had known..." He trailed off, his face stricken.

"The only people who know are Tory and my roommates," I said, my voice quiet. "I don't like talking about it. I went to California for a few weeks to help Dave with the girls while Mom recovered."

"Wow. That must have been hard."

A melancholy smile touched my lips as we continued crunching along the gravel trail. "You could say that. Though Mom's fine now, and those few weeks meant I got to spend quality time with my sisters."

"That's a relief!"

I could leave it there, pretend like that was the worst of it, but knew I couldn't. "The story gets worse, if you can handle it."

I tried to keep my tone light, but this was veering into dangerous territory for me and my emotions.

"Hit me with it." He nudged my arm in encouragement.

"I was engaged when I went to help Mom. It was that guy who didn't like nature. His name was Lyle, and I thought he'd be my forever. He quickly proved me wrong. Not long after I left, he started cheating on me with my best friend, Emily." I choked on the words but pushed forward, desperate to let someone see my scars fully. "I found the two of them making out at his apartment when I got home."

"That's—" Grey broke off, for once at a loss for words as he reached for me and hesitated, shoving his hands into his pockets. "That sucks."

"That's the understatement of the century."

"With your best friend? The gal you used to hike with?"

"Yep." The "p" gave a distinct popping sound as I said it. That was probably the part that hurt the most. Emily had been my first phone call when I'd found out about my mom, encouraging me to take the trip, promising everything would be okay. Her betrayal still tasted bitter on my tongue.

"That proves they're both dumber than I thought." Grey's words caused an unexpected warmth to settle in my chest.

We started walking again, and only a moment later he brought his hand up, nudging my pinky with his. The brave little pinky leading the charge. I accepted the invitation, lacing my fingers with his, not caring who saw, as warmth stole up my arm and settled in my cheeks at the surprisingly comforting gesture.

"They might disagree. They got married the day we left for this trip."

Grey remained quiet for a moment, processing my words before a mischievous grin crept across his face.

"I hope he gets gored by a bison on his honeymoon. Nothing fatal. Just something that might impede other activities." Grey's eyebrows danced suggestively as he squeezed my hand.

"Grey!" I laughed in surprise.

"Stampeded by a moose? Chased by a bear? Really, any of those options sounds appropriate."

I shook my head, not even trying to hide the grin Grey's words triggered. "You're assuming he's honeymooning somewhere like Yellowstone. What if he's somewhere tropical?"

"I'm sure we could come up with some appropriate alternatives. Bit by a shark? Allergic reaction to his sunscreen?"

"Sunburned where the sun doesn't shine," I said before I could think about it.

"Couldn't happen to a nicer guy." Grey nodded sagely, his face schooled into a serious expression that only lasted a moment before his smile returned. "The question is, what activities are they participating in that would result in a sunburn in that location?"

I bit back a laugh and shook my head. I'd actively spent this week trying not to think of Lyle and Emily, and now here I was, freely sharing the most painful parts of myself with Grey and finding humor in them. We'd come a long way since those first moments in the car when I had been ready to strangle him.

But what about that phone call? I pushed the thought away, choosing to stay here, happy in this moment.

"I vote for a change of topic," I said, gesturing to the scenery around us. "Would you rather live the rest of your life in the mountains or on the beach?"

"Do I get to visit the beach if I pick the mountains or am I forever stuck in a cabin in the woods?" Grey asked, following my lead and embracing the shift in conversation.

We continued hiking, making our way through the forest. The trail, while it did wind some, was mostly flat, making me wonder what kind of waterfall could wait for us at the end. Back home, most hikes to waterfalls included steep hills and sharp drop-offs. But my body, used to yoga and walking my dog, was grateful for the milder hike.

When we reached the waterfall, I could only stare, soaking in the simple beauty. While not a roaring, massive waterfall, the steady stream spilling over the cliff face to the waiting cavern and pond below was stunning in its own way. I clambered over rocks and downed trees, eager to get closer to the waterfall. The sound of the steadily rushing water filled my ears as I drank in the view in front of me.

"Wow. Not quite what I was expecting, but still, wow," Grey said.

A portion of our group had gathered near the pool at the waterfall's base, watching as water plunged down the cliff face. Grey stood to my right with Kylie on his other side. Brad and Alex had made it to the waterfall ahead of the group and were settled on some rocks, snacking on granola bars and ignoring a curious chipmunk that had skittered over to them. Tory and Trent hung back, choosing to take in the view from farther away.

"I can't even imagine how long it would take for something like this to form," Kylie said.

I nodded, continuing to take in the scene and snapping a few photos. As I turned to take a selfie with the falls in the background, Grey looped his arm around my shoulder, joining the photo with a cheesy grin. If the knowledge that he'd photobombed my picture made my smile all the wider, I chose not to question it. Instead, I captured the moment, nestled into Grey's warmth with my new favorite waterfall in the background.

Chapter Twenty-Seven

OUR GROUP RESTED FOR a while, drinking water and eating the sack lunches we had packed at the cabin. While the hike had been mostly flat, my feet were tired from the long distance we had walked, and I was looking forward to slipping off my hiking boots when we got back to the car. Already the group was talking about getting an early dinner in West Yellowstone instead of driving all the way back to the cabin to fix something. Sandwiches and granola bars only provided so much fuel.

"Grey, Tory said you're a construction genius. Can I pick your brain for a project I'm working on?" Brad called as we started the hike back.

"Of course," Grey said, shuffling our hiking order and leaving me alone at the back. He threw me a wink, and I hoped it was a promise he'd join me in the back again soon.

I didn't mind having a moment alone. I took my time walking, pausing to take pictures and enjoying the scenery a bit more before we got back to the car. I reached the turn back onto the main trail from the Fairy Falls Trail to find Kylie stretching her calves, waiting for me.

"Mind if I walk back with you?" she asked, her ponytail bobbing as she fell into step beside me.

"Of course not." I shook my head, surprised Kylie wanted to talk with me. I assumed she'd be flirting with Grey and laughing about an inside joke with Tory, Brad, and Alex. While I didn't think Kylie was intentionally trying to cut me out of the group, my lack of shared history showed.

"It's beautiful here. Is this your first time in the area?" Kylie asked.

"It's my first time hiking Fairy Falls, but I've been to Yellowstone before." My words felt stilted as I tried to figure out why Kylie had waited for me.

"That's awesome! I came with Tory in the early spring, but it was too cold to really do anything besides hang out at the cabin. We did visit Big Springs, though. There was still so much snow!"

The conversation tapered off. I tried to ignore the awkward dynamic between me and Kylie, instead focusing on the fact that at least she'd tried to strike up a conversation. Even if it fell flat.

"So, are you big into hiking?" I asked after wracking my brain for conversation topics. I had a hard time picturing Kylie, with her designer clothes and manicured nails, regularly clambering up mountains, but maybe I was wrong.

"You know," she gave a flip of her hair, gesturing vaguely at herself in biker shorts and a floral top, "this really isn't my scene. I prefer days at the spa and shopping, but every once in a while, it's nice to switch things up. Not to mention you can't be friends with Tory if you're not willing to venture into the mountains from time to time."

I bit back a grin, curious to know what Grey would think of "visiting the spa" and "shopping" being listed as hobbies.

"A change of pace is a good thing," I said.

"I was thrilled when Tory told me who was coming on this trip. I mean, we're all, well most of us, are such good friends. It sounded like a blast. Tory told me she thought Trent might even propose on this trip."

Based on the dynamics I'd witnessed between Trent and Tory this week, I highly doubted that. In fact, I'd be more surprised if their relationship survived the waves of jealousy rolling off Trent every time Brad walked into a room.

"I had some secret hopes for this trip myself," Kylie said, a sad smile teasing the corner of her lips. "I'd hoped I could convince Grey to see me as more than a friend. I thought he was just playing hard to get, and I'm competitive enough I couldn't resist throwing my hat in the ring. After watching him with you, though, I realize it's never going to happen. Everyone tried to warn me, but I didn't listen."

"I'm so sorry," I stammered, not sure how to respond to Kylie's confession. I had been prepared for some backhanded information-gathering mission or maybe snide comments questioning why Grey would choose me. Kylie's frankness was startling. Also, what did she mean by "after watching him with me"? Had she seen his interest and realized she couldn't compete? Or was something else buried beneath the surface of her observation?

She gave a small shrug. "I can't count the number of times someone told me 'he's not the relationship type' or that 'leading girls on is what he does.' For some reason, I thought I'd be the one to convince him to give a relationship a shot. He always seems happy and interested when we're together."

She paused, watching me before continuing. I was careful to school my expression, my gaze focused on my feet and the trail.

"That's part of why I wanted to talk to you, away from the group. I wanted to do for you what others tried to do for me. Be careful around

Grey. He's fun and flirty, makes you feel special and seen, but he won't commit. Though watching him with you is the most interest I've ever seen him show in someone." I felt hope at the offhanded compliment, but Kylie kept talking.

"He can't even commit to a job for longer than a year. Why on earth did I think I could get him to commit to a single woman for longer than a weekend?" She gave a self-deprecating laugh.

"What do you mean he can't commit to a job? He said he worked construction." I forced the words out, picking apart Kylie's revelation and trying to find some flaw in her logic, something that would prove her wrong. Instead, I replayed the pieces of conversation I'd overheard from his phone call back at the cabin.

"He does, right now. When I met Grey last year, he was a substitute teacher. Before that, I think he worked retail or something. He kind of just bounces around. He even lived out of state for a bit but came back after a family emergency. If his brother hadn't beat him to it, I think he would have moved as far from Utah as possible after his dad passed away. The only thing keeping him there is his mom, and that tie will only keep him there for so long. I think his brother's trying to convince him to take a job in Oregon, bring his mom with him."

I shook my head. Kylie's claims didn't make sense. They didn't align with the man I'd met, the bearded, flannel-wearing man with a big heart who liked to flirt and tease, but who also stood by his mom in times of crisis and made me feel safe enough to show my most vulnerable places. And yet, did I really know Grey well enough after less than a week to say with certainty Kylie was wrong? How did I know Grey wouldn't drop everything for the next adventure, especially if he could bring his mom?

His text conversation with his brother from our drive up came to mind. He'd said it was a message about his brother struggling to provide help for their mom from states away. That would change if they moved closer. Maybe a fresh start would do all of them some good. Not to mention he'd have help handling his mom's anxiety.

"It's sad, really. He's such a good guy. Too bad he's too busy getting lost in adventure to recognize what he's missing out on in the dating sphere," Kylie said, her tone nonchalant, her face pinched into an expression of genuine sadness. "And Audrey, I genuinely mean that. You're great, and I don't want Grey hurting you because he's too busy chasing the next shiny thing."

Even spoken in kindness, Kylie's words hit their mark, and my heart shattered. I had just started to hope, allowing myself to imagine a life after Lyle. A life with a genuinely nice guy who would value and cherish me. Who would choose me, again and again. But if what Kylie had said was true, my future dreams of a happily ever after were just as far out of reach as they had been before Grey had shown up on my doorstep with a grin and an apology.

After giving me time to process her words, Kylie changed the topic, rambling on about work or some other mundane thing, but I stopped listening. I followed her on autopilot, my feet moving but my mind still digesting Kylie's revelations and what they would mean for me. Nothing had changed, not really. Grey hadn't promised me anything. It was my fault for reading so much into his smiles and touches. Too bad that didn't make this moment hurt any less.

Chapter Twenty-Eight

KYLIE AND I WERE the last ones to make it back to the cars. She brightly greeted everyone before climbing into Brad's car for the drive back to West Yellowstone. I remained silent, following Grey, Trent, and Tory to Tory's car. Tension rolled off Tory and Trent in waves, though I pretended not to notice as their whispers filled the air with a harsh undercutting tone. I'd have to ask Tory about it later, when we were back at the cabin away from prying eyes and listening ears and men with beards and flannel who were deceptively good at making a girl underestimate them.

I'd told him about Lyle and my mom's accident. I'd let him see a side of me that I kept hidden, having previously only allowed Tory and my roommates to get that close. Yet, I couldn't really blame him. He'd made no promises. It wasn't his fault I'd read him wrong, trusting him when I should have been running away as fast as I could. Because if there was one thing I knew for sure, it was that I couldn't handle another heartbreak, not now, possibly not ever. And falling in love with a man getting ready to leave Utah for Oregon was guaranteed to destroy me.

The car ride to West Yellowstone was nearly silent, Trent and Tory stewing in the front seat and Grey seeming to pick up on my mood in the backseat.

At one point, Tory slammed on the brakes, pulling me from my thoughts, and I flinched when I looked through the windshield to see a bison inches away from the car, staring us down. Grey, who must have been watching the road more carefully than I had, had thrown an arm in front of me, as if trying to protect me from the threat outside the car. If only I'd been as cautious with the threat inside the car.

"Are you okay?" Grey asked, concern creasing his brow and filling his tone.

My heart pounded, proof that it still functioned even if it was breaking.

"I'm fine," I stuttered, a cold sweat breaking over my skin at the realization of how close we'd come to repeating my mom's accident. Except a bison would have been much worse than a deer.

"Sorry, guys. He stepped into the road without warning. Everyone okay?" Tory asked from the front seat.

"We're fine," I said, taking a deep, steadying breath. It had been a close call, but we were fine. Nothing had happened.

Grey watched me carefully for a moment longer before withdrawing his arm. I missed the contact immediately, a ridiculous reaction that I needed to rein in. I needed to forget my attraction to Grey. He would leave me behind, just like every other girl he'd flirted with and then left for the next job.

The bison moved out of our way, and Tory was able to continue driving, taking it slow as we passed the bison that had nearly made contact with our car. Once we were out of the park and away from the risk of another bison stepping into the road, my heartbeat slowed to a normal rhythm, the fear finally dissipating.

We parked on the street in West Yellowstone near one of the many stores packed with memorabilia geared towards tourists who visited the area. The storefronts displayed a variety of goods ranging from the average to the unique. One t-shirt in particular, black with a red flannel sasquatch silhouette, caught my eye. My lips ticked up in a smile that quickly slipped off my face at the thoughts of Grey it triggered.

Kylie's words rang through my mind as we walked, our group separating as we each explored the stores that captured our interests. I wandered the shops, shadowing members of our group but not participating in their discussions as I navigated the emotional landslide that was currently filling my mind. If my mom's failed relationships before Dave had taught me anything, it was that I did not have time nor space in my heart for a man uncertain about commitment. I needed safe and stable. Two things Grey was not, if Kylie's words and my own observations were anything to believe.

In one store, I paused in front of a bar necklace display, appreciating the beauty of the simple necklaces, each with a different word engraved in the metal. A gold one with the word "Wander" in cursive script caught my eye.

My first day with Grey and his reference to the now familiar quote from *The Lord of the Rings* filled my thoughts. This week I had wandered away from my routine, my safety net. Now I felt more lost than I had the day I had come home to find Lyle kissing Emily on my couch. And if it was at all possible, a part of me felt even more devastated. Which told me all I needed to know about my relationship with Lyle. In this moment, I mourned the loss of what could have been more than a real relationship I'd invested over a year of my life into.

"I think it's meant for you," Grey said, gesturing to the necklace. "Maybe I'll get a matching one." He gave me a crooked grin, no doubt expecting me to laugh or banter back.

Instead, I shook my head and put the necklace back. "Unfortunately, it's not really in the budget right now. Though you should still get one. I bet it would go great with flannel."

"I do have a certain standard of fashion to live up to." Grey struck a pose, arms across his chest and hip cocked.

I snorted. "You could give the biggest fashionista a run for her money with your lumberjack chic."

"That's all I've ever really wanted."

I sobered as our banter registered. I shouldn't be doing this, not with Grey. Not if he had one foot out the door. The overheard conversation and mentions of a new opportunity came flooding back. I was not signing myself up for more heartbreak, not if I could help it.

"You okay? You've seemed off since the hike." Grey rested his hand on my shoulder, his warmth making me hesitate for just a moment.

I shook my head and stepped back, trying to create some much-needed distance.

"It's nothing. Just had an important message come in from work. I might need to leave the trip early." The lie slipped easily from my lips before I could second-guess myself, knowing this was neither the place nor the time to ask him about Oregon. I needed to find a way off this trip and back to Utah, back to where it was safe and where there weren't bearded men who left me questioning my career goals and life choices. I just had to find a way to do it without Grey tagging along and that wouldn't devastate Tory.

"Keep me posted. If I need to pack up a couple of days early to drive you home, I'm happy to," he said, sincerity ringing in every word.

I nodded, refusing to commit to anything. The last thing I needed right now was several more hours in the car alone with Grey. I could pretend my heart wasn't aching if we weren't alone and our interactions were brief. If I had hours of uninterrupted time, who knew what I would say? If I wasn't careful, Grey could convince me to give him my heart, and I didn't think I could survive giving it to the wrong man again.

I exited the store, passing Tory at the checkout.

"Audrey, you okay?"

I gave a noncommittal noise, rushing to exit the store in my need to get outside and away from Grey. The wooden storefront had a certain rustic appeal, but the coziness of the town was lost on me as I continued to drown in my thoughts. The desire to run, to hide, to escape rang loud and clear in my ears. I didn't even care about the risk of running into wild animals on the drive home. I needed to get out of Idaho and Montana, now.

As I rushed down the street headed towards the cars, I bumped shoulders with Brad.

"Easy there," Brad's hands cupped my shoulders, holding me steady. "Where are you running to?"

"I just needed some air," I gasped out, my breaths coming in sharp, staccato beats. The world was closing in, and I couldn't get enough oxygen.

"Do you know where the rest of the group is? I was with Alex, but he wanted—"

Brad's words stopped registering as I struggled to fill my lungs, each breath coming out as a ragged gasp.

"Audrey? Audrey!" Brad grabbed my shoulders, giving me a gentle shake and pulling me back into the moment. The worry on his face indicated he'd been trying to get my attention for a few minutes.

"Audrey, I need you to relax. Breathe with me." Brad's hand rubbed gently up and down my arm, coaxing me to follow his instructions.

My first inhale rasped against my throat as I tried to follow Brad's instructions.

"Good. Now can you breathe deeper? Try counting to four as you breathe in." Brad's voice was steady and calm.

It took a moment for my brain to process Brad's instructions, but slowly, the deep breathing helped to still the rising panic in my chest. Taking one more deep shuddering breath, I sank onto a nearby bench, Brad settling in next to me.

"Better?" Brad asked, his tone wary, like he was approaching a wild animal.

"Much, thank you. I just..." I paused, unsure how to express what had happened. "I became overwhelmed," I finished lamely.

Brad nodded, as if I'd said something sage and wise instead of a lame excuse for having had a panic attack in the middle of a tourist town. "It happens to the best of us. I'm sure getting some food in your stomach will help. It's been a long, busy day, and emotions have been high."

We sat there, watching as families of tourists scurried past us, rushing from one souvenir shop to the next, arms loaded down with bags full of their purchases.

"Is she okay?" A feminine voice asked, and I looked up to find Tory standing next to the bench, concern written on every facet of her face.

"I don't know if I can make it to the end of the trip," I muttered, unable to stop the words from spilling out. "It's a long time to spend with the same group of people, and I'm starting to stress about work, and—"

Tory held up a hand, cutting me off. "Don't blame this on work. What's really going on? The fear on your face has nothing to do with your job."

She sank onto the bench next to me, forcing Brad to move to make room for her. She wrapped an arm around me, inviting me to tell her everything. I hesitated only a moment, not wanting to open up this much in front of Brad, but too exhausted to move or pretend I was fine.

"It's just everything with Grey. It's too much." I knew I owed her more, but it was all I could say at this moment, unsure how to fully explain that I was running away from a nonexistent relationship before he could leave me behind.

Tory studied my face, seeing more than I cared to admit. I silently begged her not to pry, knowing she could see straight past my excuses. I felt horrible about leaving her birthday trip early, but I would feel even worse ruining the trip with my emotions and the confrontation I knew was building between me and Grey.

"But you rode up with Grey." She spoke the words softly, as if trying to reassure an injured animal. "How are you going to get home?"

I leaned back on the bench, trying to think through my options. "Maybe there's a bus or something? If you could drive me to Rexburg, I could get a rental car. Or..." I trailed off, realizing I really didn't have many options. It wasn't like I could ask my roommates to drive five hours, pick me up, and turn around and drive back. While I had no doubt they would, I'd feel guilty for asking them to give up so much time.

"If Kylie hadn't ridden up with us, I could drive you home. We could be back to Utah before midnight," Brad said, reminding us of his presence.

"But that would cut your trip short," I protested half-heartedly.

Brad shrugged, his expression one of practiced nonchalance. "It might be better for everyone if Trent and I got some space from each other."

Pain flitted across Tory's face, making me wish we were alone so I could talk to her about it but knowing now wasn't the time.

I bit my lip, hesitating for only a moment before voicing my thoughts. "I could take Kylie's place. She could stay, ride back with Grey, and I could ride back with you and Alex."

I'd already gone on one long distance car ride with a near-stranger once this trip, why not repeat the experience in reverse with a different set of guys? These ones would be safer. They weren't bearded, snarky men wearing lumberjack apparel who were too perceptive for their own good. It was already guaranteed to be a better experience for my emotions this time around.

"Are you sure?" Brad leaned forward, gauging my expression. "I know driving at night with wildlife isn't your favorite thing."

I shrugged, surprised he'd noticed. It made me wonder if Tory had said something. "I'll survive, but only if you're okay with this, Tory. I don't want to ruin your birthday trip."

I turned to Tory, trying to gauge her reaction to this change of plans. I didn't want to cut the trip short, but if I didn't leave soon, whatever was building between me and Grey would only become worse.

Tory studied me for a moment before nodding. "I'll miss you, but we're leaving in two days anyway. I don't want you to stay if you'll be miserable the whole time."

"I wouldn't be miserable..."

"We both know that's a lie," Tory said, wrapping an arm around my shoulders and pulling me in for a comforting embrace. "Just promise me you won't leave until morning. I can run interference between you and

Grey. I just don't want to have to worry about the three of you making that drive at night."

I gave a sad, relieved smile, shifting to face Brad. "If you're still okay with it, sounds like we're heading home early."

"Let me talk to Alex and Kylie and get it arranged. First thing tomorrow, we'll head back to Utah." He gave a decisive nod, pushing up from the bench and walking towards the store entrance where the rest of our group had started to gather.

My heart might be breaking, but at least I wouldn't be trapped here with the reason for my heartbreak.

Chapter Twenty-Nine

As we arrived at the restaurant, my stomach churned with nerves and anticipation. We still needed to tell the rest of the group we were leaving early, and I knew Grey wasn't going to like it. But I couldn't bring myself to stay another day, falling in love with Grey and knowing it would just end in heartbreak. I couldn't take the risk.

We settled at our table, everyone commenting on the rustic décor that made the burger joint feel like an old-time saloon waiting for a cowboy to step in, spurs jangling like in an old western film. I glanced at the menu. Nothing sounded appetizing, but I needed to eat.

"Have you ever had bison before?" Grey asked, leaning over and pointing to one of the menu items. "Do you think it tastes different enough from cow to justify the additional five dollars?"

"Only one way to find out," Brad said, quirking an eyebrow at Grey. "I'm a firm believer that everyone needs to try bison at least once in their life, if for no other reason than being able to answer that exact question."

Our waitress arrived, carrying a tray of waters. Everyone else was ready to order, so I quickly selected something, landing on a cheeseburger topped with barbeque sauce and onion rings. I also ordered a Pepsi, needing the caffeine kick to make it through dinner and the rest of the evening.

Conversation tapered off as we waited for our food, the first awkward silence of the trip descending over our group and making me wonder if somehow they already knew what Brad, Tory, and I had discussed.

"What's on the agenda for tomorrow? Another float down the river? Campfire and stargazing? It's our last full day at the cabin. We've got to make it count!" Kylie said, grinning at Tory with clear excitement.

"Yes, to all of the above! Also, I'd love to do another hike, maybe drive up to Sawtelle for the sunset," Tory rambled.

I fidgeted with my straw wrapper, tying it into a knot and then tearing it into little pieces as I waited for the right time to share our news with the group.

"That sounds fun. Anything else people want to do?" Grey asked, trying to draw the rest of us into the conversation.

Brad took this as his opening.

"It's really up to the four of you." He gestured to Trent, Tory, Kylie, and Grey. "Alex, Audrey, and I are heading back tomorrow. That is, if you're okay riding home with either Grey or Tory, Kylie."

Alex gave an encouraging nod, having clearly talked to Brad about the decision before now. I bit my lip, waiting for everyone's reaction.

"Of course. I'm flexible," Kylie rushed to reassure.

Grey seemed the only one truly bothered by the pronouncement. Trent didn't react, and Kylie looked excited at the prospect of a change of rides. A look of shocked hurt filled Grey's face, and I forced myself to ignore it. He'd move on from me soon enough. I bet he'd find his unicorn in Oregon, probably someone who enjoyed long walks on the beach while getting caught in the rain.

"What do you mean you're heading back tomorrow? We're supposed to be here a couple more days," Grey protested, looking back and forth between the three of us, his eyes snagging on mine and holding until I finally broke his gaze, choosing to stare at the straw wrappers littering the table in front of me instead.

Brad gave a noncommittal shrug. "Some stuff has come up at home, and Audrey mentioned needing to get back too."

"Tory, you're okay with this?" Grey turned to look at her, and Tory gave a small shrug.

"I'll miss them, but if they need to head back a bit early, I understand. Life happens." I could hear the words she didn't say about how I needed space. Though I guessed having Trent and Brad in separate states wouldn't hurt things for Tory either.

I bit my lip, waiting for someone to question Brad further, to dig into his vague excuse for cutting our trip short, but they seemed to accept his reasons, though Grey appeared less than satisfied with the answer, trying to read something on my face from his position across the table from me.

Our waitress arrived with our food, and the table descended into silence, the only noise the sound of cutlery on plates. I barely tasted my food. Instead, I stared at my plate, doing my best to avoid Grey's probing gaze.

Finally, Grey broke the silence. "I can officially say bison burgers are not worth an extra five dollars."

A stilted laugh escaped from the group, breaking the tension. Soon everyone dove into conversation. It was quieter than before but served to distract everyone from our pending departure and the holes it would leave in the group.

Chapter Thirty

THE DRIVE BACK TO the cabin was quiet. The setting sun chased us home, casting shadows and making me strain to see if deer or moose lurked in the dark. I tensed at every turn, relieved when the headlights illuminated a clear roadway instead of hidden wildlife.

When we arrived at the cabin, I went straight to my room and started packing. We might not be leaving until morning, but I could still be ready to go as soon as Brad gave the word. I quickly packed everything into my duffle bag and backpack and changed into joggers and a hoodie, ready to join the group for a movie or whatever they had decided on for the evening's entertainment.

Stepping into the living room, the cabin was oddly quiet. Grey lay on the couch, typing on his phone, but no one else was in sight.

"Where is everyone?" I hung back in the hall, wary of the conversation ahead.

"Since Alex and Brad are leaving in the morning, they ran over to their family's cabin to check on a couple of things for their grandpa. Tory, Trent, and Kylie went with them to help."

My stomach clenched. Why had Tory left me alone with Grey? She knew Grey was the reason I was leaving tomorrow. I didn't want to talk to him, to risk showing him just how badly he'd hurt me after only a few days.

I debated returning to my room and hiding from Grey until the others returned.

"Come sit. We might as well wait for them together." He patted the cushion next to him, making the decision for me.

I sank onto the loveseat, reaching for the book I'd left on the floor nearby. I flipped to my bookmark, not seeing the words in front of me.

"So, is it work, the reason you're heading back?" he asked, curiosity and something else filling the deep timbre of his voice. "I thought you said you weren't going to let them ruin your vacation."

"Something like that," I hedged, not wanting to lie but unsure how to explain that he was the reason I was running. How did you tell someone you hadn't even dated that they'd broken your heart and that you were running away from them? "It'll be nice to get back to Ruby."

That part, at least, was true. I missed my dog and her familiar weight at the end of my bed and the uncomplicated way she loved me, no strings attached, no pressure.

"Are you sure that's all?" Grey sat up, turning to face me, his face stoic as he slipped his phone into his pocket. Maybe he'd been spending too much time with Trent. He was starting to adopt his facial expressions.

I told myself not to notice his arms and how his flannel shirt hugged his chest.

"What is that supposed to mean?" I crossed my arms over my chest, trying to hold in the emotions I could feel raging inside.

"Don't think I didn't notice you started shutting me out after you hiked back with Kylie. What did she tell you?"

"Nothing. We just got some one-on-one time, a chance to get to know each other." I hedged.

"There's no way that's all that happened." Grey studied my face. "She said something to you that has you running scared. Something about me."

I expelled a breath in surprise. I didn't want to share the details of my conversation with Kylie, but I knew my expression had already given me away.

"She mentioned that you're a hard guy to pin down, that's all. Something about how you're just passing through on your way to the next job out of state. Why would that have anything to do with me leaving?" I attempted to shrug it off, pretend her words hadn't stung.

Grey pushed to his feet, pacing in front of the bank of windows that reflected our current scene. I couldn't help but wonder if the Grey and Audrey reflected back at us stood a chance. If they had any hope for the possibility of a future together.

"I told you, I'm not going anywhere. My mom needs me."

"Just until you leave for Oregon, right? Or are you taking her with you?" The words spilled out before I could think better of it, and I clamped a hand over my mouth, wishing I could call them back.

"Who said anything about Oregon?" His eyebrows pinched together, confusion battling with frustration on his face.

"I heard you talking about it. Something about a good job offer." I repeated the words I'd heard in the hallway, wishing my voice wasn't filled with bitterness.

"It's...that's..." Grey stuttered, trying to find the words. "I'm not going anywhere. My brother's trying to convince me and Mom to move up there. I told him I'd talk to her, nothing else."

"And if she wants to go?" I could imagine it: his mom, a woman given the opportunity to be with both her sons, Grey finally finding help with his mom's anxiety. It wasn't an easy image to dismiss.

"Then I'll cross that bridge when we come to it. What does it matter? I'm here now."

"It matters to me!" I shot to my feet, stalking towards him. My emotion forced me to move, to pace, to process.

"Why? Why does it matter to you?" Grey all but shouted, stepping towards me, and suddenly I noticed our proximity. If I reached out, I could wrap my arms around him, pull him close.

I stumbled back half a step, and he continued forward until my calves bumped the couch, preventing my escape.

"Why does it matter to you?" he repeated, this time with a whisper that held worlds of possibility.

I bit my lip, and his eyes dropped, registering the motion.

"It...I..." I stammered, words failing me as my gaze darted to his lips. I had spent the entire trip wondering what they would feel like. All it would take was pushing up onto my toes and—

Grey's lips crashed onto mine before I could finish the thought, demanding answers I was too afraid to speak out loud. His beard rasped against my skin, tantalizing me, leaving me wondering why I'd dated men without facial hair for so long. His arms wrapped around me, pulling me into his warmth, and my hands moved to rest against his chest, grasping his shirt and steadying me in his embrace. Our mouths tangled in a dance I never wanted to end, which is why it had to stop.

Mustering all my self-control, I gave him a gentle push, hardly anything noticeable. Grey noticed, pulling back to look at me. I couldn't school my features fast enough, and I was certain he saw the raw desire on my face, but he also must have seen the fear and hesitation because he released me, stepping back and giving me space.

I pulled in great gasps of air, my lungs struggling to recover from the best kiss of my life. After a moment, I spoke, the words coming out quiet and breathy.

"I can't risk another heartbreak. I can't let you in, only for you to run away the first chance you get. I won't survive." The words were raw, a direct glimpse at my heart.

Grey expelled a disbelieving breath, shaking his head. "I'm not the one running away. I'm right here."

"For how long? I haven't known you long, but I do know you have a wanderer's heart. How long before the call becomes too great and you leave? It might not be Oregon, not now, but it'll be somewhere, someday, soon." The words felt like shards of glass as I forced them out, the pain inescapable, but my fear too great to contain.

"Don't blame this on me. I told you I'm not going anywhere. We both know this is about you. You're afraid and blaming it on me to try to justify stopping this before it begins." He reached out as if to cup my cheek, but drew his hand back, letting it hang limply at his side.

"Afraid? Of what, do tell?" I crossed my arms over my chest, doing my best to hold myself together. I could fall apart later.

"Of having fun, of living your life, of breaking from the plan and maybe wandering off course. Of possibly being happy." His voice grew soft on the last words, almost like a caress.

My breath hitched, and I reared back like I'd been slapped. "Who said I'm not happy?"

"Call it a wild guess."

"I don't need some guy I just met telling me how to live my life. Before you go handing out life advice, maybe you should take a good, close look at your own."

With those words, I turned on my heel and stormed into my room, slamming the door behind me. I stood there, frozen, leaning against the door and trying my best to breathe deep. I could see the shock and hurt in Grey's eyes at my words, but even more haunting was the truth and vulnerability in his face as he'd talked about happiness.

I pushed away from the door, trying to dislodge the sting of Grey's words and the memory of his kiss. I *was* happy. I had security and stability. I had a business degree and a steady job. I had a dog and a 401(k). I had followed the checklist. I was happy, I really was.

If I said it enough times to myself, I might even believe it.

Chapter Thirty-One

THE MORNING WAS SLOW in coming. I spent a restless night trying not to picture the heartbreak that had stolen across Grey's face as I'd walked away. I tried counting my breaths, a bedtime yoga routine, and a meditation app, but nothing had done the trick. At one point, I'd even found myself pacing my room, afraid I'd wake up the entire cabin with my anxious energy, but all had remained silent while the loud voices in my head had tried to reason through what I should do and how to move forward from here.

Darker circles than before shadowed my eyes as I forced my hair into a messy bun and slipped on a pair of joggers that had seen better days. I stumbled into the kitchen to find Tory behind the stove, looking far too happy for my taste as she cooked breakfast. The counter was already covered in various breakfast foods, just waiting for everyone to come eat.

"Good morning," she greeted with a wave of the spatula. "This is my happy place: up at the cabin, making food for the people I love." She fairly vibrated with happiness, reminding me of Dot, a direct contrast to my current state of mind.

"Morning." The words sounded strained and tired, but Tory didn't seem to notice, beaming at me before turning back to what appeared to be enough hashbrowns to feed all the bears in Yellowstone. I retrieved a Pepsi from the fridge and sank onto one of the stools at the island, telling myself it wasn't too early to drink a soda.

"I'm sad you're leaving. I'm going to miss you. But it's probably for the best that Brad and Trent won't be spending any more quality time together." Her mouth pulled into a frown as she spoke, trailing off as she pondered the tension between her boyfriend and her oldest friend.

"Tory, I hope you know Trent doesn't deserve you." I said the words without thinking. Apparently something had broken in me yesterday and now I couldn't keep my thoughts to myself.

She shook her head. "You just haven't gotten to know him like I have. He's really a great guy under that gruff exterior, I promise."

"I hope you're right." I decided to let it go, not wanting to leave on a sour note with Tory, though I was fairly certain Trent wasn't hiding a gooey center beneath his tough shell.

"I'm so glad you came. I know this week was a lot," she said, changing topics as she continued zipping around the kitchen. "What with taking time off from work, knowing Lyle was getting married, then finding out that his wedding fell apart, and then meeting and starting to fall for Grey. I can only imagine how hard it's all been."

It took a moment for Tory's words to register, but when they did, I jerked up straight, banging my shins into the island with a thud. "What do you mean Lyle's wedding fell apart?"

Tory froze, spatula in the air as she turned to face me.

"You didn't know?"

I shook my head, still trying to clear the cobwebs in my mind enough to process this conversation. I needed the caffeine to kick in faster.

"It's all over social media. Emily called the wedding off the day of, something about another guy and deciding she wanted something different from a life with Lyle." Tory shrugged, as if finding out one's ex-boyfriend had been jilted at the altar was an everyday occurrence. "She went on their honeymoon and has been posting pictures of beaches and the ocean for days."

"Why didn't you tell me?" I sat in shock, trying to process everything.

"I figured you already knew and didn't want to discuss it. Besides, what does it matter? You're over Lyle anyway."

Tory continued to babble, but I tuned her out, processing her news. Did I care that Lyle was free, that Emily had left him? No. The answer surprised me. I thought I would feel something, validation maybe, a bit of relief. Instead, I felt tired as I finally accepted that I was giving Lyle even more of my time that he didn't deserve.

"After seeing you with Grey, though...honestly, Audrey, how can you leave now?"

Hearing Grey's name grabbed my attention, bringing me back to the moment as Tory turned off the burner and deposited a mountain of hashbrowns on the counter.

"Things were going so well! I know yesterday scared you, but whatever happened, which you will explain to me soon"—she paused, giving me an arched eyebrow that would have made her mom proud—"can be worked out. Give Grey—give happiness—a chance!"

"I think you're reading too much into me and Grey." I tried to dodge her probing look, reaching for a piece of bacon to give my hands something to do.

Tory shook her head. "You forget I know you. I've seen you in a relationship and I've seen you completely heartbroken. This is the most romantic interest I've seen you exhibit in a long time. How can you just let it go?"

She settled onto the stool across from me, forcing me to look at her.

"Tory, you don't know all the factors. There are so many reasons Grey and I will never work. He has one foot out the door and—"

"Grey is one of the best men I know. If he wasn't firmly a friend, I'd give you a run for your money. Which is why I can say with full confidence that Grey isn't the one half out the door in this relationship. Don't go blaming this on him. The decision to leave is all you. I just hope you don't regret it." Tory gave my hand a squeeze before walking to the top of the stairs and calling down to the group that breakfast was ready.

My stomach churned as I pondered her words. Could Tory be right? And what did it mean for me and Grey if she was?

Breakfast passed in a blur as I did my best to avoid eye contact with Grey, who Tory had somehow managed to sit directly across from me. Instead, I attempted to listen to Kylie as she talked about work and an upcoming business trip to St. Louis.

When the last dish was washed and all the food put away, I breathed a sigh of relief, grateful to escape into Brad's car and the four-hour drive ahead. It would lack a running dialogue about fast food restaurants and classic rock, but it would also be infinitely safer than another minute in this cabin with the bison-stampede of emotions I was feeling.

I loaded my duffle bag into Brad's trunk, keeping my backpack slung over one shoulder, and turned, wrapping Tory in a hug.

"Thanks for an epic trip. It was a great break." I gave her one more squeeze, but she held on, preventing me from stepping back.

"I'm not going to lie and say I'm sorry for what I said earlier, because I'm not. But no matter what you decide, I'm still your friend and am here for you. Even if you're making a huge mistake." She whispered the words in my ear, before releasing me from the hug and stepping back.

I waved at everyone else in the group, giving Grey a tight smile as he stepped forward, a small paper bag in his hand, the kind tourist shops in West Yellowstone used to package purchases.

"I got you a little something. I didn't realize you'd be leaving, so I guess it's for the road." He gave a shrug, looking the most uncertain I had seen him this entire trip. The echoes of pain from our conversation yesterday lingered in his eyes, and I wished I could make it disappear. But doing so would require me to take a risk I wasn't sure I could survive.

"Thanks." I took the package with some hesitation, slipping it into my backpack before depositing the bag in the backseat next to where I'd be sitting.

We stood there for a moment, neither of us knowing what to say or do. When I'd climbed into Grey's fast-food-scented car, I'd had no idea the adventure that awaited me, and I hated to see it end. Yet, I knew this was how it had to be.

Grey reached for me, wrapping me in a quick tight hug. I instinctively returned the embrace, taking in his comforting warmth and familiar scent one more time. All too soon, Grey released me, stepping back without a word and heading into cabin.

I climbed into the car and waved at Tory, Trent, and Kylie, who stood on the cabin porch watching us leave. Brad put the car in reverse, and we were on our way. A tear stole silently down my cheek, and I batted it away. If I was making the right decision, why did it hurt so bad?

The drive passed quickly. Brad and Alex were the ideal travel companions, asking for my opinions on music and keeping up polite, if somewhat boring, conversation. There were no out-of-context quotes from *The Lord of the Rings* or unexpected detours. I eventually closed my eyes, pretending to sleep in an effort to escape the perfectly normal car ride around me. After a few minutes, Alex and Brad began to talk quietly, trying not to wake me. Their deep voices still carried to the back seat.

"Do you regret it?" I heard one of the twins, probably Alex, ask from the front seat.

"Regret what?" The forced tone hinted I was overhearing something I shouldn't, but it wasn't like I could leave the car.

"You know what. Going to Tory's birthday, even knowing Trent would be there."

"That dude's all wrong for her."

"You and I both know that, but Tory disagrees. Unless you tell her how you feel, you have no right being upset about the eventual outcome."

"What if I lose her along the way? I don't know if I can do life without Tory as a friend." Clear frustration filled Brad's voice.

"If Trent gets his way, you won't have much choice in the matter."

Their conversation trailed off, music replacing their words. It appeared I wasn't the only one in the car with a broken heart connected to a fear of speaking up. I just hoped Brad was braver than I was.

Chapter Thirty-Two

WE ARRIVED HOME IN the early afternoon, and I all but collapsed on the couch for the rest of the evening, depositing my bags in my room and promising myself I'd unpack later. Instead, I formed a cocoon of blankets and Ruby-snuggles, remote and Pepsi in hand. My roommates looked at me with worried expressions they tried to hide, but I could hear their whispers of concern. I'd texted both Chloe and Mallory on the ride home, telling them I was coming home early, but I hadn't shared any details. I'd also messaged work, letting them know I'd be coming back early after all. I knew if I didn't head into the office, I'd spend the entire next day sitting in a useless pile of emotions on the couch. At least at work, I could channel my anxious energy into something productive.

The next morning came too early, anxiety waking me up for a quick yoga session before I went through the half-hearted effort of getting ready. I slipped into my favorite pencil skirt and blouse combo, almost immediately hating the feel of the tight, restrictive professional clothing. I applied makeup and styled my hair, not bothering to curl it, electing to leave it straight and long down my back. Grey's comments about my appearance rang in my mind, drowning out the voice of Lyle that I had listened to for far too long.

I took one last look in the mirror before grabbing my keys and heading out the door. Might as well get the first day back over with.

My mom called on my drive, and even though I told her I was fine, I could tell she didn't believe me. Her responses were probing, searching for details I wasn't willing to share.

I bit my lip as I turned into the parking lot, debating before asking her the question that was weighing on me. "Mom, how did you know Dave was the one? How did you know he was worth the risk when he first asked you out?"

"Honey, I didn't know he was the one that first date. I almost didn't accept a second date because he was so nerdy." Affection filled her tone as she shared a part of her love story I'd never heard. "But everything in life comes with risk, and love is the biggest risk of all. One of these days, you'll find the person worth risking your heart for. Until then, you just have to keep trying and hoping."

We said our goodbyes as I parked Jovi near the back of the lot. The familiar industrial building where I had worked for the last several years felt simultaneously familiar and strange. It was still the same mix of glass and brick, the same scraggly bushes lining the walk to the front door. Yet, it felt different this time as I walked past the receptionist desk, up the stairs, and badged my way onto my floor.

I settled into my grey office chair, kicking off my high heels and depositing my purse in the cubicle drawer before turning on my computer. The familiar routine didn't bring the sense of relief I'd anticipated. Instead, the boulder of dread in my stomach seemed to increase in size until I worried I'd need to slip out and do a quick yoga session in the breakroom. Anything to rid me of this tension. I wanted mountains and open skies and a bearded man who made me feel seen, not a cubicle that wasn't even near a window.

"Late, I see." Drew stood at the entrance to my cubicle, glowering at me through the gap in the grey panels that made up my workspace. He wore his usual polo shirt tucked into slacks, his hair gelled to perfection, no trace of stubble on his chin.

A glance at my phone showed I was three minutes late, hardly a noteworthy amount. Apparently, Drew hadn't taken my hanging up on him well.

"I'll have you know, the team had to work over the weekend without you here to pull your weight." His voice was a nasal whine that set my teeth on edge.

"I was on vacation, Drew. It's not like I skipped out on mandatory overtime to go golfing or something," I said, remembering the many times I'd had to come in on a Saturday so Drew could do that very thing.

He stepped into my cubicle, crowding me.

"That's not the point. The number of calls..." I tuned Drew out as he shared his woes from the weekend, moments when he'd had to actually do his job because I hadn't been there to cover for him. Instead, I remembered all my daydreams of a career as a yoga instructor, setting my own schedule, doing work I actually loved.

That's when it hit me. I didn't have to take this. I didn't have to sit in this cubicle a minute longer. I had tried root beer milk, shared a bed with a near stranger, and jumped off a rock into the Firehole. I could stand up to my boss.

"Because of you—"

I pushed to my feet, refusing to cower as Drew no doubt had expected. Instead, I jabbed a finger in his chest and stepped closer, forcing him back and out of my workspace.

"Because I took my first real vacation in *years,* you had to actually do your job. Is that what you were about to say? Or were you going to mention how because I took *paid time off* that you approved, you came to realize just how much the team depends on me to pull *more* than my fair share of weight? Also, need I remind you, I came back early. I wasn't supposed to be here today. Technically, I could still be gone, with your sign-off."

Drew gaped at me, his skin paling at the confrontation, but I refused to back down. I was done. I just wished it hadn't taken several years and a long overdue vacation to help me see that my time here was finished.

I slipped on my shoes, threw open my drawer and snagged my purse, slinging it over my shoulder as I glanced around the impersonal cubicle. I didn't even have a photo of Ruby because Drew had claimed such decorations were unprofessional.

"Where do you think you're going?" Drew stuttered as I pushed my way past him towards the door.

"I'm leaving." I bit my tongue to keep from tacking on an "obviously" at the end.

"What do you mean you're leaving?" Drew was chasing after me now, my heels making a satisfying click with every step towards escape.

"I quit, effective immediately."

"That's not how—"

I turned on my heel and Drew froze just short of running into me. "Don't start with me. Two weeks is a courtesy you don't deserve. I've put up with hell working for you, and I'm done."

I could see other coworkers peeking around cubicle walls, watching the exchange. At my last pronouncement, I thought I even heard several gasps of surprise and someone attempting to start a slow clap.

"What about your career, Audrey? Do you think you'll be able to put this place down as a reference after pulling this stunt?" he said, clearly flustered.

"You know, Drew, for the first time in my life, I genuinely don't care." Images of me helping Grey and leading the group in a yoga routine filled my mind, and a small smile touched my lips. "I'm going to find a job that I'm actually excited about."

I exited the floor, letting the door close behind me, blocking Drew's protests.

The walk to my car and the drive home were a blur. My phone hadn't stopped vibrating since I'd left the building as different coworkers attempted to contact me. I ignored them all as I walked into my apartment to find Mallory in sweats and a t-shirt, her blonde hair in a high ponytail, sitting on the couch reading, Ruby curled up at her feet.

"Did you forget something?" Mal asked as she set her book on the recently refurbished coffee table. A fresh coat of white paint now covered the scratches and dents I'd grown used to while living here.

"My sanity," I joked, settling on the loveseat so I could watch Mal's reaction to my news. Ruby took this as her invitation and came over to sit next to me. I buried my fingers in her fur, letting the texture soothe me as I said four words I'd wanted to say for years. "I quit my job."

Mallory's mouth opened and closed a few times before a smile stole across her lips. "It's about time. I was starting to worry you'd never leave that place."

Now it was my turn for shock. "What do you mean? You never said anything about this before."

Mallory shrugged. "What was I supposed to say? 'Audrey, I think you should quit your job. They don't appreciate you and are slowly destroying your soul.' It wasn't my place."

"Chloe's going to freak out," I said, pushing down the panic that was trying to claw its way up my throat. "I don't have a job." It was the first time since I was a teenager that I could say that sentence. The words tasted odd on my tongue, bringing with them a sense of excitement and panic. I planted my elbows on my knees and buried my face in my hands. "What am I going to do, Mal? How am I going to pay rent? What about insurance?"

Mallory moved to settle next to me on the loveseat, wrapping an arm around my shoulders and giving me a squeeze. "You're going to do whatever you want. You're going to find a job you'll actually love and want to go to every day. A job that lets you go on vacation without making you feel guilty the entire time. A job that lights up your soul and makes you feel appreciated."

I took a deep breath, counting to four as I inhaled and then exhaling for four counts, letting Mallory's words wash over me. "You know, Tory thinks I should teach yoga." I paused, waiting for Mallory's reaction, waiting for her to tell me it was as crazy an idea as I feared it was. Not acknowledging that the idea hadn't originated with Tory. I wasn't quite ready for that level of vulnerability.

When she didn't speak, I sat up, turning to face her.

She bit her lip.

"What, no response?"

She let out a long breath, scooting back on the couch to better see me. "Honestly, I think you'd be a great yoga instructor. You're always going to classes at the rec center. You're kind and patient. You've led Chloe and me through more yoga flows than I can count, and we're not the easiest students."

I bit back a laugh as I remembered multiple late night yoga sessions with the two of them giggling and falling over while I patiently tried to help them find their balance.

I leaned back, letting my head fall onto the couch as I closed my eyes, blocking out all the pressure. "I've only done the most basic research into becoming an instructor."

My few internet searches were hardly sufficient to help me pursue a change of careers.

"Then I guess you know where to start. Do some research, see what's feasible, and go from there. Audrey..." she paused, resting her hand on my arm and waiting until I looked at her. "Don't worry about rent or doing the practical thing, for once in your life. This is your chance to genuinely chase what you want. Wander a bit, maybe even get a little lost."

I froze as Mallory's words reminded me of Grey's admonitions from the weekend. I tried to push his brown eyes and bearded grin out of my mind, but they seemed to underscore everything Mallory had said, causing my heart to twist as I thought about how I'd left things. It was better this way, wasn't it?

Mallory left me on the couch, mumbling something about meeting her boyfriend for lunch. While Ridge was only here for the summer before returning to Idaho to finish school, the two of them were inseparable, and I loved seeing how happy he made my roommate.

Ruby crawled into my lap, settling into a tight circle of warmth. I absentmindedly ran my fingers through her soft brown fur, the familiar movement bringing with it a level of comfort I needed.

I could become a yoga instructor, or at least learn what it takes, find out if it's what I really wanted to do in life. I could do this. It was long past time I took a real risk.

Chapter Thirty-Three

I SPENT THE AFTERNOON researching what I needed to do to become a yoga instructor. It would take time, but the more I researched, the more excited I became as I pictured the possibilities. I could work at the rec center or a local yoga studio. I might even be able to start my own studio or run my own classes. The possibility of teaching outdoor yoga at local parks or even up in Island Park sounded particularly appealing.

A little before dinner, I pushed up from the couch, my eyes tired from so many hours staring at the computer screen, planning my future. I headed to my room, rubbing at sore muscles that weren't used to such long stretches on the couch.

My duffle and backpack waited for me on the floor, still full from my trip. The group would have driven back today. I wondered if they'd stopped at the creamery and tried odd milk flavors. Maybe they'd visited Dot and Hank, eaten cookies, and listened to stories about falling in love.

Pushing the thoughts aside, I sorted through the bags' contents. Unzipping my backpack, a brown bag fell onto the floor. I'd forgotten about Grey's gift.

I weighed the unassuming paper bag in my hands for a moment, curious. It was probably something simple like an odd flavor of licorice he wanted to goad me into trying. I was fairly certain I'd seen huckleberry flavored everything in the store. Maybe they'd even had huckleberry milk, though the bag wasn't quite heavy enough for something like that.

I unrolled the top and dumped the contents into my hand. It was the necklace from the display I'd been perusing before running from the store and the complication Grey personified. The gold bar shone brightly against my palm as I read the word etched on it: wander.

Of course that was the word he'd picked. It was utterly perfect, as I thought about the week and everything I'd experienced. I really had wandered, and instead of becoming lost, I'd found myself. I hadn't even realized I had been missing, lost in all the fears from my mom's accident, the expectations of work, and the remnants of my failed relationship with Lyle.

But I'd come out the other side, a little more sure about who I was and what I wanted, though the possibilities still brought a level of fear and anxiety I was trying to block out. I wanted a job I loved and a life that fit hiking and yoga and classic rock and cooking and all the interests that made me who I was. I also wanted love, the kind of love that could handle all my self-doubt and help me be braver and stronger for it.

Thoughts of something else, or rather someone else, I also wanted in my life filled my mind, and for the first time since returning from the cabin, I didn't push thoughts of him away. An image of Grey, with his constant smile and flannel-wrapped arms, played in my thoughts. I wanted him too, but I worried it was too late. I had run away. Why would he want me now?

Yet, he'd be the first person to tell me to be brave and chase what I wanted. I just wasn't sure how he'd respond if I showed up on his doorstep begging him to give us a chance. Especially when we weren't even dating. We were two acquaintances who'd become friends on a vacation. Could we be something more?

I studied the gold chain a moment before slipping it around my neck, the bar resting on my chest above my shirt collar, right in alignment with my heart.

I was willing to take the risk to find out.

Chapter Thirty-Four

THAT EVENING, I CURLED up on the couch, Ruby resting on my feet. A cooking show provided quiet background noise as I worked on a budget that would see me through the next several months of uncertainty. I was developing a plan to chase this new dream of mine, and while I wouldn't be able to make a living initially, the excitement in my belly told me this was already a better life decision.

A knock on the door pulled me from my dreaming. Ruby jumped off the couch and wandered to the door, giving me an impatient look as I trailed behind her. Both Mallory and Chloe were out for the evening. Mallory was off with Ridge, and Chloe had said something about going to a movie with Derek, a guy who she'd friendzoned but who would very much like to change that.

The possibility of seeing Grey on the other side of the door had me opening it without looking through the peephole, even though I knew chances were slim. More likely it would be a neighbor asking to borrow something.

Pushing the door open, I froze when I saw who waited on the other side: Lyle.

He looked good, but something seemed a bit off. His thick, dark hair was trimmed, as always, though the top wasn't slicked back into perfect lines. It was slightly mussed, as if he'd been running his fingers through the short strands. His green eyes were rimmed with faint circles, and while he smiled when I opened the door, it appeared forced and uncertain. His shirt was wrinkled, the top two buttons undone.

"What are you doing here?" The words popped out of my mouth, void of pleasantries.

"Hello to you too," Lyle said.

Ruby took one look at our guest and returned to the couch, not interested. Now I stood alone, in front of the man I'd thought I loved, who had betrayed me more than anyone else in my life, and I felt nothing but mild surprise. Not hurt or anger or shock. All the emotions that I'd thought would come with a run-in with Lyle were absent. Here was the man I'd thought I would marry, and at the moment I wished he was someone else: a bearded man with sexy arms and an average body who had a tendency to talk too much but who also had a remarkable ability to help me be brave.

My fingers reached up, finding the now familiar necklace where it rested against my skin. I'd been touching it all day, as if doing so could connect me to the man who had given it to me.

"After everything you've put me through, I don't think you deserve a hello," I said, crossing my arms in front of my chest, channeling the same brave Audrey who had told Drew off.

"Can I at least come in? We have things to talk about, and I really—"

I held up a hand, the same strength that had convinced me to quit filling my voice now. "If I'm not going to tell you hello, why on earth would I invite you into my home? You're lucky I haven't slammed the door in your face."

Lyle winced. "I guess I deserve that. It's just...this isn't exactly how I pictured this conversation going."

I glanced around the breezeway, taking in the cement hallway broken up by maroon doors. "Funny, I have no idea what this conversation is, so I can't tell you where I pictured it happening. Maybe you can start talking, and I'll let you know if the venue lives up to expectations."

If I had my way, I would never have another conversation with Lyle. Unfortunately, it was too late for that wish to come true.

Lyle paused for a moment, watching to see if I was serious. When I waved a hand, gesturing for him to continue, he spoke.

"Audrey, I wasn't fair to you, and I recognize that. The way I treated you was unacceptable. This week has been"—he swallowed before continuing—"hard. I thought I was marrying the love of my life. But then Emily called off the wedding, and I was shattered. Everyone kept telling me I'd get through this. I'd figure it out. And that's when I realized the one person I wanted by my side who could help me through, help me figure things out, wasn't Emily. It was you."

With his last words, Lyle looked me straight in the eye, earnestness filling his expression.

I waited, certain this had to be a cruel prank. There had to be a punch line because there was no way my ex, the man who shattered my heart and trust by cheating on me with my best friend, was begging me to come back. When Lyle didn't so much as crack a smile, I had to bite down a bitter laugh.

"Excuse me? We haven't talked to each other in over a year. I found you making out with my best friend! And you think you can just walk over here and feed me some line about how you 'missed me' and I'll, what? Fall into your arms? Declare my undying love for you? Take you back?" I winced, realizing that not too long ago, I might have done exactly that. I had been waiting for life to reset, to go back to the safety and security I had felt as Lyle's girlfriend. A security I'd been searching for since I was a kid with a dreamer for a mom. But my mom, with all her flighty tendency, had taken risks and found her safe place to land. It was my turn to do the same.

"No. I just thought that, maybe if I explained, we could—"

I held up a hand, cutting him off. Excitement burned in my chest at the realization that the life Lyle had offered was never the life for me. I was forging a new life, one I was actually meant for.

"Lyle, you are a jerk. You're a manipulative pretty-boy who's used to women falling at your feet if you just smile, and I'm done. There is no 'we.' There is no 'us.' There is no 'Lyle and Audrey against the world.' You broke my heart, and I'm better for it because now I see that I deserve more. I wish you luck. Actually, scratch that. I don't wish you anything but the life you deserve. Now, get off my doorstep, and never come back." I stepped inside the apartment and closed the door, satisfied at the look of complete and utter shock etched on Lyle's face.

I leaned against the door, processing what had just happened. I expected to feel a small bit of loss, considering that I'd just slammed the door closed on ever getting my life with Lyle back, but instead I felt excitement. In one day, I'd quit my job and told Lyle off. What else was I brave enough to do? My fingers toyed with the necklace at my throat. I couldn't wait to find out.

Chapter Thirty-Five

I WAITED UNTIL MORNING to text Tory, though my fingers itched to do it sooner. I'd spent the night pacing and pondering my options, and now, I had a plan. It was crazy and ridiculous, but if I played my cards right, it might just be worth it.

I might also end up with my heart shattered into a million pieces, but what was life without a little risk?

TORY: *You're up early. What's up? P.S. I missed you the rest of the trip. It wasn't the same without you, Alex, and Brad.*

ME: *Would you believe me if I told you I needed to leave? I realized something huge coming home, and I don't think it would have happened if I had stayed.*

TORY: *If your realization is that you're falling in love with Grey, I know. I'm pretty sure all of Idaho knows at this point.*

ME: *Way to steal my thunder! But yes, that's part of it. I messed up, and I'm pretty sure I'm the last person he wants to see right now.*

TORY: *What are you going to do to fix that?*

I laid out my plan, hoping and praying it would work. If I played my cards right, I would be confessing my feelings to Grey before the end of the week.

—— *eee* ——

"Will you hold still? We're almost to the trailhead." Tory reached over and placed a hand on my knee, attempting to stop it from bouncing.

We were driving to the start of the Grove Creek Canyon trail under the pretense of a group hike. Tory had coordinated the whole thing, ensuring Grey would be there. What he didn't know was that, besides me and Tory, no one else was coming. In fact, the plan was for Tory to drop me off and for her to drive a couple of blocks away, giving Grey and me space to talk. I'd asked her to drive for fear that, if it was up to me, I'd bail and drive home to the safety of my cooking shows and dog.

It also gave Tory a much-needed distraction. Only hours after I'd texted her to coordinate this plan, Trent had asked her to meet up. She'd accepted, expecting their usual dinner date. Instead, Trent had dumped her, refusing to "play second fiddle" to the other men in her life. A ridiculous assertion, based on the number of times I'd seen her over the weekend actively distancing herself from Brad to make Trent happy.

Tory had driven to my apartment immediately after, and we'd spent the night eating ice cream and talking about how Tory deserved so much more than Trent and his inability to express emotions. Before Tory had left, I'd offered to reschedule our plans. But she'd assured me having something else to focus on would do her good.

Which brought us to this moment, me fidgeting in her car, desperate to find something to do with the anxious energy filling my veins.

"This is a terrible idea. Let me out here. I'll walk back or get a ride share or something." I gestured to the neighborhood we were passing. I lived several miles away, but I could make the walk. The movement would release the nerves dancing in my belly. A walk would also help me clear my head and make better life decisions than professing my feelings to a guy I wasn't sure even liked me anymore.

"Love is a Battlefield" by Pat Benatar streamed out of the speakers, a song choice that, in retrospect, might not have been my best idea.

Tory glanced at me before hitting the door lock. "I am not letting you out to run away again. If you are going to be a coward, you'll have to do the full walk of shame from the trailhead."

"A good friend would take me home," I muttered, folding my arms over my chest and redoubling my knee bouncing.

"Maybe, but a best friend would save you from yourself and force you to be brave."

I let out a huff of air, knowing she was right. It was part of why I'd made her my accomplice in my plan. Left to my own devices, I would chicken out.

"Also," Tory added as she turned onto the street that led to the trailhead, "I'm doing everyone who's had to spend time with you this last week a huge favor. No more back and forth. No more stewing. It's time to act."

"Rude!" Laughing, I gently smacked her arm. "But have I been that bad?"

Tory shook her head. "No. I'm teasing. You've actually been a good distraction for me."

Sadness flitted across her face, and I reached over, giving her arm a gentle squeeze.

"Trent's an idiot," I said, without hesitation.

"Was he? You and I even talked about it. I could see how he—"

I lifted a hand. "Stop right there. You and Trent talked. You explained your relationship with Brad and even took steps to distance yourself and set boundaries. Brad left your birthday trip early, for heaven's sake. It's on Trent that he couldn't handle your friendship."

"But—"

"No buts. You deserve better than a man who can't handle your personality and love for other people so he dumps you the day after your birthday trip."

We pulled into the parking lot, and my stomach dropped as I saw who waited at the trailhead: Grey. He looked good. His beard was trimmed, his hair was mussed from the wind. He wore basketball shorts, hiking boots, and a green t-shirt, and a part of me missed his flannels.

"*You* deserve better than questions and what-ifs." Tory gave me a gentle nudge, pushing me towards the door.

I climbed out and tugged down my blue "Pepsi kind of day" t-shirt, wondering if I should have dressed up a bit more than workout leggings and a messy bun. But I shook off the impulse and walked towards Grey, both praying for and dreading the moment he looked up and saw me coming. Did he even want to see me?

"Grey. How's it going?" I flinched at the inane greeting. Was that really the best I could do? We hadn't talked in days. Surely there was a better way to greet him. *Walk any beaches lately? How goes the unicorn hunt? Do you still hate pina coladas?*

His eyes darted to my face, taking me in for a moment, before looking away to scan the parking lot. "Audrey. I didn't know you were coming. Tory didn't say anything."

I shrugged. "I asked her not to. I worried that if you knew..." I trailed off.

"I'm not that big of a coward. Just a commitment-phobe who apparently plays with hearts and runs away to exotic destinations like Oregon."

I flinched at the unspoken accusation. I deserved that, but I hoped Grey could look past the pain I'd caused and give me another chance. "Listen, that's part of why I'm here. I want to apologize."

"Apologize for what? You don't owe me anything, Audrey. We're two people with mutual friends who happened to share a long car ride and a vacation together." Grey turned to face me, reaching to grab my arm out of habit before pulling back, as if remembering we were no longer the kind of friends who touched.

"We did also share a bed," I said before I could think better of it. I shook my head, ignoring his smirk and pressing forward. I had to get this out now, or I'd always regret it.

"What if 'friends' isn't all I want us to be?" I breathed out the words, digging deep for a boldness that felt foreign.

Grey searched my face, and I bit my lip, trying not to overthink this moment. Instead, I reached for his hand, rubbing my fingers over his knuckles and feeling the calluses that covered his palms.

My anxieties bubbled near the surface, but I pushed them down. Determined to finally say my piece, to be brave and bold and all the other characteristics Grey had claimed to see in me throughout our trip.

"I ran away in Island Park because I was scared. I told you my history. I don't like risks, and liking you, possibly dating you, feels like the biggest risk of all. Bigger even than driving up a mountain road at night. Yet, I can't imagine living my life hiding from the world and only doing what makes me comfortable. I want to lose sleep, stargazing and watching stupid movies. I want to wander, jumping into rivers and climbing mountains." My fingers brushed the necklace at my throat, and Grey followed the movement, his gaze heating before returning to my face. "I want—" My words caught in my throat for a moment, and I looked away from Grey, gathering my nerve. "I want to lose my heart to someone like you."

Grey's hands found my face, gently nudging me to look back at him. The parking lot was crowded, and people walked past us to the trail, but I ignored them, focusing on the man in front of me and the love I found in his eyes.

"I want to lose my heart to you too."

Grey leaned forward, his lips finding mine, and I bit back a groan at the familiar sensation. Soft lips contrasted with the stubble from his chin as my lips worked to meet his, movement for movement. In that moment, I knew I could wander this entire world, but with Grey by my side, I would never be lost.

Epilogue

THREE MONTHS LATER

"Where are we going?" I asked, tripping over a root in Grey's determination to drag me up the mountain.

I'd been late meeting him at the trailhead, distracted by my yoga research. I'd started classes to get my teaching certification and was constantly getting sucked down research rabbit holes as I learned about different poses and their benefits.

"We're going to miss it," Grey muttered, continuing to pull me forward.

"Miss the mountain? I don't think it's going anywhere. Though we probably should have brought flashlights. It's getting dark," I said, noting how dusk was settling in. While I was doing better at handling my fears of driving at night, hiking in the dark did not appeal for a whole slew of different reasons.

Grey growled and pulled me along faster, making me laugh and gasp a little as we continued up the trail. While I had hiked more this summer than in years past, my lungs and calves were still getting used to the steep inclines and elevation changes that came with hiking in Utah.

"Maybe we could slow down," I panted after a particularly steep stretch. My lungs burned, and a stitch in my side begged to be massaged.

"Just a little further."

I did my best to keep up but fell behind, my muscles screaming for a slower pace.

Grey suddenly stopped, waiting for me to join him before gesturing to a rock outcropping that overlooked the valley.

"We're here!"

I glanced around, taking in my surroundings. At this spot, the trail hugged the bend of the mountain, providing a wide-open view of Utah Valley below.

"It's the valley." I nodded, unsure what I was looking at and confused why we weren't continuing to follow the trail. The trees below were just starting to change colors, hinting that summer was ending. I knew from past hiking experience that another mile up the trail, we'd find a waterfall. Why Grey felt this view of houses outranked a waterfall tonight, I had no idea.

Grey grabbed my hand and led me to the rock outcropping.

"Exactly. And that," he pointed to a field a few miles away dotted with construction equipment, "is what I wanted to show you."

"Okay..." I trailed off.

"I'm working that job site right now."

"That's good." I nodded, trying to understand what the big deal was. Grey had worked on several sites since we'd started dating. He loved talking me through what he was doing and the results of his work, and I loved knowing these jobs kept him close and gave him purpose.

"That's where I'm going to build a house."

I nodded again, still not following. Grey primarily worked home construction jobs. I had no idea what made this one special.

"I'd love your thoughts on the design. I'm thinking three bedrooms, two and a half bathrooms at least. An open concept with a large kitchen, plenty of space for baking cookies. An office that could be turned into a yoga studio."

"All of that sounds amazing. The future homeowner has excellent taste."

Grey paused, a crooked grin stealing across his face before he reached for my hand. "I might be biased, but I think so."

He turned me to face him, tipping my chin up to look at him.

"Audrey, that house isn't just for anyone. It's going to be mine. I finalized purchase of the plot today."

My breath caught in my throat as his words registered. "Seriously?"

At Grey's nod, I threw my arms around his neck in excitement, pulling him down for a quick, celebratory kiss.

"That's amazing! You're going to own a house." I turned to look at the field once more, just barely able to make out the plot in the fading light.

Grey pulled me back into his chest, resting his chin on my shoulder. "If all goes according to plan, I hope I can share it with you someday."

"I could be persuaded to make that happen, when the time is right."

Someday, probably a few more months down the road, once Grey and I had a little more dating under our belts, he'd ask me a question that I already knew the answer to. A question I could picture him asking right here on one knee. It was a question we'd talked about, but Grey was smart enough to know I needed a little more time. So much had changed so quickly, and while I was doing better at being flexible and brave, I still had my moments of overwhelm. Thankfully, with Grey and his gentle coaxing, I found myself more able to meet life's unexpected turns head on.

My cheeks ached from smiling as I settled back against Grey and enjoyed the moment, the last specks of light fading and the stars coming out to wink at us. Life would bring more adventures and wandering. I'd probably even get lost from time to time, my anxiety leading me astray. But I knew no matter where life took us, for me Grey would always be home.

For a bonus epilogue, visit authorhillaryslaughter.com

Also by Hillary Slaughter

Lost Roommates Series
Love Letter Lost
Losing Sleep
Lost Daydreaming

Acknowledgements

To Mom, Dad, Lindy, and Landon, thank you for cheering me on with this second book. I could not have done it without you and your incredible love and encouragement.

Thank you to Madey. I miss you every single day and will always be grateful for my guardian angel.

Thank you to my extended family for your love and support. Grandpa, thank you for helping with the business side of things and for your patience with all of my random questions. Riley and Jayme, thank you for the many cousin trips that inspired this book. Jim, Pam, Catherine, and Will, thank you for the many Island Park adventures you've made possible. Nate, thank you for introducing me to the Firehole. That summer trip to Island Park where you acted as tour guide will forever be one of my favorite vacations.

To Dana LeCheminant, this book would not have been possible without your friendship, advice, and pep talks. Thank you for being my emotional support author friend.

To Cassy and Jessica, thank you for beta reading this book and helping me develop Audrey's story into what it is today.

To Annie Jakes, Amanda Schimmoeller, Jentry Flint, Raneé Clark, Nicole Kimzey, and the many other authors who have answered my questions along the way. I could not have done this without you.

To Lindzee Merrill Photography, thank you for the incredible headshots.

To Emily at Midnight Owl Editors, thank you for helping me polish and finalize this book.

To my book club and bookstagram friends, thank you for giving me a space to nerd out about books and for all the book recommendations.

To my arc readers, coworkers, friends, and everyone else who has had a hand in this book, thank you. Your support is felt and so greatly appreciated.

Finally, thank you, my readers, for reading Audrey's story! You make what I do possible, and I will forever be grateful for every person who decides to take a chance on one of my books.

About the Author

Hillary Slaughter is a crafting addict, avid reader, and hiking enthusiast. Born and raised in Utah, she loves exploring the mountains, especially if she can bring her dog with her. She has a Bachelor's degree in English from Brigham Young University and a Master's of Business Administration from Utah Valley University. She loves writing sweet contemporary romance with a dash of humor and is the author of the Lost Roommates Series. You can learn more about Hillary and her books at authorhillaryslaughter.com.

www.ingramcontent.com/pod-product-compliance
Lightning Source LLC
Chambersburg PA
CBHW061939170626
46813CB00006B/2466